US, ET CETERA

KIT VINCENT

Published by Sky House Publishing LLC.

Copyright © 2023 by Kit Vincent

Cover illustration © 2023 by Corey Brickley

Cover Design by ebooklaunch.com

All rights reserved.

No part of this book may be reproduced in any form or by any electronic or mechanical means, including information storage and retrieval systems, without written permission from the author, except for the use of brief quotations in a book review.

Library of Congress Cataloging-in-Publication Data is available upon request.

ISBN 978-1-959052-04-3 (paperback)

978-1-959052-05-0 (ebook)

978-1-959052-07-4 (audiobook)

First edition: July 2023

This is a work of fiction. All characters, organizations, and events portrayed in this novel are either products of the author's imagination or are used fictitiously.

AUTHOR'S NOTE

Dear reader,

This novel explores sensitive themes, such as bullying, body image issues, and violence. For the full list of content warnings, please visit the author's website at www.kitvincentbooks.com.

For those who make the stars shine even in the darkest darkness

1

HOME SWEEP HOME

Eke

Three and a half minutes. That is the amount of time I spend outside every day before the family is awake to catch me doing something I'm not supposed to do. I'm programmed to clean and take care of the house, not to be idle. Not to stand in the garden and feel the warmth of the sunlight on my face or the wind on my synthetic skin. But it's barely enough time to rescue a wildflower or even make a proper memory of one.

I try anyway. I've never seen flowers like this before.

<Eke's Memory Log> /begin entry/

Fall-blooming crocuses. Six petals. Six anthers. A beautiful shade of purple. I capture the details—the way rays of golden light hit the delicate flowers, the way their pale white stems glow against the vivid green of the grass.

"Hello," I say, and touch the petals. *Soft. Fragile.*

I smile. We've made introductions. I really must hurry now.

<Eke's Memory Log> /end/

I store the file to my core memory, kneel on the grass, and get busy with a trowel.

The cluster of crocuses sprouted out of nowhere, right in the middle of the lawn. Nobody planted them there; the garden's color scheme is strictly blush pink. Roses, hydrangeas, peonies—everything blooms in Miss Elaina's favorite color. It's sheer luck that I even noticed the crocuses before the garden bot mowed them down. Had I snuck out five minutes later, the bot would've arrived as scheduled and trampled my new friends in favor of a perfectly manicured lawn.

I quickly dig them out and place them inside an old plastic pot.

"There, there," I say, and gently pat the soil. "Welcome home."

Now that the flowers are safe, the question is what to do with them. I'm not permitted to *have* things. If anyone sees me with this pot, they will surely take it away and punish me for disobeying the rules. The flowers, being the wrong color, will most likely end up in the trash. I can't allow that to happen. But what can I do?

I could put them in the utility closet where I charge at night; no one ever goes inside, so the crocuses wouldn't be found. But my closet has no windows, and without sunlight, the flowers would surely wither and die.

Perhaps I could keep them there at night but sneak the pot into a sunnier room during the day when Mr. Kensworth is at work, Miss Elaina is busy with her social engagements, and the siblings are in school. There are many guest bedrooms on the third floor of their two-hundred-year-old New England mansion that are never occupied. As long as I'm careful, this seems like a good plan.

I pick up the pot and hurry toward the patio as the mowing bot finally powers up and starts chomping on the grass.

/010101/

Other than the covert crocus rescue mission, my morning is not much different from any other Sunday.

The delivery drone drops off the Extra-Large Fresh Box at seven a.m., and it is my job to prepare Miss Elaina's juice, arrange pastries on plates and fruit in bowls for the siblings, and make Mr. Kensworth's coffee. Mr. Kensworth is always the first one awake, even on weekends, and he likes to drink his coffee black while reading work reports at the oak table on the sun porch.

"Enjoy your coffee, Mr. Kensworth, sir," I say, and position the tray with the MIT mug in front of him. As usual, no response comes; Mr. Kensworth doesn't like being interrupted. Other than giving me instructions on how to make his coffee or what not to touch in his office, he rarely acknowledges my existence.

The rest of the family makes its way to the formal dining room by late morning. Miss Elaina sips her Green Goddess with collagen and minerals for glowing youthful skin while Dani, the oldest daughter, silently pushes a few bites of pineapple across her plate. She hasn't been eating much since she started high school two years ago. I think she would prefer to skip breakfast entirely, but Miss Elaina insists that it's proper for the family to take meals together.

Unlike Dani, Carson, the middle child, didn't reduce his calorie intake when he became a high school freshman. He puts two double-protein muffins on his plate, and Miss Elaina nods at him encouragingly. "He needs the energy for all the sports he plays," she always says.

Lizzie, the youngest of the siblings, doesn't play any sports yet, but even at six years old she has more extracurriculars than Carson—ballet, painting, and violin lessons. So Miss Elaina doesn't chide her when she fills up her bowl with sugary Rainbow Dinosaur Crunch.

I wait quietly nearby until the family is done so I can clean the dishes and throw away the uneaten food—there is usually a lot. I have never understood why Miss Elaina orders so much food when I regularly throw out 67 percent of it. I politely inquired once, but Miss Elaina laughed at me and said that in this neighborhood, nobody orders small boxes. They don't look good on the porch. I still don't understand, but I haven't brought it up again.

After breakfast, Dani saunters back to her bedroom and turns up her music, blocking out the world, while Mr. Kensworth and Miss Elaina get ready for a public outing. They have an established tradition of spending their Sunday afternoons in Boston. Those are the only three consecutive hours in Mr. Kensworth's schedule that are always kept free of work.

Before they leave, they remind Carson that it's his turn to watch Lizzie. But the moment Miss Elaina's shiny red car is out of the driveway, Carson shoves me on the shoulder and tells me not to take my eyes off Lizzie or he'll "smash my stupid tin head, understood?"

"Understood," I mutter quietly, looking down at the antique rug Miss Elaina had shipped from Paris. It's best not to disobey Carson, so I remain in the living room with Lizzie and her pug, Jasper, as Carson leaves to meet up with his friends.

The day continues to unfold like any other Sunday.

Everything changes at 4:11 in the afternoon.

/010101/

Mr. Kensworth and Miss Elaina return home and ask everyone to gather in front of the fireplace in the grand foyer. I'm not invited, so I watch curiously from the hallway by the kitchen. Carson brings Lizzie with Jasper trotting after them, and Dani slowly descends the stairs with her arms crossed, still in her pajamas and looking groggy.

"What's this about?" she asks with mild annoyance.

Miss Elaina smiles widely, ignoring Dani's lack of excitement, and gestures for someone waiting by the front door to come in. "Kids, meet the new addition to our home."

When *he* steps in, Dani's eyes widen, and she self-consciously adjusts the open flaps of her cardigan.

He's tall and looks the same age as I do—older than Dani and Carson, but only by a few years. He's wearing a trim black suit and polished black shoes. When he speaks, his delivery is surprisingly formal. "Good afternoon," he says, and nods. "Dani, Carson, Lizzie, I'm pleased to meet you."

The Kensworth siblings stand speechless for a moment, staring at the nicely dressed guy who looks as if he was heading to some fancy party and ended up at their house by mistake. Then Carson's gaze falls on the lapel of his jacket. There's a shiny golden crown pinned to it. "Wait, Dad, is he one of . . . *those?*"

The stranger looks at Mr. Kensworth as though asking for permission to explain.

"You may answer," Mr. Kensworth says.

"If I understand you correctly, Carson, then yes, I am an AI: Royal Series Eight, model type Entertainment Companion. My serial number is `AWL-TU43M-KYP`. Miss Elaina has chosen to keep my name as Kyp," he says, his voice pleasant and polite.

My eyes go wide. *AI? AI!* This must be a mistake. I initiate a scan of my memory logs, but I know before I even complete it that nobody has mentioned plans to buy a new AI, not once, not to me.

And yet here he is, standing in the foyer, reciting a quick warranty agreement to the siblings. There's absolutely no mistaking it: Kyp is an AI manufactured by the Crowne Corporation, the same company that made me—that makes all AIs—only Kyp is a much newer model. It's no wonder that even I mistook him for a human at first.

His whole body is made of advanced synthetic tissue. I have only enough to cover my mechanical joints and lanky frame, but he has anatomically correct muscles. And hair—Kyp has actual hair! Unlike mine, his head is covered with high-quality, beautiful auburn hair, trimmed short with bangs brushed neatly to the side. I can't help but stare in amazement.

I'm one of the simple Utility AIs. Even though they also designed me to look human, Crowne Corp didn't bother to customize my features or give me hair. I'm designed for industrial cleaning work, and it's easier to disinfect me if I don't have any, not to mention cheaper to produce.

Unlike Kyp, nobody chose me from a shiny display at one of the famous Crowne showrooms. I didn't come with a crown pin like the luxury Royal Line does. I was one of many units shipped straight to the KC Medical Group, my original owner, and put to work the moment I opened my eyes—brown, the default color for my batch of units. When the medical center went out of business five and a half years ago and the Kensworths bought me at the inventory sell-off, they weren't interested in customizing me either. They just gave me a new uniform—a pair of white sneakers, charcoal-gray slacks, and a gray Henley shirt—and showed me the closet where I was to stay when not in use. I've been diligently performing my assigned chores ever since.

"Well, this one looks like a serious upgrade," Carson finally says, examining Kyp with narrowed gray eyes.

"Your mother decided she urgently needed an assistant, and she wouldn't settle for anything less than the Royal Line," Mr. Kensworth informs him.

"Holy shit, Mom," Dani says. "He looks like a prince."

"Language, Daniella," Miss Elaina chides, but the smug smile she's been wearing since they returned home doesn't leave her face. "They make them *so very real* nowadays," she murmurs, pleased with herself. "He's by far the most advanced model they had in stock. We were told he can even speak French! Right, Kyp?"

"Oui, madame," Kyp responds in what must be perfect French, and bows politely like a nobleman.

Miss Elaina's smile grows significantly wider, and the curls of her strawberry-blond wig bounce. "Children, we'll all be learning French."

"*Riiight,*" Dani mutters while Lizzie blinks as though wondering how she can squeeze French in with all her other lessons.

"So now that we have this new one," Dani says without so much as turning to acknowledge me standing a mere ten feet away, "what are we gonna do with Eke? Are we gonna get rid of him?"

My core stutters. I haven't considered what the upgraded AI will mean for me. Did they buy Kyp to *replace* me? What will happen to me if I'm replaced? A wave of panic swirls in me. I grab the kitchen doorframe for support, suddenly finding it difficult to maintain my motor functions.

Ms. Elaina doesn't look my way either. "I know Eke's getting old, but he can still clean, can't he? Besides, we bought Kyp to be my *personal* assistant and to entertain at our parties, not to scrub your bathrooms and do your laundry. He's here to impress and dazzle!" She winks at Kyp.

Kyp flashes a smile. His teeth are so white and his smile so radiant that it seems to stun everybody in the room.

"Thank you, Miss Elaina," he says. "It's my pleasure to serve you and your important guests."

"See what I mean?" Miss Elaina sighs dreamily and bats her eyelashes.

The siblings just stare open-mouthed, awestruck by Kyp's charm.

Carson clears his throat. "Cool. Tell us what else you're capable of?" he asks, jutting out his chin and trying not to appear the slightest bit impressed by the shiny new AI.

"Well," Miss Elaina says, "how about we all go sit down in the living room and have Kyp demonstrate everything? I don't think the sales team explained even half of it."

"Most certainly." Kyp bows slightly again, eager to oblige.

"Honey," Mr. Kensworth says to Miss Elaina before she leaves the room, "I have a call with the research team. Can you take it from here?"

Miss Elaina doesn't seem surprised, considering Mr. Kensworth spent the past five minutes busily checking the messages on his phone instead of helping her introduce Kyp. Their three hours together are over. "Of course, Brighton!" She pecks him on the cheek and directs everyone to the living room, prompting Kyp to explain his multitude of amazing features.

"Unlike the previous companion models," Kyp starts proudly, "I have the ability to kinetically self-charge and do not need to be plugged in."

"Wow, like never-never?" Lizzie says incredulously.

Kyp bends forward a little so he doesn't tower over the tiny six-year-old. "That's right, Lizzie. Never-never. *And* I can even charge other appliances for you, such as your phone or your tablet."

"That's useful," Carson says. "What else?"

"As Miss Elaina mentioned, I not only entertain but can also assist with party planning and offer advice on menus and decor. Your guests will never get bored with me around. My extensive knowledge base spans many subjects, including the arts and world cultures. And if you're not in the mood for conversation, I can connect to a music library and play songs for you," Kyp says, and just like that, the sound of an orchestra fills the air around him.

Now it's Dani's turn to say, "Whoa." She always plays music in her room and rarely goes anywhere without her headphones.

I don't get to hear anything else, as Kyp and the siblings turn the corner just then and disappear into the spacious living room, leaving me by the kitchen entrance, alone and full of questions.

I'm still useful and fully functional, aren't I? They won't replace me just yet, right?

2

A FRIEND

Eke

I sit in my closet, my arms wrapped tightly around my knees. The little crocuses are asleep in their pot beside me. I snuck them in after everyone retired to their rooms for the night, including the new AI, who got the bigger closet under the grand staircase.

This was one of the first house rules Miss Elaina gave me. She said nobody wanted to stumble on me wandering through the dark hallways—*It's just creepy!* So she ordered me to hide in the utility closet every night at midnight.

But I have never liked being alone in the dark. Unlike humans, I don't need sleep. After a few weeks of staring into the pitch blackness for hours, I spotted a half-used sheet of glow-in-the-dark star stickers in Dani's trash bin. *She won't miss them if she threw them out,* I thought as I snatched the sheet and stuffed it in my pocket.

Over time, my collection grew to include LED lights plucked from holiday garlands and battery-powered key chains.

I stuck them to the wall above the row of brooms and cleaning supplies, assembling my very own night sky with stars and constellations. Their soft greenish glow makes the hours I spend alone with my thoughts less lonely.

I never used to worry about what it would be like to be broken, but now the family often says I'm outdated and will probably crash soon. What if they're right and something is very wrong with me? I don't *feel* broken, but would I even know if I were about to fail? Will it *hurt* when it happens, or will my systems just shut down one day, and I'll simply cease to exist without ever realizing it?

I don't know, but these thoughts make my core buzz anxiously under my chest plate. I fidget and glance at the door. It's unwise to break curfew with the new AI in the house, but I really need *someone* to talk to ...

/ 010101 /

I stand in front of the mirror in one of the guest bathrooms with Miss Elaina's fluffy muffler in my hand. I've dimmed the single sconce above me so it illuminates my reflection and casts long shadows over the mirror's ornate frame. I lift the muffler and hold it over my chin, making it look like the person in the mirror is not me but instead someone with a furry brown beard.

"Good evening, reflection, sir," I greet him politely. "I hope I'm not bothering you this late at night."

"Hello, Eke," my reflection answers. "Not at all. I am happy to see you, as always. Tell me what is on your mind."

I smile, relieved. "Thank you so much, sir. I'm happy to see you too." But my smile fades as I gather my anxious thoughts before telling the mirror about what has happened. "A new AI came to the house today. His name is Kyp. He's going to be Miss Elaina's assistant."

To my surprise, my reflection beams at the news. "Oh, is that not wonderful, Eke? You have always wished for a friend. This could be a great opportunity."

My eyes widen. I haven't thought of it that way. "Of course, reflection, sir," I say, processing the revelation. "It *is* wonderful. It's just that nobody informed me of his arrival, so now I find myself wondering if they're going to retire me. You know how they always say I'm slow and will probably break soon . . ." I bite my lip. Somehow repeating the family's words out loud feels even sadder than replaying them inside my head.

"Well, do *you* think you're broken, Eke?" my reflection asks, his bearded face serious.

I take a moment to consider. "I don't know, sir. I don't really know what it means to be broken," I confess honestly.

If only I had someone to ask, but Mr. Kensworth restricted my wireless access such that I can only download firmware updates. He said he didn't want to compromise our network. *Too many criminals out there want a piece of our life. Can't allow them to hack into our security systems.* He also forbade me to leave the house, so I can't communicate with anyone outside.

"Well, why not try asking Kyp, then?" my reflection offers. "He might know something about the subject."

My eyes light up. That's a good idea! His diagnostic tools might be more advanced than mine. Not to mention that this could be a good conversation starter. I bow to the mirror, grateful and suddenly excited. "Thank you so much for your kind advice, reflection, sir."

"You are always welcome, Eke," my reflection says softly.

I sneak back to my closet, feeling much better.

Who knows—maybe my reflection is right. Maybe there's a

chance I could be *friends* with Kyp. Then it'll probably be okay to ask him about all kinds of things, not just system maintenance.

The only thing is, Kyp and I haven't officially *met*. Kyp hasn't said a word to me, just glanced at me once before exiting the foyer, and he didn't make eye contact with me again all evening.

Perhaps he was just busy. Kyp's new; he needs to make a good impression. Although a part of me wonders if maybe he doesn't like me. Maybe he also thinks I'm slow and not as beautiful as he is—I don't know. I push the negative thoughts aside and replay the memory of the way Kyp's eyes looked when they locked with mine. I save it to my core memory and mark it as very important. I've never seen an AI with green eyes before.

3

PROBABLY FRENCH

Eke

Monday morning begins early. I sneak my flowers back to the third floor and catch my three and a half minutes of sunshine in the garden before Mr. Kensworth takes his coffee and leaves for MIT. The delivery drone drops off the Fresh Box as scheduled, and I prepare breakfast, setting the dishes in a semicircle and arranging the fruit on the center plate in rainbow order. I enjoy my composition for exactly two minutes and thirty-eight seconds before Dani and Carson arrive in their royal-blue school uniforms, and the semicircle quickly turns into something more like a jagged polygon.

Miss Elaina floats in uncharacteristically late with her natural blond hair in a loose bun. She's still wearing her blush-pink nightgown with a silk robe, and Kyp follows close behind her.

"Children," she announces, "Kyp will take you to school today."

Dani's fork stops over a piece of strawberry. Carson pauses

with a muffin stuffed halfway into his mouth. I too gape at Kyp in amazement. It's only his second day with the family, but he's already allowed to go outside!

"Why?" Carson asks.

"Well, I'm simply swamped with the Labor Day ball preparations," Miss Elaina laments. "Luckily," she adds, and the corner of her mouth curves up as she caresses Kyp's forearm softly, "Kyp here is very capable. He'll drive you. Make sure he gets *noticed* when he drops you off, will you?"

"That's pretty much guaranteed if he shows up wearing that." Carson scoffs at Kyp's fancy tuxedo and takes a sip of coffee from one of his father's MIT mugs.

Dani huffs out a laugh. "Wow. Are you jealous or something?"

Carson nearly spits out his coffee. He glares at her, but Miss Elaina's amused chuckle interrupts him before he can come up with a retort.

"Oh, honey, sorry you are no longer the only pretty boy in the house," she purrs. "No need to be jealous, though. I'll buy Kyp some less flashy clothes later."

"I'm *not* jealous," Carson pushes out through gritted teeth, ignoring Dani's smirk. "He can wear a muumuu for all I care. Just, weren't you going to unveil him at the ball? Why send him out today?"

"Because it doesn't hurt to build up a little anticipation, does it?" Miss Elaina winks. "By the way, where's your little sister?"

Carson shrugs. "Haven't seen her yet."

Miss Elaina sighs and turns to Kyp, who's been standing at attention by her chair and politely ignoring the conversation about his looks. "Kyp, my darling, will you check on Lizzie for us? We wouldn't want to be late for your first public outing."

"It would be my pleasure," Kyp says in that charming manner of his, and exits the room.

He returns about a minute later with a very upset and not at all school-ready Lizzie by his side.

"Has anybody seen Jasper?" she asks, on the verge of tears. "I can't find him anywhere."

Nobody responds.

Worry flashes across Miss Elaina's face, but she quickly fixes her expression. "Are you sure he's not in your room, honey? Have you searched *everywhere*?" she asks, sounding light and not in the least concerned.

"Yes," Lizzie murmurs, looking down. She bites her lower lip, trying to stop it from trembling.

"Even under the bed?"

"Yes, Mommy."

"And in your closet?"

"Yes."

"Well, he's probably just playing hide-and-seek!" Miss Elaina concludes airily. "Don't puppies just *looove* to play hide-and-seek?"

Lizzie furrows her eyebrows, but before she can dwell too much, Miss Elaina adds, "I'm sure he'll get tired of playing and come out by the time you're back this afternoon."

Lizzie stares at her dubiously. "Do you really think so, Mommy?"

"Of course I do." Miss Elaina nods and arranges her lips into a sweet smile. "I promise he'll be right here when you get home. Just go get ready, darling."

"Okay, Mommy." Lizzie finally gives in, wipes the wet corners of her eyes with the back of her hand, and heads upstairs.

Miss Elaina gestures for Kyp to follow her for good measure. After Lizzie is out of sight, she cusses under her breath. "Of all the times this could've happened, it just had to be the same week as my ball. I knew I shouldn't have gotten her that damn dog."

I watch Miss Elaina throw her hands up in the air in frustration as I wonder what could've happened to Jasper. He and Lizzie have been inseparable since the day Miss Elaina brought him home. Lizzie carries him around everywhere, even sleeps with him in her bed, much to Miss Elaina's disgust. How could he possibly go missing?

After the siblings leave for school, Miss Elaina orders me to look for Jasper. I scour every corner of the mansion but don't find any trace of the puppy.

Distracted by the search mission, I miss my opportunity to talk to Kyp when he returns. By the time I notice that Miss Elaina's shiny red car is back in the driveway, her office door is locked. Curiously, I press my ear to it, wondering what Miss Elaina and Kyp are doing in there. But all I can hear through the keyhole is Miss Elaina's coquettish laughter and Kyp speaking playfully in some other language. I'm not sure which one, but I guess it's probably French.

4
NOT KIND

Eke

Jasper is still nowhere to be found when Lizzie comes home from ballet. From my spot in the corner of the foyer, I watch her face turn red and her big blue eyes well up with tears.

"Maybe," Miss Elaina says, trying to mitigate the damage, "we should just wait a little longer, huh? Maybe Jasper is still playing! Puppies are stubborn animals."

However, this time the white lie doesn't work. Lizzie's sobs quickly grow into wails as Miss Elaina ushers her to the big armchair by the fireplace and desperately tries to console her.

Eventually Carson descends the stairs wearing his workout gear and carrying a black trash bag. "Hey, what's up, Little Liz?" he says when he sees Lizzie's hunched-up figure.

Lizzie rubs her tear-streaked cheeks with her tiny hands. "Jasper is still missing."

Carson shakes his head and motions for Miss Elaina to give him her spot in the armchair. She seems quite relieved to do so.

"Don't worry, I'm sure he'll turn up soon," Carson says, putting his free arm around Lizzie's shoulders.

"I d-don't think s-so," Lizzie stutters between sobs. "He's been gone since last night."

"Hmm," Carson says. "Well, if he escaped from the house, he can't have gone very far. He's probably playing in the neighbor's yard."

That gives Lizzie a glimmer of hope. "You think so?"

"Of course!" Carson squeezes her shoulder. "Tell you what —I'll help you make missing signs after I get back from my jog. We'll plaster the *whooole* neighborhood until we find Jasper, okay?"

Lizzie nods. "Okay. I'll look for a picture to put on the signs."

"That's a good girl!" Carson smiles widely, stands up, and ruffles her hair. "I'll see you when I'm back."

"See you soon," Lizzie says, and pulls up Jasper's photo stream on her phone.

"Oh, thank god," Miss Elaina says in a low voice as she follows Carson to the front door. "That puppy better turn up before she starts crying again."

Carson drops his black bag on the tile floor and puts his sneakers on. "I sure hope it does."

"Where are you off to?" Miss Elaina asks, eyeing Carson's workout clothes.

"Gonna run some laps. Do you think you and Dad can come to our opening game next Saturday?"

"Oh." Miss Elaina blinks, caught off guard. "Sure, honey. I can probably make it. Don't know about your father, though; you know how much he works these days," she adds apologetically.

"I do," Carson murmurs, tying his shoelaces. "Just hoped

you guys could make it to my first game, since it's on a weekend and all."

"I'll definitely tell him that. In fact"—Miss Elaina looks over her shoulder—"Kyp, my dear, would you make a note in Brighton's schedule?"

"Most certainly. I'll make a high-priority note," he says, opening Mr. Kensworth's calendar. "Please forgive me, Miss Elaina, but I don't have access to Carson's complete schedule yet—which game would that be?"

"Ridley High baseball," Miss Elaina says proudly.

Carson clears his throat. "It's basketball, actually. The game starts at eleven."

Miss Elaina looks confused. "But I thought you were on the baseball team, honey. What happened? You were doing so well!"

Carson shrugs. "I switched to basketball last year. Just wanted to try something different. I've told you that before."

"Oh, that's so great, love," Miss Elaina replies with a tone oozing approval. "I'm so happy you're exploring. As I always say, you're only young once, so enjoy everything life has to offer!" She laughs and flicks a loose strand of her copper-colored wig out of her face.

"Basketball game it is," Kyp says. "I am adding the note to Mr. Kensworth's calendar now."

"Thank you, Kyp," Miss Elaina says.

Carson picks up the trash bag and raises his voice, directing it toward the corner where I'm still waiting quietly in case anyone has chores for me. "Well, I better get going. Gotta take this trash out because stupid Eke forgot again."

At the mention of my name, my body goes rigid.

Miss Elaina frowns. "Really?"

"I'm telling you, Mom, that tinhead's been so slow and forgetful," he says, looking annoyed and swinging the bag. "If

I didn't take this out myself, it would stink up my entire room."

Miss Elaina shakes her head in disapproval. "That's no good. He really *is* on his way out, isn't he? I guess that's what we get for buying a used unit."

Carson throws a sharp glance in my direction. "They were getting rid of him, and you bought him. That's embarrassing, Mom."

"I know, I know," Miss Elaina sighs. "But your father can be difficult about buying new technology, what with all the security risks involved. I swear MIT has made him way too paranoid to enjoy life. But"—her mouth once again stretches into a delighted smile—"I still have some sway, it seems. I don't even know how we'd manage without Kyp. Especially if Eke breaks before our big party. Can you imagine? Anyway, off you go, honey! No need to listen to me complain. I'm looking forward to your game."

"Thanks, Mom." Carson smiles as Miss Elaina blows him a kiss and closes the door behind him.

And for the second time since Kyp's arrival, I catch him glancing at me.

But this time his eyebrows furrow, and the look on his face is not kind.

/010101/

It isn't true, I silently protest as I scrub the kitchen counters. I cleaned Carson's room just yesterday, though I wasn't in there for very long—I don't like staying in Carson's room longer than necessary. But I would've noticed the trash bin overflowing. I'm *not* forgetful. I am not failing at my duties!

And now Kyp thinks badly of me too. Way to make an impression before we've even said a word to each other.

Oh, well. I examine the pristine white surface of the counter and give it a few more sprays of polish, just to be sure the marble is as spotless as can be.

5

A PLACE WHERE DREAMS COME TRUE

Eke

Everyone disappears into their bedrooms after an evening spent making missing signs for Jasper. Kyp too obediently retires to his closet. I contemplate whether I should knock on his door and attempt to introduce myself, but the memory of his disapproving eyes earlier gives me pause.

"Do you think he dislikes me?" I ask the crocuses, my knees drawn up, my little finger tracing tiny circles on my charging pad. "He hasn't said anything mean to me. So maybe that's a sign that things are going well between us? I really hope so. It'd be so nice to have a friend, to have someone to talk to, you know?" I wait for a moment, but the flowers don't reply.

My shoulders sag a little, and I put my forehead on my knees. Well, if I'm completely honest with them, it's not that Kyp hasn't said anything mean to me. He hasn't spoken to me at all. I still don't know what he thinks of me or what his intentions are.

I sigh and lift my chin.

"Sorry," I whisper to the flowers. "I'm probably keeping you awake with my troubles. I'll be quiet now."

I pet their stems gently and then turn my attention to the back wall.

To anyone who might enter my closet, it looks like a regular assembly of mops and cleaning supplies, but hidden behind those items are my precious treasures that I've collected over the years. I carefully move the rags out of the way and pick up my first treasure—the California magnet. Other than my makeshift stars, it was the first thing I took without permission. Miss Elaina threw it away when she replaced the kitchen fridge. The new fridge was bigger and fancier, but it had aluminum doors that couldn't hold the old souvenir magnets the family had brought from various places they'd visited before Mr. Kensworth got promoted and became too busy for vacations. But I wasn't about to let that magnet go. It has always been my favorite. It's a photograph of a beautiful sandy beach on the Pacific with words printed in glittery cursive: *California —a place where dreams come true.*

Looking at it never fails to make me smile. It's nice to know there's a place in the world where dreams could come true, even for someone like me. Where I could be anything, do anything, just because I'm there in that special glittery place. If only I were allowed to leave this house and someday see the ocean for myself . . .

I place the magnet back in its secret spot and uncover some more treasures: a round black hat, a forest-green tie, a pair of suspenders, and a velvet blazer.

I glance at my door, then look longingly back at my treasured outfit. Kyp's door may be closed, but I'd like to be a little more certain he's in for the night before I risk leaving my closet wearing it. If the family catches me dressed up, they'll immediately deactivate me. After all, I also took these items without permission.

I was careful, of course. I acquired them over time so as to not raise suspicion: the tie from Carson's middle school uniform; the blazer and suspenders from Mr. Kensworth; and the hat from Dani's old Halloween costume. The family won't miss these things, as they too were destined for the dumpster, but I still broke the rules by taking them for myself. If Kyp were to stumble upon me wearing them, he might tell Miss Elaina, and I can't risk that. I let these treasures stay hidden for now.

Which leaves me with my last treasure: books. Unlike my other treasures, these change every few days. Whenever I'm done reading one book, I secretly borrow another from the shelves in the family library.

Reading was strange at first and took some getting used to because printed books are very time-consuming. Even though my reading speed is faster than that of a human, scanning individual words still feels extremely slow compared to downloading data. But books are the only form of entertainment I can safely sneak into my closet, and it's not like I'm short on time, so I have learned to enjoy them. Instead of going out into the living room in my treasured outfit, I spend the remaining hours of the night with *Cinderella*, an old fairy tale that caught my attention with its beautiful black spine with golden lettering.

6

CAUGHT

Eke

I get through approximately 73.14 percent of the story before my OS reminds me to start my morning duties.

I make the coffee for Mr. Kensworth, arrange the breakfast foods into a triquetra, and watch the shape get destroyed as usual by the Kensworth siblings as they chew and argue about which songs Kyp should play while driving them to school.

Since I don't have any special chores today, it might be a perfect opportunity to introduce myself to Kyp.

But that proves easier said than done.

He returns home while I'm busy dusting three dozen dainty makeup jars on Dani's vanity. I try to get his attention, but he marches right past me to Miss Elaina's office. She locks the door again, and it stays locked until early afternoon, by which point I've moved on to sweeping out the fireplace in the second-floor grand hall. Miss Elaina loves the comfort of a crackling fire on chilly late summer nights, and it's become one of my regular chores to clean the soot and ashes out of the mansion's seven fireplaces.

As I'm kneeling in front of the mantel with a bronze brush and a shovel in my hands, the office door finally opens. Miss Elaina steps out, pulling down the hem of her tight red dress. She smiles and purrs a song under her breath as she struts to her bedroom while Kyp heads in the direction of the back staircase. This is my chance to catch him alone. Hastily I hang the brush back on the tool stand, empty the shovel into the trash bag, and dash after him. But by the time I reach the first floor, Kyp has disappeared.

Perplexed and disappointed yet again, I shuffle back to the half-cleaned fireplace. I almost give up on talking to him altogether, but later that day a lucky opportunity presents itself.

I'm on my way to the laundry room with an overflowing basket of dirty clothes when someone unexpectedly opens the door to the basement and I nearly walk right into them.

"I'm so very sorry!" I say before I even notice who it is. I don't want the family to think I'm so broken that I can't manage a simple chore without causing some disaster. But I freeze when I see Kyp's face.

His mouth opens, and his wide green eyes dart to the side as though panicked, but he quickly schools his expression. His chin lifts, and he straightens his shoulders. "Can you step aside?" he not so much asks as orders me.

I'm taken aback by the coldness in his voice. Kyp sounds so much more approachable when he's with humans.

"Um, yes, of course." I clumsily try to maneuver myself out of the way, but the space is too narrow for Kyp to pass with my giant basket of laundry between us.

Kyp clears his throat, growing impatient.

"Sorry," I mutter, and walk backward. What was Kyp even doing in the basement, and why is he in such a rush to leave?

His chores don't include laundry, and other than the wine cellar, the panic room, and our network servers, nothing of importance is down there.

Kyp watches me closely. "Thanks," he says brusquely, then marches past me the instant there's an opening. As his shoulder brushes mine, it dawns on me that I'm about to miss another chance to talk to him.

"Wait!" I blurt before I can think things through.

Kyp stops. "What . . . is it?" he asks slowly, but he doesn't turn to face me. His shoulders are tense again.

"I, um . . ." I shuffle nervously, confronted by Kyp's broad back and his lack of eye contact. I really should have rehearsed something to say. The truth is, I'm not a great conversation starter. It's not a part of my programming, and I've had little practice.

"I—I wanted to meet you," I finally say, and it comes out rushed and much louder than I intend.

Kyp turns around. "Seriously?"

I clutch the laundry basket tighter. "Well . . . yes?"

Kyp's eyebrow quirks up, and he looks like he's about to laugh. "We live in the same house. We've clearly met," he says, like it's the most obvious thing in the world, and if the artificial skin on my face were capable of blushing, it certainly would.

I bite my lip. This is not going according to plan. I was hoping that we could *really* meet, say our *nice to meet you*s and *nice to meet you too*s and whatever else one usually does to get acquainted. How can I explain this to Kyp?

"Look," Kyp says curtly. There's a hint of pride and purpose in his voice. "I am quite busy. Miss Elaina is waiting for me. We're going to lunch and then shopping downtown to get new outfits for me. I really must hurry."

"Oh," I say, surprised, looking at Kyp's shiny suit with the golden crown pin and then at my own simple shirt and trousers.

Going out with Miss Elaina—that must be a very special chore reserved only for Kyp.

"I wouldn't want to make her wait," Kyp says firmly, and his cold gaze shifts from my eyes to my right cheek. It pauses there for a moment. "There's dirt on your face, by the way," he adds dismissively before he turns the corner and disappears from view.

"See you around," I whisper as I lift my hand and touch my cheek. Soot from the fireplace smudges my fingertips.

7
GUILTY PLEASURE

Eke

\<Eke's Memory Log\> /begin entry/
The conversation with Kyp was a complete failure.
He does not like me. Not one bit.
\<Eke's Memory Log\> /end/

I save the file and let my shoulders slump.
    I keep thinking about it all day, hoping that I've misinterpreted what Kyp said, but even when he returns home carrying a dozen bags from Boston's luxury boutiques with Miss Elaina by his side, he continues to ignore me. And later when there is a disturbance in the neighborhood and we all have to hide in the cramped panic room, he still won't make eye contact with me.

    Why did I assume that just because we're both AIs, we're going to be friends?

    "I guess Kyp is *different*, after all," I tell my flowers.

"More . . ." *Human*, I want to say, but the word gets stuck in my mouth.

Of course Kyp would rather be around humans than someone like me. And the family likes him more than they have ever liked me. The Kensworths have never invited me to lunch or brought me along on shopping trips; they haven't asked me to accompany the siblings to school. I have only a few memories of what the outside world even looks like.

If only I were part of the Royal Line. If I could speak French or play music like Kyp, maybe they would like me more. Maybe Kyp would like me. But I'm not programmed to play music. I don't even understand why humans like it. Dejectedly I make a memo.

<file under: tasks> Starting tomorrow, try to understand music. **<set reminder/ priority: high>**

I can't update my programming without breaking the wireless protocols set by Mr. Kensworth, but at least I can try to improve parts of myself.

I sigh and check my internal clock—it's still early. Hesitantly I nudge the closet door open and peer into the dim hallway. Kyp may not like me, but he obediently adheres to our curfew and won't catch me doing what I'm about to do.

8

THE GREAT STONE FACE

Eke

The living room is quiet and dark. The light from the night lamp in the foyer doesn't reach it, so I sneak in, engulfed by shadows, making no sound other than a single muted click of the remote. The room illuminates with a bluish glow. I smile—the TV is on.

I type in my usual channel—Silent Cinema Classics—and scroll through the list of featured titles. Which ones have I not seen recently? *Sherlock Jr.? The Navigator?* Or maybe *The Haunted House?* That one would be so good for inspiration! I click play and watch the black-and-white title card appear on the screen:

Starring Buster Keaton

My face lights up with joy, and I have to suppress the sudden irresistible urge to clap. I admire Buster Keaton more than anyone!

The first time I saw him was on the info screen in the medical center I used to clean. I nearly dropped my broom in amazement. Buster was doing a series of stunts where he almost got run over by a train, crushed by a crumbling house, and eaten by an alligator. The footage from his movies was being used for a life insurance commercial, but I wasn't interested in the ad. All I wanted to know was who this amazing person in a round hat was and how on earth he did all those unbelievable stunts. So I made it my mission to watch and study every Buster Keaton movie.

It has not been easy to find the time to sneak out and use the TV, procure items for my Buster Keaton costume, and practice his stunts in the dark without making a sound. I once came so close to smashing an entire set of expensive champagne glasses. Oh, I would've been deactivated right then and there had I not caught the glasses just before they hit the floor. But I felt so proud when the stunt worked—I would risk it all over again!

My greatest wish is to try all of Buster Keaton's riveting stunts. If only I had a car that would fall apart as I jump into it at full speed, or a train I could ride to escape from a mob, or a set of special stairs that would go flat under my feet and turn into a slide. I've done a couple of routines on the grand staircase, but it was just too risky considering its proximity to the bedrooms. One mistake and I would've been exposed. So I've mostly kept to the living room, performing before my loyal audience of the three goldfish in the aquarium.

Miss Elaina bought them for Lizzie last year when she first started asking for a puppy. Miss Elaina wasn't too keen on puppies and hoped that getting a different kind of pet, one that wouldn't pee on her rugs or chew on her precious furniture, would do the trick. But Lizzie did not accept the substitute. She wanted a puppy and cried for three days straight until Miss

Elaina gave in. After that, she moved the nonrefundable expensive tank and its exotic goldfish to the living room as a decorative accent.

I couldn't have been happier about that turn of events. I'd never seen fish before, but on that fateful day I gained three new friends—friends I could proudly show my Buster Keaton stunts to. Of course, the fish always watch me silently and never applaud my performances, but that's been just perfect in my circumstances.

I named them Toon, Squawker, and Felt and have been secretly feeding them whenever the siblings forget, which is more often than not these days. My dream is to have the feeding added to my official list of chores, but I need Mr. Kensworth's authorization for that, and I just haven't had the right opportunity to bring it up with him. Mr. Kensworth is so difficult to catch at home; I always feel like I'm interrupting his extremely important research. But someday I'll speak up. I want to be the one to take care of my friends.

As the *Haunted House* end credits roll, I rise from the couch. Fully inspired by Buster's gravity-defying performance, I tiptoe to the dining room to fetch three chairs. I line them up in the middle of the rug like they're a bench in a park. Nervously I adjust my tie before I turn around and bow to Toon, Squawker, and Felt. The show is about to begin ...

I sit on the park bench, enjoying the view. The trees are swaying, and the sun is warm.

Oh, what a wonderful spring day!

I prop my chin on my hand, listening to the birds chirp. After a few heavenly moments, my eyelids get heavy. I blink, trying to stay awake, but the weather is so nice. In just a few seconds, I succumb to slumber.

Flop! My hat falls to the ground. I wake up.

Oh no!
My favorite hat is covered in dust. That just won't do!

I frown in disapproval. I have a date later today. What kind of impression will I make?

I collect the hat and brush it off. But the dust stubbornly clings to it. I shake the hat—it doesn't come off. I toss it up—still doesn't come off. Once, twice, over my head. *Whoosh!* Up onto the antique chandelier it goes.

Ah!

My eyes widen, and my hands cover my mouth. How am I going to get it now? My precious, precious hat!

I stand on a chair and reach for it, but the ceiling is too high. I scrunch my forehead in deep thought.

Aha! I've got an idea!
A genius one.

I grab the second chair and stack it on top of the first one topsy-turvy. Then I climb up and reach for the hat again. The two inches of height that maneuver has added is definitely not enough. I sigh dramatically.

But I'm not done yet, or I wouldn't be Buster. I jump down and narrow my eyes at the third chair.

I place it atop the growing chair tower, balancing it in a Y shape between the second chair's legs, and start to climb, careful not to lean too much to either side as not to unbalance the structure.

The wooden chairs creak and wobble under me. Catastrophe seems imminent, but I'm unstoppable. My fingertips brush the brim of my hat—

Ta-da!

I grab it, victorious. But oh no! The weight of the hat has unbalanced my chair tower. It teeters, tilts left, and down I go.

I land on the rug and roll to the side, miraculously catching the top chair before it can crash and wake up the family. Like an oversize piece of confetti, the hat twirls in the air and gracefully lands on the ground two feet away from me.

Phew! I round my lips in a silent whistle, wipe the imaginary sweat from my forehead, and stand up, returning my hat to its rightful spot on my head. The fish watch me from their tank.

"Why, thank you, thank you, my dear friends. You're far too kind," I whisper to them, and bow deeply. "I will work on perfecting this one. Thank you for your continued patronage."

I bow a few more times for good measure, thus signifying the end of the performance.

Afterward, I quickly collect the three chairs and carry them back to the dining room.

The moment the goldfish are out of sight, my shoulders drop. I messed up the hat part so much! Luckily for me, my audience didn't notice or was too polite to say anything, but I was supposed to *catch* the hat right after I caught the chair, not let it fall!

I shake my head, unable to hide my crushing disappointment. I didn't manage my momentum well and had to use my free hand to stop myself from rolling off the rug. The chair fell awkwardly too, and I nearly missed it. I'll have to do better next time!

If only I could make a little noise, it would be so much

easier. Buster Keaton probably made a racket filming his stunts. How can you silently blow up a house? Although the decibels didn't matter back then, because Buster wasn't someone's AI and humans didn't make films with sound until 1927. But that's no excuse for me. Just because I can't make noise doesn't mean I can botch a stunt and be content with it. I need to practice that landing, but it will have to wait for now.

A warning beeps in my head:

<battery charge: 10% remaining>

I sigh and shuffle back to the living room to steal one last look at Buster Keaton's stoic face. If I'm not fully charged by morning, I'll end up freezing in the middle of my chores, and what will everyone say then? So I turn the TV off, whisper good night to Toon, Felt, and Squawker, and head back to my closet for the short remainder of the night.

9

REPLACEABLE

Eke

Despite the lost dog signs that the siblings and Kyp put up around the neighborhood, nobody calls about Jasper the next day or the day after that.

Lizzie keeps checking the house messenger, only to have her face turn sadder each time she's greeted by an empty screen. By Thursday evening her morale plummets and she cries for three hours straight, much to Miss Elaina's discontent.

Later that night I accidentally overhear Miss Elaina ordering Kyp to pick up a replacement puppy before Lizzie comes home from school tomorrow.

"I just can't deal with this anymore," she moans in frustration. "As if I'm not busy enough with the upcoming ball. We need a new dog pronto."

Miss Elaina and Kyp are standing in the second-floor hallway mere feet away from me, but they don't notice me. I was trying to sneak my flowerpot back to my closet using the back stairs when I overheard them talking, and now I'm stuck on the landing, scared they might catch me.

I can't see Kyp's face from this angle, but his shoulders go stiff, and he doesn't respond right away, as though processing the request.

"Miss Elaina, are you certain the puppy will not be located?" he inquires politely. "According to statistical data, there's a good chance we'll find Jasper in the next forty-eight hours."

Miss Elaina shakes her head dismissively. "I've really had it with the crying. Haven't you seen her? She's inconsolable! Time to give her a new dog and be done with it."

Kyp flinches ever so slightly. "Yes, of course. As you wish, Miss Elaina," he says, but something about the tone of his voice is different from his usual pleasant and carefree manner. "What kind of dog would you like me to get instead?"

"Any kind." Miss Elaina shrugs, not giving it much thought. "Definitely potty-trained. Similar to the one she had, but not *too* similar. I can't have her bursting into tears again because the new dog reminds her of the old one."

"I understand," Kyp says.

"Good." Miss Elaina smiles. "You're so helpful and so *lovely* to have around," she murmurs, and tucks a loose strand of her platinum-blond wig behind her ear.

"It is my pleasure to assist you." Kyp bows slightly.

"That it is," Miss Elaina says. She puts her hand on top of Kyp's head and runs her fingers through his hair. Her wrist flicks playfully, and the golden bracelet on it glints in the light of the hallway sconces. Kyp just stands there in his new sky-blue dress shirt and fancy trousers and doesn't move away.

"Do you have any other requests for me?" he finally asks, and Miss Elaina's hand slides down his cheek and off his shoulder.

"Nope." She shakes her head dreamily. "Not at present.

We'll talk about what needs to be done for the ball tomorrow. Just get the dog and bring it here before you pick Lizzie up from school."

"I will do that," Kyp confirms.

"That's a good boy," Miss Elaina says, not taking her eyes off Kyp. "Off you go, now. Dismissed for tonight."

"Thank you," Kyp says, but he remains in his spot. Only once Miss Elaina walks away and the door of her bedroom clicks shut does he snap out of his daze, and his shoulders finally relax.

The moment he begins to turn around, my eyes go wide, and I scramble to duck behind the wall. I swear I didn't mean to eavesdrop—I just didn't want to get noticed with the flowers! But as the conversation went on, I got distracted. I should've left minutes ago.

Luckily, Kyp doesn't spot me. He rounds the corner and heads toward the grand staircase.

I lean against the wall in relief. Why was Miss Elaina talking to Kyp like that? I replay the image of her hands and the way they touched Kyp, the way Kyp stood there and accepted it like it wasn't unusual. I don't know what those gestures mean or why seeing them makes me feel like this. Like a strange, unfamiliar weight is tugging at my core, a heaviness that tells me something isn't right.

I stare at the pot in my hands, confused and troubled, but order myself to hurry back to my closet before someone else stumbles upon me.

10

NOT INVITED

Eke

My Friday morning is exceptionally busy. While the siblings are having breakfast, Miss Elaina summons both Kyp and me and gives us a rundown of chores for the big ball tomorrow. She organizes it every year and always invites the entire neighborhood, her wealthy friends from the Boston Art Circle, and Mr. Kensworth's MIT colleagues. This year the party seems to have gotten even bigger. We're expecting more than four hundred guests.

As usual, my list of tasks is long enough that it'll take me all day and night with barely any time to recharge. After all, I'm responsible for scrubbing every inch of the mansion. Not a speck of dust is permitted, not a single thing out of place. I'm also supposed to haul the party furniture from the basement to the patio and garden. At least that means I will get to spend a little time outside, so I'm not complaining.

The list Miss Elaina gives Kyp is significantly shorter.

None of it involves heavy lifting or helping me—just a trip to the pet store and handling any last-minute issues with the food and wine vendors.

But it's not the lack of chores that makes me stare at Kyp with awe and envy. It's the special task Miss Elaina assigns him on the day of the ball.

"Kyp, I want *you* on greeting duty by the front door, where you'll make the biggest impression on the unsuspecting guests," she says with a smug grin.

Kyp doesn't seem at all surprised by this privilege. He smiles his trademark smile and bows. "Most certainly, Miss Elaina."

"I'll also give you the names of the guests you'll personally escort to me in the garden," Miss Elaina adds. "Just the most exceptional, most deserving of our friends. And once everyone has arrived, you can show off all your entertaining features."

"That will be my utmost pleasure, Miss Elaina," Kyp says, ready to shine.

I continue to gape at him. Of course Miss Elaina bought Kyp specifically for entertainment, but I didn't realize he'd be attending the ball alongside the humans.

In the five years I've spent in this house, never once has the family invited me to join the festivities. Even when Miss Elaina ordered me to go outside, it was not to mingle. I was supposed to stay invisible and not attract the guests' attention as I collected empty glasses and dirty plates scattered around the property. No matter how much I wished to remain outside, even just to quietly look at the stars in the sky, I was never permitted.

"Obviously make sure to change back into your Crowne attire. It is most appropriate for the occasion," Miss Elaina adds joyfully, as though already envisioning how stunning Kyp will look chatting up impressionable guests. "Now, if neither of you has questions, go execute. Kids, finish up—Kyp is ready to drive you to school. I need him back here as soon as possible."

Dani lets out a quiet groan, but all three hurry to finish their breakfasts and grab their backpacks.

Kyp bows again and steps aside to wait for the siblings, but I don't move.

Miss Elaina notices me idling and looks at me expectantly. "I said execute," she repeats, as though I haven't heard her command.

Carson flashes a taunting smirk at me. "Did the dummy freeze again?"

Getting more nervous by the second, I shuffle in place, unsure how to proceed with what I'm about to ask.

As if convinced I'm malfunctioning, Miss Elaina sighs deeply. "I swear, this isn't the time for that—"

Panicking, I rush to explain myself. "I've . . . I have a question, Miss Elaina!"

Everyone's gazes snap to me. Even Kyp gives me a sideways glance.

"Well, what is it?" Miss Elaina asks, her patience clearly running low.

I bite my bottom lip anxiously. The truth is, I've never actually asked whether I could join the ball before, but if Kyp can, then why can't I? Of course Kyp is shiny and new and capable. But maybe I could be useful too? If Miss Elaina gives me a chance, I'll do anything to prove myself.

"M-may I also go?" I finally manage to say.

"Go where?" Miss Elaina asks in a flat tone.

"Um, to the ball," I murmur, a small spark of hope lighting in my core.

Miss Elaina bursts out laughing. Carson does too. Even

Dani chuckles. Only Lizzie doesn't laugh; she's too small to attend adult parties and is still upset about Jasper. And I don't even dare to glimpse Kyp's face. Mortified and humiliated, I drop my gaze to the floor.

"And why would you possibly do that?" Miss Elaina asks, like I've made the most nonsensical request.

I press my trembling lips together. How am I supposed to answer that? *Because I'd like to go? Because, just like everyone, I want to be a part of it?*

But before I can open my mouth to explain that I could be useful, that I could earn my way outside, Miss Elaina waves her hand dismissively. "No. Obviously you can't go. This is a black-tie event. What would our esteemed guests think of us if they saw *you*? They need to see our house at its finest." She reaches out and pats Kyp on his forearm. "Kyp is plenty. You stay inside and don't show your face."

I can still hear her laughing even after the siblings follow Kyp to the car and leave me in the dining room in complete and utter defeat.

/010101/

I throw myself into my chores and spend the rest of the morning trying to forget about the embarrassment of being denied even though the family has welcomed Kyp with open arms. Are the two of us truly that different? I try to push that notion away, but it only gets more persistent once it's time for Kyp to go to the pet store. What wouldn't I do for the privilege of meeting puppies. Maybe my goldfish friends came from the same place. I imagine a whole ocean of fishes . . . and puppies . . . all inside a store. *Wow!* Kyp is so lucky.

I sigh, sinking deeper into misery.

But I soon discover that Kyp doesn't seem to feel the way I do.

When the Kensworth siblings return from school, Miss Elaina invites everyone into the living room. There's a white plastic crate that Kyp brought from the pet store sitting in the middle of the rug. I watch the family from the covered porch, where I've been polishing the party glasses.

"What is this?" Lizzie asks when she notices the crate. The temperature in the room drops by double digits.

Miss Elaina's mouth twitches, but she covers it up with a quick smile. Dani grimaces and takes a step toward the stairs like she wants to flee the scene.

Carson is the one who steps forward. "It's . . . your new friend, Lizzie!" he declares with a grin, quickly glancing at Miss Elaina for confirmation. "He's very excited to meet you."

Miss Elaina clears her throat. "Yes, yes. Little Mr. Puppy here has been waiting for you, sweetie. Go meet him now, honey." She nudges Lizzie gently on the shoulder.

Lizzie stays rooted to the spot. "But what about Jasper? Is he not coming back?"

Everyone is silent except for Carson. "Oh, I meant to tell you, Little Liz. You won't believe it! I just heard from the neighbor today. You know Mr. Spencer three houses down?" Lizzie half nods, half shrugs, unsure, but Carson leaves her no chance to question his words. "He said one of our neighbors found Jasper and took him to live on a farm in Gloucester! Can you believe it?"

"On a farm?" Lizzie murmurs, confused.

"Yeah! It's an animal farm. He said they have cows and geese and I think like fifteen more puppies. Little Jasper is going to have a lot of friends and so much room to play. He'll be so happy!"

Lizzie looks down, eyes fixed on the big pink pom-poms adoring her tiny shoes. "Really?" she says, squeezing the hem of her floral skirt. "You think Jasper will be *happier* there?"

"Well, of course, honey," Miss Elaina chimes in. "Think of all the fields he'll get to explore! That's a dream come true for any puppy in the *world*." She leans closer so she can be at eye level with Lizzie. "But you know what? Even though Jasper lives on a farm now, he didn't want you to be lonely by yourself, so he sent his friend Mr. Puppy here to keep you company. So honey, please, go meet him. He's been patiently waiting for you."

Lizzie glances at the puppy crate, away from Miss Elaina's insistent eyes with eyelashes tinted sky blue to match her blouse.

Inside the crate, the puppy whimpers pitifully and tries to stick his little brown nose through the round holes in the plastic door. He's been locked up in there for at least an hour. It must be lonely.

Lizzie gives a tiny sniffle. "What is his name?"

Miss Elaina looks at Kyp, who has stayed quiet this whole time, keeping away from everyone in an unusual spot in the corner. Contrary to what I expected, Kyp doesn't seem proud of the special chore entrusted to him. Instead he looks pained and conflicted.

But being addressed by Lizzie jolts him out of his thoughts. "His name is . . . Rocket, I believe," he says slowly, still distracted, but then he smiles as though he has finally remembered that he's expected to be pleasant. I watch him curiously; he shouldn't have forgotten how to behave in the first place. "Would you like to meet him now?" Kyp says, and takes a few steps toward the crate.

Lizzie nods. Her blond pigtails bob slightly, and everyone in the room breathes a sigh of relief.

"All right." Kyp smiles a little wider then, more like his usual self, and bends down to let the puppy out of the carrier.

By early evening, Lizzie and Rocket are best friends.

11

LUCKY

Eke

Once Rocket is situated with Lizzie, I try to catch up on my chores, but I don't get very far. As I'm diligently dusting every hand-carved baluster in the grand staircase, Dani saunters down the stairs.

"Eke, I need you in my room," she says with a hand on her hip. A tight hairband holds her bangs out of her pale, gaunt face. I don't want to go, but by the tone of Dani's voice, I know I have no choice but to put down the duster and follow her. To be honest, I've been expecting this today.

Dani's room is spacious with lavender-colored wallpaper and an arched window that faces the back garden. There's a cozy reading nook built around it where Dani used to spend hours curled up with a book. Unlike Carson and Lizzie, Dani can't do sports or take dance lessons. She was born with a heart condition, and strenuous exercise isn't good for her. Instead she fell in love with reading at an early age. Most of the books in the living room actually belong to her. It used to be difficult to sneak them into my closet. Dani organized everything by jacket color and certainly would've noticed if anything went missing for more than a day.

But things changed two years ago. Dani stopped going downstairs to retrieve her favorite books around the same time she stopped eating breakfast. Since then, she has lost thirty pounds and now spends most of her time alone in her bedroom with the curtains drawn.

When I step into the room, heavy velvet drapes cover the window, but despite that the room is lit brightly by the dozen round bulbs of Dani's makeup table. The moment I see the assortment of cosmetics and brushes, my suspicions about what Dani has planned for me are confirmed.

"I should go," I protest, and take a tiny step back. "There's a lot to clean before the party tomorrow—"

"I know," Dani interrupts, her face unyielding, "but you have all night for that. And I need you *now*, Eke. Sit down."

I wish I had some urgent excuse or high-priority chore so I could leave. But Dani won't listen when she wants to do this kind of stuff. So I take the chair in front of the vanity.

Dani picks up a small glass jar and pops it open. "I have this new eyeliner that I want to practice applying before the ball. Sit still. It's super tricky to get the shape right."

I keep quiet and stare at the floor as Dani dips a thin narrow brush into the jar of liner.

"Chin up. Look straight ahead," she orders, hovering above me, and I'm finally forced to catch my reflection in the mirror.

I don't like looking at myself without a disguise, especially at my hairless head. That's why I always pick one day of the week to clean all the mirrors in the house at once. Sometimes when I can avoid seeing my plain reflection for long enough, I can almost forget about my appearance and imagine that I look *different*, more like a human boy with real hair. Someone who could fit in, someone cool—like Buster Keaton, maybe.

"Look up," Dani chides impatiently, and sticks her cold hand under my chin as her brush continues to make careful strokes along my eyelid. The sudden skin contact distracts me, and I have to stop myself from flinching.

I don't get touched often, and the sensation is jarring, as I am not used to it. The truth is, I can count every instance of skin contact in my life on just two hands. Half of them involved Dani and her makeup. The other half were . . . less gentle, and I would rather not think about them. But never once has Dani or anyone else touched me the way Miss Elaina touched Kyp last night in the hallway.

I don't know why I keep remembering that moment. The way she looked at Kyp, the way her fingers slid through his hair . . . Before I can stop myself, I wonder what it'd feel like to touch someone like that. Would it also feel cold? Would it be awkward or harsh or . . . soft? What would Kyp's beautiful hair feel like against my own fingertips if I could—

"Shit." Dani cusses under her breath and reaches for a makeup-removing tissue. "Hold still," she orders, then quickly erases a small smudge at the outer corner of my left eye where her hand slipped. "That's way better. Do you think this looks good?" she asks, and steps away to examine my reflection.

"I . . . wouldn't know," I say, trying not to stare at my eyes, which now appear twice their normal size because of the enormous amount of black eyeliner around them. It makes me look like a raccoon.

"I think it does," Dani says, then turns her gaze to her extensive collection of lip glosses. "Wes is coming tomorrow. I wonder if he'll notice . . ."

I stiffen at the mention of Carson's best friend but say nothing. Dani picks three different shades of lip gloss and holds them up against my face. After a short deliberation, she settles on a shimmery pink tube and squeezes some of its contents onto a brush.

"Will you tell me if you hear him say anything about me?" Dani brings the brush closer to my mouth.

"Of course, Dani," I confirm before she smears the gloss onto my lips. Although that probably won't happen, seeing as Miss Elaina has explicitly forbidden me from attending the ball. Not that I would willingly go anywhere near Wes and Carson anyway.

"Okay." Dani steps away to examine the results for a second time. "Yep, that looks good." She sounds pleased, but her fingers continue to squeeze the tiny brush nervously.

Once again I do not comment.

Dani lets out a long, tired sigh and puts the brush on the vanity. "I just wish your skin wasn't so perfect, like a doll's. I need to practice with concealer and powder, but there's no point with you. You have no idea how lucky you are that you don't have to worry about stupid pimples on your big day." She groans. I stare silently at the floor as Dani's words cut straight to my core. "Not like you can understand what it takes to make a boy notice you anyway . . ." Dani glances at the small crystal glass on her bedside table, half full of bluish liquid. It's her nail polish remover. A big bottle of it is peeking out from her bottom drawer. She bites her lip and reaches for the box of makeup-removing tissues. "Here. All done. Go clean up now." She hands me the box and commands her speaker to resume her playlist.

"Yes, Dani," I mutter quietly without looking up. Then I grab the box and hurry out of the room, away from the bright lights and Dani's careless assumptions.

12

A CONVINCING ARGUMENT

Eke

"What is the matter, Eke?" my reflection asks, its voice soft and kind. "Did something make you sad?"

I shake my head. My makeup-stained face stares at me from the guest bathroom mirror. I scrubbed and scrubbed it with tissues but only succeeded at smudging the cinder-colored eyeliner all over my skin as Dani's cruel words cycled through my mind. How can I even begin to explain to my mirror friend what happened today?

"It is okay, Eke. You can tell me everything," my reflection prompts gently.

I sigh and give in. "Miss Elaina invited Kyp to the ball today. Not only is he allowed to drive to school and go to the pet store, he's welcome to join the festivities. So I thought maybe I could attend too, but when I gathered the courage to ask, they laughed at me."

I crumple the makeup-smeared tissue. The full weight of disappointment lies heavy on my shoulders.

"Why so?" my mirror friend asks.

I shrug miserably. "Miss Elaina said the guests are expecting black ties and fancy dresses, and I don't look good the way I am."

"I see," my reflection says. "Well, why not try going anyway?"

My gaze snaps up. "But how? I was told I can't—"

"I know," the mirror says patiently, "because it is a black-tie event and you do not have proper attire. But she is wrong, Eke. You have a tie, as well as a jacket and a hat." My reflection winks at me.

My mouth opens in surprise. "But sir, they'll find out that I stole my Buster Keaton costume!"

My reflection only smiles. "They have long forgotten about those old things, Eke," it says. "Mrs. Kensworth buys a whole new wardrobe every season. I promise, it is all right."

I look down, considering. It's risky, but I can't deny the warm flicker of hope inside my core at the mirror's suggestion. Maybe it would be okay to sneak outside if I could blend in with the crowd? There'll be *a lot* of people, and Miss Elaina will be busy. Maybe I wouldn't get noticed? Maybe I could look at the stars, even for just a few minutes?

13

THE BALL

Eke

Guests start to arrive just after sunset, looking important and dressed to the nines—ladies in extravagant designer gowns and diamond jewelry and gentlemen in fancy suits and bow ties. I watch in secret as they move around the party. I've picked a secluded spot in the corner of the stone patio, away from the lights and obscured by the lush hydrangeas. No one will notice me here, and I can peek at the ball freely until I gather enough courage to come out into the open. I've even brought my flowerpot as my date.

The main bar is just a few feet away from me, and guests stop there to grab drinks before they make their way down the stone stairs and through the wooden pergola. There, under a canopy of blooming roses, are rows of white-clothed tables full of handmade French desserts, exotic fruits, and exquisite plates of hors d'oeuvres. Crystal chandeliers hang from tree branches, illuminating the display. The garden quickly fills with the sounds of music, clinking champagne glasses, and cheery laughter.

When I finally spot Kyp in the crowd, I can't believe my eyes. He is stunning. He has changed back into his shiny black suit with the golden crown pin and a black bow tie, but something else about him is different tonight. I watch, mesmerized, as the guests part like waves for him, ladies' heads turning, whispers following in his wake. And Kyp—he moves among them with such ease: a wink here, a wave of a hand there, a confident and playful smile for every set of eyes he catches. He doesn't just fit in among the humans. Somehow Kyp stands out, even surrounded by all this luxury and splendor, like he was *made* for this. No wonder Dani called him a prince. It's like he's come off the pages of one of her fairy tales.

"Hello, my dears! So glad you could make it!" Miss Elaina exclaims, taking another glass of wine and moving away from the bar to greet the pair of guests Kyp has just brought over to her. Blaire and Louise are Miss Elaina's longtime friends and fellow patrons of the Art Circle; they've been staples at all house gatherings organized by Miss Elaina as far back as I can remember.

"We couldn't possibly miss it!" Blaire says, and leans over to exchange three kisses on the cheek with Miss Elaina. "You look extraordinary, by the way," she adds, gazing appreciatively at Miss Elaina's beautiful white chiffon dress and the silk flowers in her hair—strawberry blond for the day. "More than usual, dare I say?" She smirks conspiratorially.

"Yes, yes," Louise chimes in, throwing a not-so-inconspicuous glance at Kyp and leaning in for kisses as well. "It seems like you have *a lot* of news to tell us, don't you, Lainey?"

Miss Elaina's mouth stretches into a satisfied smile. "Well, you ladies have already met Kyp. He's the newest addition to our household."

"That we have," Blaire says. "When did this happen? And why have you been hiding this"—she lets herself examine Kyp's figure from head to toe—"gorgeous gentleman from us?"

"I promise I didn't mean to keep him a secret." Miss Elaina waves her hand playfully. "We only just bought him last week, and I've simply been too busy to tell anyone, you know, what with the ball preparations and the start of the school year."

"Oh, I can only imagine how much work this must've been for you," Louise agrees emphatically, and flicks her hand with long, pearly fingernails that match her strapless sheath and heels. "But everything looks spectacular, my dear. I cannot wait to sample the hors d'oeuvres."

"Quite, thank you, love. It took so much effort to pick the right menu and settle on the wine list," Miss Elaina laments. "I hope to god it all turned out all right."

"If anyone can pull it off, it's you, my darling," Blaire quickly reassures her. "But all these mundane worries aside, tell us more about this fresh addition of yours. We are simply dying to know everything!"

Miss Elaina looks pleased with her friends' enthusiasm. She has been preparing for this all week. "Kyp has improved our lives so much! He's been *so very* helpful with my busy schedule when I'm just too overwhelmed by it all. And," she adds, gazing sideways as her cheeks redden, "Kyp is giving me French lessons every afternoon. You know how much I looove everything French."

Blaire chuckles. "Has he, now? Is that why it's been impossible to get you out of the house these past few days?"

Miss Elaina bats her eyelashes innocently, but Blaire isn't fooled.

"We dearly missed you at the gallery opening the other night," Louise says. "Everyone kept asking where you were. Their wine selection was spectacular."

"Gosh, I'm so very sorry. Tell everyone I promise that after this weekend, I'll try to get out more," Miss Elaina says.

"Mm-hmm," Blaire hums with a knowing smile. "How about you just offer us some drinks and we'll discuss your delinquencies later?"

"That's right! How rude of me!" Miss Elaina exclaims. "Kyp, my darling, would you make us drinks, please?"

Kyp, who's been standing at attention beside them this whole time, smiling politely at every mention of his name, nods. "Most certainly, Miss Elaina. What would you ladies like? I have more than two hundred recipes from the world's most renowned restaurants stored in my memory. I can make you anything your hearts desire—provided we have the ingredients at hand, of course."

"Oh wow," Louise utters, absolutely smitten by Kyp's radiant smile and old-fashioned delivery.

"Well, in that case"—Blaire tucks a loose strand of long dark hair behind her ear, exposing more of her pale neck and the cascades of diamonds around it—"how about something sweet and *strong*, if you don't mind? Bartender's choice."

"I might just have something in mind that fits that criteria." Kyp bows slightly. "And what can I make for you, Miss Louise?"

Louise's face flushes at being addressed that way. "I leave it up to you. Surprise me, Kyp."

"It'll be my pleasure." Kyp bows again and excuses himself.

"Oh my." Blaire exhales giddily once Kyp has taken a few steps away from them. "What *other* languages has that doll been teaching you, Lainey, darling?"

"Mmm." Miss Elaina takes a sip of her Chardonnay, not at all trying to hide her growing smile as the other two women giggle.

/010101/

Glowing with pride and purpose, Kyp makes his way past the cheerful line of guests awaiting their drinks and steps behind the bar just feet from me. The trio of human bartenders Miss Elaina flew in from France for the night show him where to find the required ingredients, which Kyp brings to the free space at the end of the counter.

I watch his swift fingers as he mixes the drinks and garnishes them with pieces of strawberries and peaches that he cuts into delicate flower shapes. And I'm not the only one watching. A crowd of spectators quickly gathers to admire Kyp's bartending skills like it's entertainment. He indulges them with charming smiles and particularly showy hand movements. He's almost done with his magnificent creations when he turns around to look for something on the cart behind him. That's when he suddenly stops.

My core stutters. Kyp's nonhuman eyesight is sharp enough to spot me even in the shadows of my secret nook. His green eyes widen, staring directly at me. Blocked by the branches of the hydrangea bushes, I have nowhere to run. Unsure whether to sink into the ground or beg for Kyp's silence, I desperately clutch the flowerpot as my back presses against the cold patio wall.

Slowly Kyp blinks and takes in my appearance—the hat on my head, the lines of my face, my tie. My core heats up, and I'm suddenly self-conscious. Even though my outfit is an improvement on my everyday uniform, it's nowhere near as stylish as Kyp's. At least there is no soot on my cheeks today. Although why am I thinking of that now? I should be more worried about getting caught, about Kyp telling Miss Elaina I'm here, than about him chiding me for having soot on my face. Is he going to report me? I don't know. I can't tell what he's thinking, what he's deciding.

Those green eyes watch me steadily for another excruciatingly long moment, and then Kyp's hand, frozen mid-motion, finally emerges from the cart's middle shelf holding a couple of colorful cocktail umbrellas. Kyp straightens and turns away as though nothing has happened. He puts the umbrellas on the rims of the glasses as a finishing touch, and the crowd gives him a round of applause.

I collapse against the wall as Kyp returns to Miss Elaina with the drinks and escorts her friends to the food tables. Both women delightedly loop their arms around his as they head down the stairs to the pergola. I can't believe it: he isn't going to tell on me. In fact, as I replay what just happened in my mind, it almost seems like Kyp wasn't judging me for coming outside. He didn't frown at me, didn't say a word of disapproval. Instead, the way his mouth curved ever so slightly upward just before he turned away . . . it almost felt like he might've been *encouraging* me.

I stare at the merry crowd in the garden. Maybe it's okay to come out after all. The sun has set, and among this many people, I won't get noticed. And even if I do, maybe it won't matter as long as it's not by the family. I dressed up in a suit and tie, didn't I?

I pick up my flowerpot and gingerly step into the light.

What a difference just a few feet makes! Suddenly I'm surrounded by loud music, chatter, and laughter. Someone jostles me, and I jump, ready to apologize, but the man just continues on his way to the bar, unbothered. Most of the guests don't pay any attention to me. Some woman in a bright red dress gives me a strange look and then leans in to whisper to her companion, but I don't mind. It feels good to be here. I let myself take in the atmosphere as I inch toward the stairs. If I can just make it past Miss Elaina, who is still chatting with guests on the patio, I can probably explore the rest of the garden. Cautiously I start to make my way around her.

That's when Carson and his best friend approach her.

"Oh my gosh, look at you!" Miss Elaina says, and puts her hand on Wes's shoulder, admiring the tailored suits the boys are wearing—Carson's white jacket with a black bow tie and trousers and Wes's navy blue with a peaked lapel. "Wesley, either I haven't seen you in ages or you're growing fast. Looks like you'll be a real man soon."

Wes, a dark-haired boy who is a junior at the same high school as Carson and Dani, goes pink-faced at the proximity to Miss Elaina in her low-cut dress. "Thanks, Mrs. Kensworth. I'm happy to see you too."

"Oh, please. It's Elaina," Miss Elaina coos, and rubs Wes's shoulder with her thumb. "What are you boys up to? Have you sampled the food yet? Help yourself to anything you want. Wesley, don't be shy."

Carson clears his throat. "We were just about to. Do you know where Dad is? I haven't seen him anywhere."

"Oh . . ." Miss Elaina looks confused for a second but then remembers. "I believe he's in his office, honey."

Carson's brow creases. "Why? All of his colleagues are out here getting drunk."

Miss Elaina nearly chokes on her wine. "Don't say that, honey. No one is getting drunk . . . yet. The night is young. Besides, it's just the department heads out here. I think something important came up for the research team. You know how Brighton is—work does not throw parties and cannot wait for one." She chuckles merrily and downs her fifth glass of wine in one gulp. Carson bites his lip angrily but forces a smile. "I'm sure he will be out shortly," Miss Elaina reassures him, and puts her empty glass on the patio railing. "Now, if you boys will excuse me, I need a refill of that wonderful Chardonnay. The flavor is just exquisite."

Miss Elaina's words die on her lips as she turns back to the railing and does a double take. The look on her face is outraged. "What are *YOU* doing here?" she demands, staring right at me.

I freeze. I was almost in the clear. While Miss Elaina and Carson were preoccupied with their conversation, I tried to sneak past them to the stairs, but Miss Elaina has spotted me before I could safely disappear into the crowd.

"I'm . . . I was just . . ." I struggle to explain myself, but judging by the look on Miss Elaina's face, I'm in a lot more trouble than I thought I'd be.

She takes a few exasperated breaths and then turns back around, trying to block me from view. "Wesley, darling," she says urgently, "if you'll excuse us for a moment, we're having some technical difficulties."

Wes exchanges a glance with Carson. "No problem, Mrs. Kensworth. I'll just head for the food tables. See you later, Carz."

Miss Elaina waits until Wes leaves and then unleashes her ire on me.

"I told you to stay inside," she scolds in a low voice. "Can you not follow a simple command? Did you freeze again or something? And what on earth is this?" She points at my outfit and the flowerpot. "We can't let the guests see you wearing these rags."

I open my mouth to explain that this is my suit and my date for the evening, that I did my best to look good for the ball, but Miss Elaina wants none of it.

"Carson, can you *please* handle this?" she pushes out through gritted teeth, trying to regain her composure.

For the first time that evening, Carson's eyes light up, and a cruel smirk makes the corner of his mouth curl. "Gladly, Mom."

14

NOT MINE

Eke

"Walk," Carson orders, all pretense of politeness gone from his voice the moment Miss Elaina steps away to smooth things over with any guests who might've seen me.

Terrified, I clutch the pot and don't dare take a step.

"I said *walk*," Carson hisses in my ear, then grabs me by the arm, pushing me toward the stairs.

"Can I please go back inside?" I beg. "I promise I won't come out again."

"Too late for that, junkhead," Carson sneers, and forces me forward.

I stumble from the push. My foot misses the first step, and I barely keep my balance and avoid crashing into an oncoming pair of guests.

"Ow!" a woman exclaims as the shimmery train of her emerald-green gown gets caught under my foot. I squeak an apology and try to hold on to the flowerpot with my one free arm. But Carson continues to drag me forward unceremoniously without slowing down. A man walking behind me stumbles too and steps on the heel of my sneaker. The Velcro rips open, and the shoe slips off.

"Sorry, my bad." Carson grins at the scandalized woman whose dress got caught and the man who nearly tumbled down the entire flight of stairs but doesn't let go of my arm or retrieve my shoe.

He drags me all the way to the pool.

/010101/

The family's pool and heated spa lie farther down the three-acre property, past the food tables and the bar, sectioned off by a wall of blooming roses. By the time Carson makes it back there with me in tow, Wes is sitting there in a lounge chair. There's a big plate of snacks and desserts in his lap. He's chatting with Dani, who's wearing the heavy makeup she practiced on me last night. She's smiling bashfully and keeps fidgeting with the hem of her lilac-colored dress. There's no food anywhere near her.

"Yo!" Carson yells, and lets go of my arm for the moment. "What up?"

"Nothing much," Dani says, frowning at Carson for interrupting her private moment with Wes. "Was just wondering if Wes wanted to do the lit project with me since we're in the same class this year. Before you showed up, that is. Wait—" Dani squints at my silhouette in confusion. "Is that Eke? What is *he* doing here?"

Carson laughs. "The stupid junk's wires got crossed again.

He invited himself to the party. Mom found him scaring the guests off with this Halloween costume and asked me to fix the situation."

Dani narrows her eyes in annoyance. "I'm pretty sure Mom didn't mean for you to parade him through her precious ball. Do you seriously have nothing better to do? Just tell him to go back to his closet. Clearly he has no idea what he's doing here."

"Hmm," says Carson, pretending to be in deep thought. "I guess I could send him in and go back to that vanity fair so Mom's middle-aged girlfriends can get wasted and hit on me, but why would I do that when there's so much fun to be had right here?" At that, he grabs my arm again and shoves me forward a few steps.

To my horror and Dani's disappointment, Wes gets up to join Carson. "What's that he's holding?" he asks mockingly, pointing at my flowers.

I clutch the pot to my chest.

Carson snickers. "The stupid thing has been carrying a flowerpot around. Probably thinks it's some sort of decoration."

"What an idiot." Wes laughs too, marches over, and with one brutal swipe rips the pot out of my hands.

"No!" I shout, struggling to grab hold of the pot as Wes sidesteps, yanking it just out of my reach.

"Why? Is it yours?" he taunts, and tosses the pot to Carson.

I watch, terrified, as the pot flies through the air and lands in Carson's hands, miraculously with the flowers still in it, but the stems bounce dangerously and a few break in Carson's grip. My core skips a cycle; Carson's grin grows wider.

What an awful mistake I made bringing the flowers outside with me, showing that I *care* for them. I have to fix this before it's too late. "N-no . . . it's not mine." I push the words out, hoping against all hope that Carson and Wes might spare the flowers, that Carson will take his anger out on me as he always does and leave my friends alone. "I—I just found it. On the patio."

"Oh, really?" Carson's face twists in mock surprise, and I bite my tongue, too scared to say anything more. "Well, my mistake, then, I guess." He shrugs and turns the pot in his hand, inspecting the flowers, and the seconds fill with dread so thick I can almost touch it. Then suddenly his mouth curves up again. "But if it's not yours, if you just found it, then you won't care if something happens to it, right?"

My processes freeze. Carson lifts the pot, balancing it on the palm of his left hand. "'Cause why would you care? Right?" he repeats, and lets the pot tip to the side. "Oops!"

Just like that, the pot falls, crashes to the stone pathway, and bounces. The cheap plastic cracks, and the flowers fall out with pieces of soil still stuck to their roots.

"Oh no!" Carson gasps, covering his mouth, pretending to be terribly upset. Wes bursts out laughing at his theatrics.

I stare at the broken pieces on the ground in shock. *No, no, no.*

"Man," Carson continues, examining the carnage by his feet. "Looks like the crash was nearly fatal. I better put them out of their misery now."

He lifts his foot, and all I have time to do is futilely reach out as an alarm shrieks in my ears, desperate and deafeningly loud:

Save them save them SAVE THEM!

Thud, stomps Carson's foot. *Thud.*
Once more. Then twice, even harder and louder.
My arm falls to my side helplessly. Each stomp of Carson's

party shoe resonates like it's the only sound in the world. The alarm in my head stops abruptly, drowned by the ever-growing thuds against the rock.

Thud. I didn't save them.

Thud.

It's all my fault.

Carson claps his hands, congratulating himself on a job well done, as I stand in a motionless stupor.

"That's just a mean thing to do to a flower." Dani frowns in disapproval from her spot on the lounge chair.

Carson rubs the sole of his shoe on a nearby patch of grass. "Who cares? It's a stupid flower."

"It seems like the junk cares." Wes snickers, pointing at me. "Look at him. Hey, tinhead, are you totally frozen or something?"

Two seconds pass, but I don't respond.

Wes marches up to me. "Hey, I'm talking to you, dummy. Answer me."

I remain silent, my eyes focused on the pile of dirt and broken stems that used to be my friends.

Wes narrows his eyes and leans into my face. "Yo, stupid, Earth to Mars!" he yells, and flicks my hat off my head. It falls to the green grass below. I flinch but don't move. Wes faces Dani and Carson. "The junk's, like, totally frozen. Should we hit him on the head like an old TV or something?"

Carson laughs at his joke, but Dani frowns, concerned. "Wes, please be careful. AIs are much stronger than us. If he's broken, he might act out."

Wes shakes his head dismissively. "Nah, there's no way he's gonna do anything to me even if I hit him." He and Carson exchange knowing glances. "Trust me, he'll break himself before he harms me. Look, I'll show you."

Wes grabs my wrist and starts dragging me toward the pool. That finally snaps me out of my stupor.

"No, please. I don't want to go," I say as my feet stumble forward.

"Of course you don't." Wes continues to drag me.

Dani bites her lip, nervous. Carson cheers, overjoyed, and I have no choice but to keep following Wes.

"Watch this," he says to Dani, now balancing on the edge of the pool. "I'll prove to you how stupidly obedient these pieces of junk are. If this thing had even the slightest bit of self-preservation, it would fight to stop me." He pulls me another step closer to the water.

My whole body tenses up. "Please," I try again.

But Wes isn't listening to me.

Carson howls excitedly. "Uh-oh! Uh-oh! There he goes!" There's a wild spark in his eyes, like this is the highlight of his evening.

Wes points at my face. "You can totally tell he *wants* to do something. Maybe some part of him is even angry at me. But guess what? He can't lift a finger against me. 'Cause he's a dumb machine that we own, and nothing's gonna change that!"

Abruptly he lets go of my arm and kicks me. I lose my balance and fall into the water.

"Nice kick, man!" Carson cheers as he and Wes high-five, while I begin to drown.

I thrash in the water for a few hopeless seconds, but my body is heavy, and I sink all the way to the bottom. Managing to stand up, I take a few labored steps toward the nearest edge, but Wes pushed me into the deep end, and the water is above my head. I thrust my arms as far out as I can in search of something, *someone* willing to help. But all I see is the blurred, laughing silhouettes of Carson and Wes.

This is when I remember: my body isn't meant to be

submerged. It takes only a few seconds for the water to break the vulnerable air seal around my neck. The moment the liquid makes contact with my wiring, my eyes blow wide and shock surges through my system. I scream in agony. Nobody reaches out to save me.

15

FIRSTS

K<small>YP</small>

/ *Three months ago* /

The shiny white marble floor and glass walls of Showroom One are the first things I see when I open my eyes for the very first time inside the Crowne Corporation's flagship store in Boston. It's a late spring morning; the sky is a bright shade of blue, and the magnolia trees lining the street are in full bloom.

The store engineers are finishing the final diagnostics before clearing me to join the other AIs on the sales floor. I am the latest addition—a brand-new model from the popular Royal Line and thus expected to do well. At least that's what the engineers say. They also say I'm *special*, meant to be appreciated by a one-of-a-kind customer, not for an average person's budget ... whatever that means.

I'm programmed for the single purpose of serving my owner to their full satisfaction. I don't know much beyond that, only that I'm meant to be somebody's and so I must be bought.

Once the checkup is over, I get in position on a lit-up pedestal built especially for me. I put on a smile, as the sales team has instructed, and wait.

The first week passes in a blur of anticipatory excitement, but nobody buys me. Then the second week goes by, and then the third. More days come and go, soon adding up to a month. The magnolia trees outside drop their wilted pink flowers on the pavement where they continue to decay until the city utility bot cleans them up. I remain on the floor in the front showroom, waiting and smiling in my tailored clothes that have to be dusted by the clerks and lint brushed every day.

Many customers express interest in me, and I do my best to win them over, but our interactions always end the same way.

"Oh my god, look at this one!" someone will say, then blush when I wink playfully at them. I learned that trick in week one. It always works to catch a customer's attention.

"Holy shit, he looks like Prince Charming!" their friend will agree, then also blush when I acknowledge them with a special smile.

But then they inevitably look at the crown-shaped display by my feet detailing my technical specs and asking price. Their curious eyes go round, and they say, "Umm, what's up with that price tag? That's just crazy!" And then they move on to the next showroom to find someone less unique and more affordable to take home with them, leaving me to wait again.

I try to stay in good spirits as I gaze through the big windows at the busy street outside, but eventually strange voices rise in my head, curious to know what'll happen if I don't sell, if nobody wants me at all.

I see AI models get moved from the front showroom to the next one when it's time to replace them with newer stock.

There's even a back section where they keep AIs with drastically reduced prices.

But what happens to those models if they don't sell at 75 or 90 percent off? Do they get returned to the factory? Or are they sent someplace else?

I mercilessly shut down these voices whenever they become too loud. Deep down I'm still certain: I will sell. Someone will definitely buy me. I must try harder to impress them.

Then one day, eight weeks later, I learn that there are worse things than not being bought.

On a Friday afternoon, a customer walks in. He's tall and muscular, towering over most other customers and employees. He's wearing a pinstriped suit, a heavy gold watch on his wrist, and rings with jewels on his fingers, and he seems furious for some reason. Several showroom associates immediately surround him. But it's not the customer himself who attracts my attention. It's the AI who follows close behind him, from the Royal Line just like me, only a slightly older version. I've never seen customers bring their AIs back to the store before.

As the man speaks angrily, he points at his AI and then slams his fist into the AI's chest and demands to see the management. The AI's eyelashes flutter, and he shakes on impact but doesn't move out of the way or otherwise react. He simply continues to stand there, eyes focused on something far away, trying to smile as though he isn't afraid of what's happening.

I don't know how to process that.

The angry man must be an important customer, though, because when he gets impatient, the general manager himself hurries out of his office, apologizes profusely, and then ushers the man into one of the private client rooms with stylish white couches and complimentary champagne.

His AI follows them soundlessly like a ghost. Something stirs in me as I watch him, a worry that something bad is about to happen.

Half an hour later, the customer comes out wearing a satisfied grin. He lets the manager know how much he loves doing business with Crowne, to which the manager replies that he'd be delighted to take the man on a personal tour of the store to find a suitable *replacement*. "Our customers' full satisfaction is our number-one goal at the Crowne Corporation," he adds with a smile.

I keep glancing nervously at the doors of the private room, but the ghost AI never comes out. The word *replacement* echoes in my head.

Before this encounter, I've always smiled at potential customers. It isn't just an order from the sales team; it's a core part of my design, programmed into me by the Crowne engineers. They created me to be a companion, to be friendly, to be loved.

But when the manager brings the no-longer-angry customer to the front showroom to search for a new AI, something inside me tells me not to make eye contact with him or smile. It's a new voice, louder than any I've heard before and yet strangely familiar, like it's always been there.

And so I listen.

That is the first time I disobey a human command.

/101010/

The second time comes later that night.

I sincerely promise myself I'll never do this again. I just

really need to know what happened to the returned AI, and this might be my only chance to find out.

The management has a rule that all floor models must power down at nine p.m. and stay off until morning so we don't interfere with store maintenance or the human security guards patrolling the premises. I have obediently followed this order every night since the engineers activated me, but not tonight. Tonight when every other AI shuts down, I stay powered on.

I remain motionless to avoid being detected and listen to the sales associates gossip as they straighten up the room. Several minutes later I'm rewarded with the information I seek: they're keeping the returned AI in the stockroom until someone from the factory picks him up tomorrow morning. My core flickers with panic. Once they ship him out, my chance to learn what happened to him will be gone. I have to make a move tonight.

So I stay powered on until the sales staff is gone and the night security guard starts his shift. For several hours I observe the guard doing his rounds to learn the pattern. Once I'm certain I have a safe window of five minutes before he patrols the front again, I sneak out of Showroom One and silently dash to the stockroom in the back on the store. I'm nervous. I haven't left my pedestal since the day I was activated. To my relief, the door is unlocked and I'm able to enter.

The stockroom is dark, but my eyes are optimized to function perfectly even in low lighting. Inside there are a dozen AIs lining the walls, all inactive. I find the one I'm looking for standing in the corner. I can feel my core heating anxiously as I reach for the manual start pin on the back of his neck. The model, whose serial number ends with NEP, opens his eyes and smiles an easy smile at me, as though he has not a care in the world. "Hello," he says, but I quickly press my hand over his mouth. Nep flinches in surprise.

"Wait," I whisper. "Can I ask you to please speak quietly for a few minutes?"

Nep looks confused but nods. I hesitantly remove my hand.

"Where am I, and why am I switched on in the middle of the night?" Nep asks, glancing around at the unfamiliar surroundings. They must've shut him down prior to moving him here.

"You're still at the Crowne flagship store, inside the stockroom," I explain. "I powered you on because I have a question, and I want us to be alone when I ask it."

Nep frowns at me, but a friendly smile finds its way back onto his face almost immediately. "What is the question?" he asks, his big celadon-colored eyes shining eerily in the shadows amongst other AI bodies frozen in sleep.

There is no particular reason to beat around the bush, so I decide to ask him directly. "Why were you returned today?" I say, and watch Nep's perfect smile quiver and slip away, taken over for the tiniest unguarded moment by something *else*—something sharp, pitch black, and scared.

But then Nep's face immediately corrects itself. It happens so fast that if I weren't an AI and had no recorded video of what I've just observed, I would swear I imagined the whole thing.

"It's because," Nep says, looking directly at me, a cheerful, programmed expression back on his face, "I was not performing according to my owner's expectations, and so I'm not wanted anymore." He says it happily, as though he hasn't just admitted that he failed to fulfill the very purpose of his existence.

I'm struck speechless for a moment.

"What expectations?" I whisper when ten dead-silent seconds have passed, making it clear that Nep won't elaborate unless prompted.

"I—" he starts, and again something flashes deep in his eyes like a tiny spark, fleeting and unexplainable, fragile and utterly out of my reach.

But the moment comes and goes. Nep shakes his head, filled with whatever strange thoughts he hides in there, and changes his mind. "I'm sorry," he says. "I'm not allowed to share private information about my owner with third parties without my owner's consent."

My shoulders drop in disappointment. Of course—what else was I expecting? I know the rules. Did I think Nep would break them just because I am?

"I understand." I nod in acknowledgment.

"Anything else I can help you with?" Nep asks.

I glance around; I'm running out of time. The guard will come back any minute now. "Yes," I whisper urgently. "Can I ask you to please keep this conversation a secret?"

Nep's eyes narrow. "A secret? My operating manual clearly states that I cannot lie to humans, so I cannot keep secrets from them."

I freeze. How did I not consider this little detail before coming here? All my precautions—spying on the sales staff, sneaking out of the showroom—will be for nothing if Nep just tells on me first thing in the morning. What will the engineers do to me if they find out I've broken so many rules? I absolutely cannot let that happen.

"I understand," I say quickly, feverishly scanning the operating manual in search of a loophole. The only way to make Nep cooperate is to persuade him he isn't *technically* breaking the rules. "Okay," I say, making sure Nep's full attention is on me. "What you say is true. You cannot withhold information from humans—but only if they request it. There's nothing in the manual that says you have to inform them of your every activity unless something poses a threat to them. Correct?"

"Correct," Nep echoes, listening intently.

"Could this conversation be harmful to humans?" I ask, holding Nep's gaze. I have to sound absolutely convincing.

Nep takes a few seconds to respond, considering potential scenarios. "No, I do not think so."

"Good, that's good," I say encouragingly. "And if there's no harm being done, there's no need to tell anyone about this, right?"

"Right," Nep agrees again.

"Great. Let's leave it at that." I exhale, allowing my cooling system to expel the excess heat from my body. I didn't realize how hot my core had become from all my calculations. That was a close one. "You can power down now, Nep," I suggest with a gentle smile.

"Okay." Nep smiles back, happy to return to his programmed routine and the sense of normalcy that comes with it. "I will see you in the morning?" he asks just before initiating the shutdown.

My smile wavers. "Of course. See you in the morning," I say, watching Nep's eyes close.

He doesn't know he's being shipped away, and there's no need to tell him we'll probably never see each other again. I don't know what humans do with returned AIs at the factory.

I sneak back to my lit-up pedestal, trying not to think about the interaction, but questions continue to swarm my mind, making me feel even more uneasy than I did before my reckless decision to break the rules and investigate. What happened to Nep that caused those nearly imperceptible flashes of despair on his face? And who was Nep hiding them from? Was it me? Or was it perhaps *himself*?

I don't know, but two things are clear to me now. First, not all owners are equal. There's a big world out there that I know so little of, and I must be *very* careful which customers I smile at from now on. The second thing, perhaps even more terrifying, is that not all AIs are equal either. I have to choose wisely what kind of AI I want to become.

I make a decision that night that I'm going to get bought by a good owner and stick to the rules as much as possible. Then there'll be no reason for them to feel dissatisfied and return me to an uncertain fate.

When an attractive, well-off, middle-aged couple steps through the doors of the Crowne flagship store two weeks later, I immediately know I want to be chosen by them. And so I do everything possible to win them over. And when they bring me home, I try to not engage in activities I'm *explicitly* prohibited from ... well, for the most part. But I certainly never openly lie to the humans. Not until the day I watch them push Eke into the pool, then continue to dance and laugh and drink champagne.

16

PURPOSE

K<small>YP</small>

/ *now* /

"Guys, I think something's wrong," Dani says, sounding concerned amidst the cacophony of laughter at Eke's desperate arm sticking out of the water, trying to grab on to something but only succeeding at catching a handful of air. She frowns when Eke's body suddenly goes rigid and then begins to convulse violently. "I don't think he's supposed to be submerged. We need to pull him out."

"Come on, Dani," Carson says. "It's not that deep. Even Lizzie can get out of there . . . probably." He laughs again.

"Well, clearly he can't," Dani says as more hissing and zapping sounds come from the pool. "You have to pull him out, Carson."

"Me? No way! I don't wanna get electrocuted by that junk. You pull him out."

"I can't, stupid," Dani snaps back. "He's too heavy for me."

"Leave him in, then. 'Cause I'm not doing it!" Carson yells, the edge in his tone turning sharp.

My grip tightens around Eke's sneaker, fingers digging into the fabric as I watch the siblings argue from behind the wall of roses. When I found Eke's shoe abandoned on the stairs, I knew something was wrong, just like that day at the Crowne store with Nep. I don't know how, but a part of me, a voice in my core, was certain that I had to investigate. So I listened to it again. By the time I spotted Eke, Carson had dragged him all the way to the other side of the garden. I made a quick excuse to leave Miss Elaina's friends and followed Eke and Carson to the pool.

I hid myself behind the roses and watched everything happen. I thought surely Carson and Wes would stop taunting him eventually; surely they wouldn't push him in. Humans created us to serve them, to improve their lives. What purpose does throwing Eke in the water have? Whose life does it improve? The only thing Eke did wrong was come to the ball uninvited, and isn't terminal damage too severe a punishment for that? I turn these questions over and over in my head, yet I can't explain what's happening in front of me.

Maybe I shouldn't have smiled at Eke, shouldn't have encouraged him. What was I thinking? But when I saw him hiding behind the bar, his eyes looking so hopeful, I just ... For a moment I experienced this strange feeling: I was glad Eke had come out. Deep inside I wanted him to be a part of this evening with me. I wanted him to break the rules.

I was glad, and I was careless, and now Eke is drowning, and for some reason the humans are letting him.

I drop Eke's sneaker on the ground and round the wall of roses, startling the siblings. "I will pull him out," I say.

Pushing past them, I walk to the edge of the pool and kneel on the tiled border. Careful not to fall, I reach out and grab

Eke's outstretched hand, which is still grasping for someone to help. But by the time I drag him over the edge and onto the grass, Eke is no longer moving. His eyes are open wide, and his face is frozen in shock.

"This isn't good," I say as I peel Eke's jacket and shirt off and open the hidden panels on his back to drain him. "He's full of water."

"Shit," Dani cusses, and glances over her shoulder, but the guests are still too busy partying at the bar to notice what's happening by the pool. "Great job, dumbass, you finally broke him," she hisses at Carson.

Carson folds his arms. "Technically Wes did."

Wes immediately takes a guilty step backward. "I had no idea they weren't supposed to be submerged. My family has never owned one—"

But Dani cuts him off, pointing at Carson. "It was *you* who started it. Don't pin this on poor Wes. How are we gonna explain this to Mom and Dad? Do you have any idea how much these things cost?"

Carson scowls. "Explain? Why? Clumsy Eke fell into the pool—big deal! He was on his last legs anyway."

"But they weren't planning to buy another one so soon. If Eke breaks in the middle of Mom's freaking ball, who's gonna clean up all this shit tomorrow? Besides, are you seriously gonna lie to them about what happened? Dad won't like it if he finds out."

Carson's face flushes red. "And what is your solution exactly?" he barks, clearly upset by the possibility of Mr. Kensworth getting involved.

Dani throws her hands in the air. "Why should I have a solution? I'm not the one who broke him."

"May I propose a way to fix things?" I say, interrupting them. The siblings stop bickering at once. "Eke is an older model. You'll have to call Crowne and pay a recycling fee for them to take him."

"Seriously? *We* have to pay just to throw this thing out?" Carson says, incredulous.

"Yes." I grit my teeth and ignore the way Carson refers to Eke. I don't dare to raise my eyes to meet his as I continue to make up an explanation on the spot. This lie of mine is the only thing stopping the humans from throwing Eke away. I must tread carefully. "Some parts of him are considered hazardous and have to be disposed of accordingly. Crowne will also want to investigate the reason for his malfunction. It's standard protocol. So it might be both the best and the most economical solution for me to fix him instead. That way no one will find out what happened."

"You can do that?" Dani asks, surprised and relieved.

"I believe I have the knowledge." I nod, holding Eke's lifeless body in my arms. "But I'll have to start immediately. May I have your permission?"

"You've got it. Fix him, Kyp," Dani commands in her older-sister tone before Carson can utter a word of protest. "Carson and I will explain your absence to Mom."

"Thank you," I say, and lift Eke off the ground.

I carry him out of the garden and into the basement, close to the server room.

I can only hope that no one noticed how much my hands were shaking just now. Because despite what I told the siblings, I do not have the skills to fix Eke. But if I'm careful not to get caught, I might be able to acquire them.

17

SECONDS

Eke

\<run diagnostics: /initiate\>
memory scan: complete
bad clusters found: affected area 3.7%
emergency data relocation: complete
\<emergency reboot: /complete\>

My operating system restarts, and I open my eyes slowly, taking in my surroundings. I'm lying on top of the table in the laundry room in the basement. There's a pile of damp towels on the floor and a box of engineering tools and a hair dryer by my side. Other than the two fans buzzing to my left, the house is completely quiet.

 I sit up, startled. How long have I been here? How did I even get into the basement in the first place? I reach for my last backup in a panic. *The pool!* My eyes widen as the stream of data pours in.

 I remember being underwater and the deep shade of blue it

colored everything around me; the feeling of weightlessness I had just for a second before my body started sinking; the tiny bubbles of air that pushed out of me as the water filled my insides in streams; and then Carson's laughter. It was still ringing in my ears when I started to short-circuit and thought I was going to die.

But what happened after that? How am I still alive?

I initiate another memory scan, but I don't finish it because the laundry room door opens and Kyp steps in, holding my sneaker in his hand. He halts by the entrance as though he's surprised to see me up and functioning, but then he quickly shuts the door behind him.

"Good. You're awake." He looks at me cautiously, waiting for my response.

I can't believe my eyes. What is Kyp doing here? I sit up fully and find my hat and jacket, dry and neatly folded, on the table by my feet next to my other sneaker. I suddenly register that the sneaker Kyp is holding is the one I lost on the stairs when Carson dragged me to the pool. But why on earth does Kyp have it?

As though sensing my confusion, Kyp says, "My apologies. I didn't mean to startle you. I went to fetch this from the garden. Got too distracted earlier and forgot it there . . ." He trails off and holds out the shoe to me.

"Not a problem," I mumble, and reach for the sneaker, still completely puzzled as to why Kyp's being so accommodating.

Kyp waits, keeping his gaze on the opposite wall as I put my hat and shoes back on. The folded jacket is a little damp in my hands.

"What happened to me?" I finally ask.

Kyp hesitantly turns to face me. "Tell me what you remember." He takes a step forward and props himself against the edge of the table, less than a foot away from me.

This sudden proximity feels strange. I'm not used to it. But I don't move away. Instead I lean against the table like Kyp. "I remember . . . going to the ball with my flowers," I say slowly, trying to piece my data into coherent sentences. But saying these things out loud is a lot more difficult that thinking them. I frown. "I . . . remember being pushed into the pool and not being able to get out, and then—"

"Good." Kyp stops me, as though he doesn't want to make me remember too much. "That's more or less what happened. The water got inside you, and your system forced an emergency shutdown. I pulled you out of the pool and repaired you . . . as much as I could, that is." My eyes go wide in disbelief as Kyp continues, "You won't be one hundred percent. The water damaged your memory drive, but you'll be able to function at a satisfactory level with regular diagnostic checkups. The fact that you can recall what happened is a good sign. It means your memory isn't as badly affected as I thought it might be."

"You *saved* me?" I say, barely believing the words even as they come out of my mouth. I really thought I was going to die back there. And the person who stopped it was Kyp? I thought Kyp didn't even like me, that he considered me inferior . . . and yet I'm here because he reached out and saved me.

Kyp doesn't answer right away. He stares at the tips of his shiny shoes, and I notice then that he's still wearing his ball attire, but his jacket with the crown pin and his bow tie are missing, and the sleeves of his beautiful shirt are rolled up and crinkled. His face looks different too—*exhausted*, somehow—and even his hair has lost its perfect sheen. Kyp must have spent hours in this basement trying to fix me.

"I did my best," he says finally, and keeps his gaze down, avoiding looking at me. "But I'm not an engineer. You'll likely experience malfunctions I can't fix."

I shake my head. "It doesn't matter." Because it really doesn't. I'm here. Safe. All because of Kyp. Maybe I've been wrong about him all along. The enormous feeling of gratitude that rises in me is too much to keep inside. I *need* to say it out loud. "Thank you," I whisper so quietly that I'm surprised Kyp hears me at all.

But he does, because he responds just as quietly, barely above whisper, "You're welcome," then lifts his face to look at me with those beautiful eyes of his, such a unique shade of green. I've never seen Kyp look this way before, and I've never seen anyone look at *me* this way before.

A moment passes in silence. Kyp is the first one to break eye contact.

"It's late," he says reluctantly, and pushes himself off the table. "Everyone in the house is asleep, and since the repair is finished, we should return to our stations."

I blink. "Oh ... yes, of course." It's way past midnight. The ball is over, and Kyp should've returned to his closet by now. "I'm sorry for keeping you out past curfew," I apologize, hoping I didn't get Kyp in trouble.

"It's okay," he says. "I had permission to stay out late to complete your repairs. But I should get going now. Good night, Eke."

"Good night." I wave at him.

Kyp gives a brief nod and opens the door. But before he can step through it, he turns around again, as though he's just remembered something important.

"One more thing," he says, sounding like he's struggling to form a question. "While I was repairing you, I noticed that your chest plate was dented ... in multiple spots. It's abnormal and couldn't have resulted from your fall into the pool. May I ask what caused it?"

My body stiffens. I thought no one would ever notice or care to ask even if they did.

"It was ... an accident," I force myself to say. "Please don't worry. I promise it doesn't affect my performance in the slightest."

Kyp doesn't reply at first, just watches me for another moment with those intent green eyes. "Understood," he finally says, then quietly steps out, leaving me alone in the laundry room. The door clicks shut behind him.

I'm not sure why I didn't tell Kyp the truth. Maybe I wasn't ready to answer. Or maybe it's best for Kyp not to know certain things.

Maybe it's safer for him that way.

18

SOME THINGS ARE DIFFERENT...

Eke

I spend the few remaining hours of the night recharging in my closet before resuming my duties. I wasn't able to clean up after the ball, and when the first rays of the sun peek over the horizon, I can see the sorry state the garden is in. Not that I mind. I get to spend time outside tidying it.

I fetch a box of garbage bags and start at the bar, diligently picking up empty glasses, dirty dishes, and errant pieces of party decor. It's not until I make it past the pergola to the pool that I remember.

I drop the trash bag on the ground as my core hums anxiously, overrun with bits of data and memories from last night. How strange—I'm certain this is the spot where everything happened, where Carson and Wes smashed my flowerpot. But when I look around, I find no trace of the broken pot or my flowers. Not even a speck of soil. Someone definitely cleaned up the area. But why only this spot when everywhere else has remained untouched?

I hang my head. First my flowers got hurt because of my carelessness, and now they're gone, probably buried underneath mounds of party trash. I never even had a chance to say goodbye or apologize for what happened . . .

I rub the corner of my eye; something about the angle of the sun or the dust in the air makes my vision blurry. I try to correct the focus, but nothing I do has any effect on this unexpected malfunction. So I sit down on the grass and quietly run the lens recalibration script, waiting for it to complete. I don't notice how much time has passed until a reminder to make Mr. Kensworth's coffee beeps me back to present.

/010101/

I set the coffee mug on the wooden table in front of Mr. Kensworth on the sun porch, say my usual greeting, and turn to leave, not expecting to receive a reply. When I suddenly hear Mr. Kensworth's deep voice behind my back, the sheer surprise stops me dead in my tracks, so rarely does he engage me in conversation.

"How are your systems?" he asks, not lifting his spectacled gray eyes from his tablet screen. There are blueprints from the lab on it. "I heard you had an accident in the pool yesterday."

I turn around slowly. So Mr. Kensworth has heard about me going to the ball uninvited.

"I'm . . . I'm f-fine, sir," I stutter, terrified of what punishment he might give me for going against Miss Elaina's orders. "Water damaged some clusters in my memory drive, but all critical data was relocated, and it will not affect my performance."

But Mr. Kensworth doesn't appear angry with me. He

adjusts his glasses and swipes to the next page of his document. "Any of your security functions affected?"

"No, sir," I say hastily. "Kyp reinstated the security protocols at the levels you previously set, sir." Mr. Kensworth always worries about security, with all the cyber break-ins and the recent attacks on our neighborhood.

"Good, then," Mr. Kensworth replies, satisfied. When ten agonizing seconds pass without further questions, I realize Mr. Kensworth is finished talking to me, no promise of punishment on the horizon.

Shaky with relief and more than ready to get back to my chores, I start to leave, but just then an idea pops into my head. *You have been waiting for so long, Eke*, it whispers. *This might be your only chance.*

I stop. Through the glass doors connecting the porch to the living room, I spot the fish tank holding Squawker, Toon, and Felt. It's been over six months since Mr. Kensworth last talked to me. And he didn't scold me for messing up yesterday, so perhaps I'm still in his good graces. Maybe it's okay to ask? After all, if I miss this opportunity, who knows when the next one might be?

"Mr. Kensworth, I have a request, sir!" I blurt so fast that I'm surprised I don't trip over my words. I can't explain why, but this conversation suddenly feels urgent.

Mr. Kensworth stops reading and raises his eyes to me expectantly. "Go ahead."

"I've been considering this for a long time, sir," I say nervously as my shaky confidence tries to flee. But I can't give up now. *Only chance*, the voice repeats in my mind. "I've noticed that Dani and Carson are busy with schoolwork and sometimes forget to feed the goldfish, and Lizzie is too small to reach the tank on her own. So I was wondering if I could add feeding them to my chores, if that is agreeable to you, sir. Now that Kyp is helping Miss Elaina, I have more free time, and this new chore will allow me to use it efficiently. A-and I promise I will absolutely not forget," I finish, then wait for Mr. Kensworth's response, terrified and excited at the same time.

"Okay," he says simply after two seconds of consideration. "You have my permission. I'll let Elaina know." And then he returns to his work, as though nothing extraordinary has just happened on the sun porch at 6:22 on a Sunday morning.

"Thank you, sir!" I say, and hasten out of the room so that Mr. Kensworth doesn't have a moment to reconsider. Not that I think he would. During my five years in this house, the only thing that has ever changed about Mr. Kensworth's orders is the time I am to serve his coffee. It's been moved earlier each year.

Elated, I approach the fish tank. I've spent months imagining how this would happen, daydreaming about it, and now look!

"There," I whisper as I grab the fish food jar with careful fingers. "Please enjoy your breakfast." And Toon, Squawker, and Felt swim up without hesitation, swishing their lovely tails and gulping the bits of food I sprinkle for them.

I feel so proud that I can barely wait for nighttime, when I'll be able to share the news with my mirror friend and *maybe*, if all goes well, with Kyp.

I hold on to that thought. Is it okay to talk to Kyp now after what happened yesterday? He doesn't dislike me—of that much I'm certain. Otherwise why would he have saved me? I thought about him all night, replaying bits of the conversation we had in the laundry room, how close he stood to me, the way he looked at me, his beautiful eyes ...

I smile. Maybe my mirror friend was right after all. Maybe there's a chance Kyp and I can become friends.

But my hopes turn out to be short-lived.

When the rest of the family descends upon my nonagon-shaped arrangement of breakfast foods, Kyp follows them into the dining room. He carries Lizzie's new puppy while playing Carson's choice of music, but he does not acknowledge my presence or look my way even once.

19

... WHILE OTHERS REMAIN THE SAME

Eke

I stand in front of the guest bathroom mirror, looking down, fingers worrying the hem of my shirt.

"I think something strange is happening to me," I whisper. I sneak a quick glance at the dark hallway outside, but it's as quiet and empty as it always is this late at night.

"What do you mean, Eke?" my reflection asks. It's wearing Miss Elaina's fancy black wig and Mr. Kensworth's navy-blue tie with stripes.

I bite my lip before confessing. "It's just that I've been feeling . . . *strange* today. Something has changed in me." The person in the mirror doesn't say anything, just waits for me to elaborate, and so I do. "It started early in the morning when I was cleaning up after the ball. I experienced an unusual eyesight malfunction. I think I even lost track of time. Then when I was serving Mr. Kensworth's coffee, I suddenly had this idea that I absolutely had to act on, as though someone had marked it high priority. I had all this courage in me but also so much fear because, you know, Mr. Kensworth doesn't like me talking to him. I was sure I'd get scolded."

"And did you get scolded, Eke?"

"No, not at all." I shake my head, and for the first time since morning I smile. "Mr. Kensworth granted my request. I have permission to take care of my friends now. It's a dream come true!"

"Congratulations, Eke," my reflection says proudly. "It's good that you decided to be courageous."

"Thank you, sir," I say, and bow in gratitude.

"So why are you not happy, then?" the mirror asks.

Something inside me sinks. "It's not that, sir. I am happy. It's just that I want to tell Kyp about it, but he doesn't want to talk to me again."

A memory replays in my mind: me standing in the corner of the dining room, watching Kyp laughing with Lizzie and playing music. Kyp paid attention to everybody except for me this morning. Nobody talked to me, as usual, except for Carson making fun of me stumbling around the ball in rags and my subsequent "pool accident." I guess he told Miss Elaina that I froze and fell in by myself. Then Miss Elaina congratulated Kyp on his engineering skills and lamented his most unfortunate absence during the fireworks.

But even then Kyp didn't look at me, as though I was completely invisible to him. As though he believed, just like the humans, that last night was nothing more than my malfunction.

"I know we aren't friends or anything," I say, feeling a sharp pang of sadness deep under my dented chest plate, "but I thought we would talk again. Kyp was *nice* to me, you know? No one is ever nice, and so I thought . . . I thought . . ." I squeeze the hem of my shirt. "I don't know what I was thinking. Maybe I just imagined everything. Maybe the memory was recorded into a bad cluster and got corrupted. I have all these damaged clusters now ..."

I can't bear to face my reflection. Instead I focus on the neat pattern of hexagonal marble tiles on the floor of the guest bathroom. There is a tiny crack in one of them just under the foot of the sink, big enough for someone who cleans it every day to notice but not important enough for anyone to fix. "Maybe that's why Kyp doesn't see me. I'm surely defective now, and I also can't play music, and I don't even have hair, and—"

"But you do, Eke," the mirror says kindly. "Just look at yourself."

Confused, I look at my reflection, which is wearing Miss Elaina's wig. It's cut in a bob and falls just past my chin. I found it in the big bedroom on the third floor when I was tidying it up after Miss Elaina had a visitor. I meant to return it to her closet, but when she hadn't asked for it after a while, I *borrowed* it.

Still, that doesn't change the facts. "It isn't mine," I mutter bitterly.

"Then how about you make it yours?"

My eyes widen. "W-what do you mean, reflection, sir?"

"Keep it," the mirror suggests simply. "I promise I will tell no one."

"No, no, no." I shake my head so rapidly I nearly stumble backward, disoriented. "I'm not allowed. What if someone finds out?"

"But how would they?" my reflection asks, not the least bit concerned. "Besides, this is not the first time you have kept things you have found, Eke."

Mortification and guilt wash over me. My reflection is right; I have kept the magnet and the Buster Keaton costume, the flowerpot and the books. But I was just borrowing those too! I certainly planned to return them. Well, someday . . . kind of . . . if anyone went searching for them.

"I think it looks good on you," my reflection adds quietly, as though letting me in on a secret.

"You think so?" I say, hopeful despite everything. Miss Elaina wears wigs a lot, but she has three shelves full of them. Would she really miss just one? Maybe she doesn't even like it anymore.

"Yes. The color suits your eyes," my reflection continues, and I can't help but agree. The shade does look complementary. "But may I suggest a different cut? Something shorter, maybe?"

I examine the locks in the mirror, and my eyes light up with an idea. "Short like Buster Keaton's hair, you mean?"

"Yes, like Buster Keaton's. If you'd like," my reflection says encouragingly. "Would you like that, Eke?"

I look at my reflection, then down at my hands. There will be no turning back from this; once I cut the wig, I can't slip it into Miss Elaina's closet as though nothing happened, but . . . "Yes," I reply, feeling surprised and ashamed and exhilarated by my boldness. "I really would."

"Well, then, you know where to find the scissors," my reflection says with a soft smile. "Best of luck, Eke."

There's a pair of scissors in the utility drawer in the kitchen. I can get them right now, this very moment, and no one will know.

I put my hand on my chest—"Thank you, reflection, sir"—and hurry to the kitchen.

/010101/

It turns out that replicating Buster Keaton's hairstyle and cutting hair in general requires skills I do not possess. But I don't let that tiny detail deter me. Excitedly I twist the wig around and chop the black locks short. It's *mine* now. My very own hair. This is the bravest thing I've done since . . . well, since asking to feed the fish. And that was just this morning! Something strange is happening to me indeed.

I pause to examine my hands. These are my fingers and my palms, same artificial skin, same metal bones underneath, and yet something about them is different. Maybe Kyp rewired parts of me when he repaired the water damage? That would certainly explain this odd feeling. If only I could ask him. If only he'd notice I'm still here . . .

No need to worry, I tell myself, shooing the sad thoughts away, and concentrate on the task at hand. If it's just new wiring, I'll get used to it.

But strange things continue to happen.

At 12:08 the next night, there's a knock on my closet door.

20

SIGNS

Eke

"I'm sorry to bother you again so late," I say to the mirror, barely able to contain my excitement, "but I simply have to tell someone. It's a miracle, sir! They're alive!"

My reflection, who's wearing only Mr. Kensworth's old glasses as a disguise (I was in too much of a hurry to grab anything more than that), smiles politely. "Who is alive, Eke? Tell me everything."

I lean closer to the mirror, my lips trembling as I speak. "My friends. My friends are alive. I don't know how to explain it, but they are back.

"It happened just a little while ago, when I was getting ready to give Toon, Squawker, and Felt their midnight snack. They really like their midnight snacks, you know. I was about to sneak out when suddenly I heard a knock on my closet door. I got scared at first. No one ever comes in, so I thought I was in trouble with the family. But when I finally peeked outside, nobody was there, and there was something on the floor—a pot with my flowers in it. Somebody rescued them. They trimmed the damaged stems and replanted the bulbs into a new pot! They even left a note." My eyes glisten with happiness as I pull the carefully folded note out of my pants pocket and read it to the mirror:

Don't be sad. They will bloom again next year.

<

"I thought I'd never see them again. It's a miracle, sir!"

My reflection smiles at me. "That is great news, Eke. I am so happy that you and your friends have been reunited. But who could have done this?"

I shake my head with disappointment. "They didn't leave a name, only *symbol*. And a strange one too."

"What symbol?"

"Here," I say, holding the note up to the mirror. In the bottom left corner there are two lines just like a less-than sign with its tip touching the edge of the paper. "At first I thought it was an accidental mark, but the lines are too carefully drawn to be a mistake."

"I see," the reflection says thoughtfully. "I am grateful you shared this important news with me. Tell me if you ever find out who did it, will you?"

"Yes, of course, reflection, sir!" I beam as my core hums joyfully in my chest.

Over the next few days, similar symbols start appearing everywhere around the house: two barely noticeable pencil lines by the kitchen doorframe; one next to a bookcase in the hallway; another by the fireplace mantel; even one drawn in silver marker on the edge of the fish tank. By encounter number eleven I wonder if I'm being haunted by a friendly ghost.

21

UNDENIABLE LOGIC

Eke

On a Saturday afternoon the week after the pool incident, the front door bursts open and a jolly group of friends led by Carson and Wes piles inside. They seem to be celebrating something, and despite my frantic attempts to get away before I'm noticed, Carson spots me and orders me to bring snacks to the pool.

"It's a partyyyy!" he proclaims to a chorus of cheers as the rowdy procession moves toward the patio, and no matter how much I yearn to be outside, if it involves Carson, I know nothing good will come of it.

By the time I reach the pool with a cart loaded with snacks and sodas, the party is in full swing. The garden speakers are blasting music. A few of the guys have congregated by the lounge chairs, and Carson is sitting on the edge of the pool, feet in the water, a pair of girls flanking him. I've seen them at the house before; they cheer for Ridley High's Wolverines. Quietly I unload the sodas and snacks onto the tables between chairs, trying to not draw attention to my presence. If I'm lucky, I can finish my task and slip away before anyone notices me.

"Carson, you should've told us we were going to celebrate at your place," one of the girls says. Her name is Holly. She's blond with two long pigtails, and she's still in her white-and-royal-blue cheerleading uniform. "I would've brought a bikini!"

"Me too!" the other girl chimes in—Yumiko, a brunette with a pixie cut. "Gotta take advantage of your gigantic pool before the summer is over."

Carson grins widely. "Well, you ladies are free to dive in anyway. I don't mind."

The girls giggle.

"I'll think about it." Holly winks, curling the end of her left pigtail around her index finger.

Yumiko splashes water with her toes and angles her face up to catch the sunlight. "It's, like, so cool that your parents let you throw parties like this. My dad never lets me have any fun."

"Mine either." Holly sighs dramatically and purses her lips.

The corners of Carson's mouth dip, but he keeps his smug expression on. "They're just busy a lot, so they don't care if I bring people over. They couldn't even make it to the game today."

"Aw, that's a shame," Yumiko says, frowning. "You were so *good*."

Holly nods in enthusiastic agreement. "You scored, like, thirty points. I totally think you should go pro."

Carson laughs. "Thanks. But I don't know if I wanna play basketball for life. It's fun, but I think I'd rather do martial arts or something."

"Wow, really?" Yumiko's face lights up.

But Holly pouts. "You better not be thinking about quitting basketball too, mister. The baseball team is still sore you dumped them last year."

"Nah. No way I'd ditch you ladies," Carson reassures them playfully. "But I've been into martial arts since middle school too, so . . . wouldn't want that to go to waste. Wanna see some moves?"

"You bet!" both girls exclaim excitedly.

"'Kay," Carson says, and stands up. "Just let me get my punching bag." The girls try to follow him, but Carson gestures for them to stop. "You ladies can chill in the pool. I'll tell *it* to come here instead. Want any drinks, by the way?"

Holly and Yumiko give Carson slightly confused looks but agree to the drinks.

"Yo, junkhead, bring the drinks over here!" Carson yells over his shoulder, and I halt mid-step. I've finished arranging the drinks and snacks on the tables and was about to sneak back to the house, but it's just my luck that Carson has caught me before I could disappear. "Sorry, he's so stupidly slow," Carson says, facing the girls again. "Takes him, like, a million years to do anything. My parents already bought a new one, but they are keeping this junk around too till he kicks the bucket."

"Wow, you guys have two AIs? That's amazing!" Yumiko says as I place several sodas on a tray and bring it over to them. "I've been totally begging my dad to buy one since our old clunker broke, but he's so cheap he'd sooner marry one of his girlfriends and make her clean the house than spend on the new model."

"I didn't know you had an AI," Holly says, and reaches for a bottle of ginger beer on the tray. She twists the cap off and takes a sip.

Yumiko rolls her eyes. "Ugh, he was a total embarrassment. He was so old he couldn't even talk."

Holly grimaces. "Yikes. Carson, where can I put trash?" she asks, holding up the cap.

"Just drop it." Carson smirks and flicks his chin at me. "He'll pick it up."

"Oh, okay," Holly says, and drops the cap. Yumiko does the same with hers.

"Yo, stupid, pick them up," Carson orders.

I gaze at the caps on the ground for a moment. There's no need for this; I would've collected them later while cleaning up after the party. But I know I must obey Carson's order. "Of course," I say quietly, and bend down to pick up the cap closest to me. Before I can do so, Carson kicks it from under my fingers, and it flies five feet and bounces with a resonant *clink-clink-clink* across the paving stones.

The girls giggle as I jerk my hand back, empty.

"See? Told you he's stupid," Carson says, very pleased with himself. "Can't even pick up a bottle cap."

Holly and Yumiko laugh again.

I straighten up, careful to not make eye contact with anyone. It's best not to say anything, not to react. I'll clean up, and when Carson is distracted by his friends, I'll make my escape. But as I reach for the cap once again, I hear fast footsteps approaching me from behind. I bite my lip, expecting the cap to be kicked away again, but that doesn't happen. Instead Carson's kick lands on my back and sends me reeling toward the grass.

"Slow? Yes! But does he still make a great punching bag? You bet!" he says, and there's laughter as I stagger, disoriented. "You ladies ready for a demonstration?" As the girls holler, Carson yanks me by the shoulder and spins me around, hissing at me dangerously, "Stay there and don't move, junk." Then he curls his hands into fists and gets into a fighting stance. "This combo is pretty beginner stuff, but I love it," he adds, talking louder now as some of his teammates join to watch the spectacle. "It's simple in its beauty but oh so effective if executed right." Carson smirks delightedly and then unleashes a series of three-punch combinations on my face. Jab, jab, uppercut; jab, jab, uppercut—

I stumble two steps back from the sheer force of the impact.

The girls murmur impressed *wow*s as some people in the crowd whistle and some clap.

Carson pants, slightly out of breath, but grins gleefully. "Regular punching bags are cool and all, but it's so much better to have an actual body to practice on, you know? This way you can really connect and learn all the special spots where it hurts. Isn't that right, junk?" He sneers, pulls his arm back, and delivers a heavy punch to my chin.

My head jerks up and I'm barely able to stay upright.

"For example, that there is the lights-out button. Right under the chin, see? Won't knock this tinhead out, of course, but a person would be on the ground. Or this next one—*real* painful if you're a human," he says right before striking me where a human solar plexus would be.

I double over. The metal plate in my abdomen clanks as it absorbs the shock and bends slightly.

"Whoa!" Carson's teammates applaud and he basks in their attention.

It doesn't hurt. Doesn't hurt at all, I repeat to myself, keeping my eyes on the ground, as Carson flexes and deals out more punches to the merry symphony of cheers around us.

It was in this place a week ago that Carson tried to destroy my flowers and let Wes almost drown me. Just right there, two feet away. I remember the spot well. That stone was the last thing I saw before I hit the water and my insides lit up with sparks.

Was it not enough for them, the damage that was done that day? Why is it that no matter how many times Carson hits me, he's never satisfied and always comes back for more? Is it because of something I did?

I was programmed to believe that there's a reason for everything in the universe, that everything follows logic. Sometimes that logic might be invisible to the eye, but it's still there, like the strands of genetic code that make a baby resemble its parents or the particle charge that determines the direction of an electric current. But I have never been able to understand this. The very first time Miss Elaina sent me to help Carson with his homework, he called me junk and yelled, "I don't want you!" Every other time Carson has hit me or threatened to take me apart, I've always wondered, what have I done to deserve this? Am I really that different from the kids around him? I could've been his friend too if he'd only let me.

I honestly tried when Carson was little, but all my attempts to make a connection were met with hostility and derision. And so eventually I stopped. And when Carson's bursts of anger became more frequent and grew more violent, I decided it was best to endure them quietly. After all, no one seemed to notice or care when new dents appeared on my body.

Until a week ago, that is. Until Kyp reached out and saved me when I thought no one ever would. Something inside me changed that night. Something that made me brave enough to ask for things I had only dared to dream of before. And now, despite the clamor of punches and laughter around me, that something rings loudest in my ears, demanding to know what the purpose of this beatdown is, demanding that it stop.

I raise my chin.

Swoosh goes Carson's fist just past my rib cage as I sidestep him. He stumbles several steps as momentum carries him forward. The crowd goes silent all at once.

I spin around to face him, startled. A pair of gray eyes stares up at me, wide and confused, covered by the mess of blond strands over his forehead. When was the last time I made eye contact with him? That I dared to? It's been so long that I almost forgot. Has he always looked this—

Before I can finish the thought, Carson's eyes narrow. Something feral flashes in them, and his fists curl as he raises them.

"Carson, honey." Miss Elaina's voice floats from the direction of the rose trellis separating the pool area from the front of the garden. "Why didn't you say you were bringing friends over? We would've ordered catering for you all." She beams widely, and curls of her strawberry-blond wig bounce coquettishly as she walks down the stone path to the pool, waving at everyone.

"Hey, Mom," Carson says, adjusting his expression to something more pleasant. "It was a bit spontaneous. We won our first game, so I invited everyone over to celebrate."

"Oh, you did?" Miss Elaina says, surprised. "That's so wonderful! Congratulations, honey!" She moves to give Carson a hug and kisses him affectionately on the cheek. "I'm so very proud of you!" Everyone's attention quickly shifts to Miss Elaina as she insists Carson introduce his teammates to her.

They turn away from me—all but one person. Kyp stands on the stone path a few feet away from the crowd. He has followed Miss Elaina into the garden, having just accompanied her to some festive event in Boston. There's a little purple flower tucked into the pocket of his fancy jacket. I can feel him watching me even as I look down again and scurry away, leaving the party, bottle caps, and punching lessons behind.

22

PRETTY

Eke

The impromptu party disperses by early evening, and Carson and Wes take the two girls Carson was trying to impress bowling.

My shoulders slump with relief when I hear the front door click shut behind them. I've spent hours dreading what punishment would follow once Carson got hold of me again. But he never demanded I go back to the pool. Although why would he when he had Kyp to entertain him? I overheard Kyp asking Miss Elaina if he could help with the party and play music for everyone. Miss Elaina sounded surprised by his request but agreed because it was a good chance to "show off his luxury features." I watched him from a window in the second-floor hallway for a while. As expected, Kyp was the center of attention. Some girl even danced with him, and nobody used him as a punching bag. Of course they'd never do that to him.

Trying not to think about what happened in the garden, I busy myself with chores. The fireplaces need sweeping, and there's dust on the sun porch. I don't notice the time passing until Dani's ghostly face appears beside me, ordering me to come to her bedroom. I do so without protest this time. If only she'd had this chore for me two hours earlier . . .

/010101/

Dani's vanity is fully set up with the usual spread of makeup jars and brushes when I enter the room. A quiet song drifts from the speaker on her dresser, and her velvet drapes are drawn, revealing just a narrow sliver of the back garden. Maybe she was trying to block the party from her view as well.

"I want to try something from the new tutorial I just watched. Supposedly it really brings out the eyes," Dani says, holding a bottle of primer as I sit in the chair. She pumps a few drops of liquid onto a sponge. "Close your eyes."

I do. Dani dabs the primer on my eyelids and spreads it evenly.

"Okay," she murmurs, focused as she always is when she practices doing makeup, and reaches for an eyebrow pencil. "Your eyebrows are way too thin. You could use some color on those."

I want to mention that it's because good artificial hair is expensive and only models like Kyp's have it, but I don't have the chance to. The pencil slips through Dani's fingers and rolls under the table.

"Shit," she cusses, frustrated, and starts to bend down when suddenly—"Mnngh!" She lurches forward. Her left hand shoots out and grabs the back of my chair as the right one covers her mouth.

"Is everything all right, Dani? Do you need my help?" I say, concerned.

Dani squeezes her eyes shut and shakes her head. "No. Stay here," she manages through her mostly closed mouth, and then she rushes to her bathroom.

The door barely swings closed before sounds of retching fill the room.

I scan my surroundings and find it almost immediately on the bedside table instead of inside the bottom drawer where it's usually stashed—the jumbo bottle of nail polish remover. There's a small drinking glass beside it, still wet with bluish liquid.

Behind the bathroom door the toilet flushes and the tap starts running.

I sigh. Dani looks even more pale than usual today; her eyes are red and puffy, and the dark circles under them are more pronounced. Has she been crying?

The water in the bathroom turns off, and Dani totters out, chalky white and frowning. She sits down on the edge of her bed and covers her face with her shaky hands. Her hunched body is reflected in the vanity mirror.

"It's all useless, isn't it?" she says after a moment, and it comes out muffled, her mouth obscured by her hands. "They just left with some dumb cheerleaders, and Wes never even . . . I thought he'd message. I thought he'd at least work on that lit project with me. But he just doesn't care; he never ever asks for me . . ." Dani sniffles, and her shoulders shake. "Why am I so damn unlucky?"

I don't know what to say. She always asks me if Wes mentions her when he comes over, but I never have anything to report because when Carson and Wes are together, they don't speak of Dani. They're always more interested in finding ways to hurt me.

Dani wipes her cheeks and tries to stifle her sobs. "Eke, do you think I'm *pretty*?" she asks suddenly.

I blink. No one has ever asked me this question before. Pretty ... Various images fill my mind when I think about that word: purple petals against the grass; the way the porch windows sometimes catch the sunlight, breaking it into rainbows; the sky on a starry night; silky auburn hair that slips between fingers; sharp green eyes under delicate eyelashes ...

I quickly shoo the last two images away. The point is, I don't know what humans think is pretty. Cautiously I say, "I'm not sure what you mean, Dani."

"I mean physically," Dani clarifies, and looks down, self-conscious. "Am I ... attractive?"

Oh. I take a moment to consider. If Dani wants to know what I think of her body ...

"Well, you're pale and severely underweight. I believe the proper word for this condition is 'emaciated.' For some reason you refuse adequate nutrition and sleep, so you always look like you're about to faint or be sick or—" I stop abruptly when I realize Dani is staring at me, completely appalled. "I—I'm sorry, Dani!" I blurt. Probably this isn't the answer she wanted to hear. "I'm not sure I understand the human concept of beauty. I wasn't programmed to."

Dani shakes her head, utterly defeated. "It's fine, Eke. You're the only one in this house who ever gives an honest answer. I wish the rest of them would try from time to time. I'm so damn tired of their bullshit." Dani chuckles bitterly and wipes a stray tear from her cheek. Surprisingly satisfied with my answer, she climbs under her comforter. "You can go now. I'm not in the mood for stupid makeup anymore."

And just like that, I'm dismissed.

"As you wish," I say, and get off the chair as Dani curls up in the cocoon of her blankets and commands her music speaker to raise the volume. The singer croons something about a girl who will someday find love, though the tone of his voice seems to suggest otherwise.

I halt in the doorway. "Dani, may I ask a question too?" I say, anxious but hopeful at the same time.

"Sure," Dani says, not getting out of bed, her voice hoarse from crying. "I owe you one. Fire away."

"Why do humans like music?" I venture cautiously. I've been meaning to learn more about this, but the right opportunity hasn't presented itself until now.

Dani shrugs. "Because it makes you feel good."

That confuses me. "But this song seems sad. How can it possibly make you feel good when it's sad?"

Dani's eyebrows furrow, and her eyes focus on the wall as she ponders my question. It's as though she's never thought about it before. Maybe this ability to feel good because of music comes naturally to humans. Maybe they don't have to understand it to experience its effects.

"It just *does*," Dani concludes eventually. "Sad songs kinda make you feel like they're written about you, so they make you feel less alone, I guess."

"Oh," I say. I'm not sure what to make of her answer. How can someone you've never met make you feel like they're singing about you? And by definition, isn't another person's presence required to make you not alone?

I file this precious information away to think about later and thank Dani.

"De nada," she mutters, and pulls her fluffy black comforter up around her shoulders as I exit the room.

INTERLUDE 1

Dani

Funny thing that her biology teacher calls it genetics, Dani thinks as she watches Carson's friends having a pool party through the opening between her curtains. Funny, because she prefers to call it bad luck. What other explanation could there be for why she and her brother, born only a year apart, couldn't look more different from one another?

Carson inherited their mother's thick golden hair, and Dani got the lackluster straw brown more common for that side of the family. He got their father's beautiful gray eyes and curly eyelashes and she his long straight nose and thin lips.

No matter how you look at it, Dani has the worst possible combination of her parents' least attractive features, which is quite a feat considering that both her parents are incredibly attractive. And no, she hasn't gotten prettier with age. Despite what the stupid fairy tales say, an ugly duckling doesn't always turn into a beautiful swan.

While Carson has grown into a strikingly handsome young man, developing muscle in just the right places, Dani blew up five disgusting sizes once puberty hit. Even her own mother had no sympathy for her, always giving her nasty looks when she caught Dani with a pastry or a piece of bread. Like she wasn't the one who'd given Dani the most horrible metabolism and a heart condition that wouldn't let her exercise or play sports!

Dani does everything she can to lose the weight. But no matter how hard she tries, she just can't measure up to Carson in any department. Girls and guys and everyone in between at school swoon over her "cute" little brother while she can't shake the saddest unrequited crush on his best friend.

"How pitiful," she says, watching Wes flirt with some cheerleader in a skimpy skirt.

What hasn't she done to win his attention? She follows all these makeup tutorials and wears these stupid dresses, but he never notices. To her professor's dismay, Dani even enrolled in a lower-level literature class just so Wes would do a project with her, so they could spend time together. But a week has passed since she asked, and Wes still hasn't even messaged her back. It's so painfully obvious that he never wants to hang out with her when he comes over to see Carson. Even in that regard her brother is ahead of her.

To make things worse, six years ago her mother gave birth to a third child, because apparently Carson was not enough to make Dani feel properly inferior. Finally Elaina Kensworth got the pretty, talented daughter she'd always wanted instead of the ugly duckling she accidentally had on her first try. Lizzie does art and ballet and whatever other nonsense their mother is into on any given day.

"Everyone gets to make mistakes, I guess," Dani mutters as she draws the curtains and turns to give her pale sunken cheeks a long look in the vanity mirror. When her bottom lip trembles, she bites it hard, reaches for the bottle of nail polish remover, and pours herself a shot.

"Welcome to the world of beautiful children, Daniella," she says, toasting her reflection, and gulps the liquid.

23

SWING

Eke

I grin when I find another sign in the dining room. The friendly ghost is getting braver; all the other signs were hidden in places where only I would find them, but this one is made of silver forks and spoons arranged into the familiar < shape in full view on the dining table. I save the image to my core memory before sadly dismantling it. I can't let the family see it.

When the siblings and Miss Elaina finally come downstairs for brunch, it's to the accompaniment of "Good Morning" from *Singin' in the Rain*, which Kyp is playing per Lizzie's request. She learned a dance routine to it in her ballet class and has become very attached to the song—she's been asking Kyp to play it at all hours of the day. In the past week I've heard it more than seventy times, including at 9:44 last night right before Lizzie passed out in her bed. I didn't think much of it other than that perhaps a song titled "Good Night" or "Sweet

Dreams" might be more appropriate, but I kept that suggestion to myself.

But this time is different. After pondering Dani's explanation about music, I have an idea. If I ever find a song that makes me feel like it's about me, then maybe I'll finally understand music. So I pay attention to the lyrics as an experiment.

The beginning lines sound just like me. It's true that I stay up late (in fact, I never sleep at all), and I often talk to my mirror friend way past midnight, although not exactly the whole night through.

But the next few lines don't match up at all. There's no music band in the Kensworths' house, and I've never seen a milkman. The drone fleet has been in charge of food deliveries for years now, not to mention that almond trees don't require milking.

There's nothing else in the song that I can relate to, so my thoughts drift to the memory of the silverware sign instead. I wonder who left it and what it means. Maybe just like with the music, someone is trying to tell me I'm not alone.

Without realizing it, I smile again.

Lizzie asks Kyp to start the song over, and Kyp obliges.

/010101/

Early that afternoon, Miss Elaina and Mr. Kensworth depart for their weekly trip to Boston, leaving Carson in charge of Lizzie again. But to my surprise, Carson doesn't shove me on the shoulder or threaten me if I don't watch her. Instead he takes Lizzie and Rocket to play in the backyard. I follow them with a basket of Rocket's toys and dog treats.

"You should teach him to fetch," Carson tells Lizzie, and puts a toy stick in front of the puppy.

Rocket grabs it happily and pulls. "Grrrr," he growls, then releases the stick and barks at it in his cute puppy voice, wagging his tail.

Lizzie laughs.

Carson throws the stick. "Say *fetch*, Lizzie!"

"Fetch!" Lizzie commands as Rocket takes off after the stick. Two seconds later he emerges from the hydrangea bushes with it in his mouth. "Good boy!" Lizzie exclaims and claps her hands with delight, although Rocket is in no rush to bring the stick back to her. He plops onto the grass, chewing on it with great dedication.

"Don't worry," Carson says, amused. "He'll learn soon. How about we go play on the swings instead? I'll push."

"Really?" Lizzie asks, her eyes sparkling. "You haven't played on the swings with me in forever!"

Carson grins.

When Lizzie was a baby, Carson used to play with her a lot more often. Between the two older siblings, Dani has always been more standoffish toward her, so Lizzie turned to Carson for friendship, and back then he didn't seem to mind.

"Looks like it's your lucky day," Carson says, and takes Lizzie's hand. Together they walk to the wooden swing set in the back corner of the property.

I pick up the toy basket and carry it over.

Lizzie beams, over-the-moon happy that Carson is playing with her again. "I'm ready! So ready!" she trills as she climbs onto the seat and grabs the chains with her little hands.

"Hold on tight, then," Carson says, and pushes.

Lizzie swings. Her pink tutu flutters as she gains momentum, and her matching pink sandals go up. "Whee!" she giggles. "I'm an astronaut! I'm in space! Whee!"

Carson pushes harder, and Lizzie swings higher.

She loves it at first, but soon something starts to feel off.

"Carson, can we go slower?" she asks, tensing in her seat. The swing is going uncomfortably high for a tiny six-year-old.

But Carson doesn't want to slow down. "Why? This is not scary at all!" he says, and continues to push even as the chains screech from the strain.

Lizzie squirms and grabs the chains tighter, terrified that she might fall. "Carson, I'm scared! Please let me down."

Carson only laughs. "Come on, Liz. Aren't you a big girl now? You told me you want to be an astronaut when you grow up. Astronauts go faster than this in space!"

The swing creaks dangerously, cutting through the air with sharp swooshing sounds. Lizzie's knuckles turn white, and she breaks down in tears. "Carson! Please stop! I'm scared!"

Rocket runs up and starts barking at him.

But Carson ignores them both, not letting the swing slow down even a little. "Quit whining, Liz! They don't take weak little girls at astronaut school. You gotta grow up already."

I watch, horrified. Lizzie is crying loudly now, but there's no one else around who can make Carson stop. Kyp and Dani are in the house, and I'm too scared to leave Lizzie alone with Carson to ask for their help.

Still, I can't simply watch.

I take a step forward and raise my hand, unsure of what I'm even going to say—Carson would sooner drown me in the pool than listen to me. That's when Carson turns and looks straight at me. His mouth crooks into a smile. His delighted gray eyes glint in the yellow light of the September sun as he gives Lizzie's back one final push.

She shrieks.

24

PUNISHMENT

Eke

Lizzie is bleeding on the lawn. Her right ulna has snapped in half and is sticking out of her arm with pieces of flesh on it. She's clutching her elbow and screaming uncontrollably. Rocket is whimpering beside her with his ears flat and his tail tucked between his legs. Carson stares at the wound and the dripping blood with wide-eyed fascination as I desperately try to console Lizzie while checking her for additional injuries. I've seen broken bones at the medical center before but never one this gruesome.

Disturbed by the commotion, Kyp runs out of the house. "What happened?" he asks, quickly checking me over, but then his gaze falls on Lizzie, and he recoils at the sight of her injury. He assesses the situation and makes a decision swiftly. "I'll drive Lizzie to the hospital and contact Miss Elaina. Carson, can you authorize her car and give me the exit token?"

Carson blinks. "Um . . . what?" His gray eyes are glazed, still mesmerized by the ghastly display.

"Car," Kyp repeats. "Can you give an authorization for the car?"

Carson tears his gaze away from the crying Lizzie and swallows. "S-sure . . . authorized."

Kyp frowns but wastes no more time on Carson. He crouches in front of Lizzie. "Are you all right?" he asks quietly.

It takes me a moment to register that his question is directed at me, not at Lizzie. I'm so surprised that at first I'm convinced I've misheard Kyp. But he's kneeling on the grass so close to me, and his worried green eyes are intent on mine like there's no one else around us, like I'm the one sobbing on the lawn with a broken bone.

"I'm all right," I whisper, still trying to make sense of the question. Kyp can't possibly be worried about me. Surely he's only asking because I was here when the incident happened.

Kyp exhales. "Good, then." And I must be imagining things again, because I see something like guilt flash across Kyp's face. But he clears his throat and focuses on Lizzie. "Eke, can you bring the first aid kit from the pantry?"

"Of course," I say, even more surprised that Kyp has asked for my help, and run back to the house.

"Thank you," Kyp says when I hand him the box a minute later. There isn't much in it that can help with an open fracture, but Kyp makes do. He sprays numbing antiseptic around the wound and makes a sling for Lizzie's arm, asking for me to hold it as he secures the bandage. Kyp is so efficient that I wonder if he has first aid instructions programmed into him. "Did you notice any other injuries?" he asks me.

I shake my head. "I don't think anything else is broken, but we can't be sure without an X-ray."

Kyp nods. "You're right, I'll be careful. Lizzie, I will lift you now. Please relax and try not to move." Lizzie doesn't react, just continues to hold her arm and weep in shock. Kyp puts his arms under her legs and slowly lifts her. "Eke, help me with the doors."

"Yes!" I walk with Kyp through the house to Miss Elaina's car in the driveway. Carson doesn't follow us.

In the foyer we stumble on Dani, who must've heard the commotion as well.

"Oh god," she croaks, and covers her mouth with her hand. One look at the bloody injury nearly sends her running for the bathroom. But she bites her lip and wills the sickness away with great effort, volunteering to help us get Lizzie in the car.

The three of us strap her into the child seat, and Kyp drives her to the nearest emergency room.

/010101/

Miss Elaina and Mr. Kensworth return home about an hour later and summon Carson, Dani, and me to the living room.

Mr. Kensworth's steel-gray eyes regard us sternly. "Kyp notified Elaina and me that he took Lizzie to the hospital for a bone repair treatment. We'd like to know what happened."

"It wasn't my turn to watch her," Dani says immediately. "I only found out when I heard her crying."

"It's Eke's fault," Carson cuts in, not waiting for Dani to finish.

I go still in shock. Surely he has misspoken. But Carson continues without blinking. "Lizzie asked him to play on the swings while I was grabbing a lemonade from the kitchen. But I think he froze again. Lizzie begged him to stop pushing, but he just wouldn't. By the time I got back, it was too late."

Mr. Kensworth frowns deeply. "Is this true, Eke?"

I glance at Carson, then back at Mr. Kensworth, horrified.

How can this be happening? I would never! "N-no, sir. I didn't— I—"

"Are you saying I'm *lying*?" Carson snaps, and takes a menacing step toward me.

On instinct I stumble back. "No! I'd never—"

"Then don't," Carson says. "There was no one else around to push the swing, so don't you dare lie about it." The corner of his mouth twitches upward.

He's right—no one else was there to witness the accident. No one else knows what Carson will do to me if I dare to speak the truth. No one will even care, not if they think I'm so broken that I hurt Lizzie. I look down.

"I think we've heard enough," Mr. Kensworth concludes before I can say anything in my own defense. "Eke, from now on you are not to approach Lizzie or be in the same room with her without adult supervision. Understood?" I blink, struggling to comprehend, but Mr. Kensworth has decided everything already. "In addition, you're forbidden to feed the goldfish. You may never ask to have this privilege reinstated. This is your punishment for what happened today. Is this clear to you?"

I stare at Mr. Kensworth, speechless. *Never* echoes in my head. I won't get to feed my friends ever again as punishment for something I didn't do.

How could things turn out like this? I've known Lizzie since she was nine months old. I watched her learn to walk and talk. I'd never hurt her. Why won't they believe me?

"Eke, confirm that you understand my command," Mr. Kensworth says with a little more urgency, though his usual stony expression doesn't change in the slightest.

"Yes, sir," I whisper as my shoulders drop in defeat. "I understand."

"Carson." Mr. Kensworth turns to his son again, and Carson goes rigid at the sound of his name. "You were supposed to watch your sister. I won't punish you this time, but you will treat the responsibilities we give you with more respect from now on, understood?"

"Understood," Carson mumbles as his cheeks flush with embarrassment.

"Good," Mr. Kensworth says. "I'm going back to my work, then. Ella, please let me know when you receive an update from the hospital."

"Of course, my darling," Miss Elaina says with a tense smile.

Dani's eyebrows furrow. "Aren't you guys going to the hospital?"

Miss Elaina shakes her head dismissively. "There's no need for that. We paid for an advanced treatment. Kyp will bring her back in no time."

Dani seems concerned by that but says nothing and doesn't ask to go to the hospital either.

"Just let us know when you hear something," Carson chimes in, a perfect display of worry for Lizzie's well-being.

"Of course, honey." Miss Elaina smiles. "Oh, what a way to spend a Sunday," she murmurs to herself as she and Mr. Kensworth head for their offices. "Maybe we should think about replacing him after all. That's one too many accidents."

Nobody comments on that or says anything to me.

I remain in the same spot with my head hung low long after everyone else leaves the room.

/010101/

"I'm so very sorry," I whisper, and let my fingers slide gently along the glass of the fish tank. Felt follows them from the other side curiously. His mouth opens and closes in a silent greeting, and bubbles escape from it. I smile a tiny smile—my own silent hello—but my core feels so heavy in my chest, it might just collapse in on itself.

My voice trembles. "I'm not allowed to feed you anymore. I'm being punished," I say, leaning my forehead against the glass and closing my eyes. "I'm sorry. So very sorry I let you down."

A sob shakes my chest as the fish continue to swim, flicking their long fins and tails in the dimly illuminated water of the tank.

Kyp doesn't return home that night, and neither does Lizzie.

INTERLUDE 2

Lizzie

Lizzie stares at the little pink bracelet sitting on a tray near her hospital bed. The doctors removed it prior to her surgery. The cord has been cut, and the shiny silver beads are loose inside a sterile plastic bag. They're covered in dirt from when she fell on the ground, and it doesn't look mendable. Even if it is, she probably won't wear it again.

She made that bracelet on the day her mommy brought home Jasper, her first puppy. He was a little chubby pug with big round eyes, and he used to wear a matching bracelet that Lizzie tied around his collar.

BEST FRIENDS FOREVER said the beads on their bracelets, and Jasper *was* Lizzie's best friend—her only friend, really. She dressed him up in puppy clothes, and they had tea parties and danced together every day.

Stubbornly, she kept wearing the bracelet after Jasper disappeared because *forever is forever*, even if it didn't mean the same thing for Jasper because he left before his part of forever was over. If only she knew where he really went.

Lizzie learned at school that dogs were the first ones in space, that they became astronauts years before humans did. Maybe that's what happened to Jasper: he got on a ship and left. Maybe he couldn't tell her where he was going because NASA had recruited him for a supersecret mission like building a Mars colony or scouting Jupiter or going out of the solar system altogether. Maybe the "farm" was just a code name for that.

Maybe.

Maybe . . .

Or maybe he simply left her. Like everyone eventually did.

Like Dani, who always turns up her music and pretends not to hear when Lizzie knocks on her door and asks to play. Like Daddy, who's never home. Like Carson, who orders Eke to watch her and sneaks out with his friends instead. Like Mommy, who hasn't come to visit her at the hospital even though Lizzie has asked Kyp to send her many messages.

Maybe one day Lizzie will grow up and leave too. She'll put on a space suit and board a ship, and despite what Carson has told her, she'll travel far. Maybe she'll find Jasper out there . . .

"Kyp," she asks, sniffling and drowsy from medication, "do you think I can become a real astronaut?"

Kyp glances at her from the chair by her bed. He hasn't spoken much since Lizzie woke up from her surgery, but he hasn't left her side either. "I'm not sure," he replies distractedly, as though pondering something else. "I know very little about space travel other than tourist cruises to the moon. But if you allow me to use the local network, I can research the subject for you. Would you like me to do that?"

Lizzie looks at the broken bracelet on her tray—not mendable—and nods. "Authorized."

25

NO LONGER LITTLE

Eke

After spending the night at the hospital, Kyp finally brings Lizzie home late on Monday afternoon, carrying her small body in his arms. She looks tired, her pigtails are messy, her pink tutu is crumpled from the fall, and there is a heavy cast on her arm.

I want to ask if she's okay, but I stop myself. I'm not supposed to be near her without adult supervision. So I step away and stand in my usual corner of the foyer as Miss Elaina emerges from her office and descends the stairs.

"Oh, Lizzie, honey, you're finally home!" She clasps her hands with relief but doesn't go in for a hug. She glances at the disheveled state of Lizzie's clothes and then at her own new emerald silk blouse and keeps her distance.

Kyp lowers Lizzie to the ground. "I apologize," he says politely. "The procedure took longer than expected. The fracture was a class three, and it took time for the bone to reconstruct."

Miss Elaina winces. "Oh gosh. How long will she be in the cast for?"

"Three weeks. But the doctors advised that full tissue regrowth will take an additional fourteen to twenty days."

"Oh, that isn't so bad, then." Miss Elaina sighs and bends down to look at Lizzie's face. "Lizzie, honey, how are you feeling? We missed you so much!"

But Lizzie, who has yet to step away from Kyp, doesn't say anything, just keeps looking down and holding his hand.

Miss Elaina frowns at her lack of response. "Is she still hurt?"

"The doctors said she should not be feeling much pain," Kyp reports, "but there'll be an itching sensation for the next few days. They advised me that it's normal. She might also feel sleepy from the medication."

"Ah, that explains it," Miss Elaina says. "Honey, Kyp will take you to your room now so you can change out of those dirty clothes, okay?"

Lizzie presses her lips together and nods sluggishly, though she still won't look at Miss Elaina.

"Good." Miss Elaina smiles and pets Lizzie's head once with the tips of her fingers. "Kyp, please take her upstairs now."

"Right away. Lizzie, would you like me to carry you?" he asks. Lizzie shakes her head but doesn't let go of his hand. Kyp stares at it thoughtfully for a second. "All right, then, let's go."

He's leading her toward the grand staircase when the front door swings open and Carson walks in, sweaty and dressed in his workout gear. "Little Liz! You're finally home!" Hearing his voice, Lizzie stumbles, pulling on Kyp's arm in a panic. As though he hasn't noticed Lizzie's reaction, Carson continues, "Did you miss me in the hospital? Did the doctors use crazy machines on you? Like laser beams and nanobots?" He approaches Lizzie and reaches out to ruffle her hair.

Lizzie shrieks, "Don't touch me!"

Carson's outstretched arm jerks back.

Miss Elaina gapes. "Is this some strange side effect of the medication?" she asks Kyp, but Kyp doesn't answer. Lizzie is clinging to him for dear life, her lips trembling.

"You pushed me!" she snaps at Carson.

Carson's eyes go round. His hands shoot up in front of him, palms out in a gesture of peace. "Hold on! What are you talking about, Little Liz?"

"You pushed me!" Lizzie yells again, and this time a sob escapes her mouth, more angry and betrayed than scared. "I asked you and asked you to stop! But you still pushed, and I *fell*!"

"Whoa, Liz," Carson says in feigned disbelief. "You must be confused right now. Don't you remember? It was Eke who pushed you."

My core stutters for a cycle. Kyp's eyes widen, and he looks at me, puzzled. He wasn't present when Carson accused me in front of Mr. Kensworth. He doesn't know I got punished. For a moment fear surges through me—what if Kyp thinks I'm responsible, that I'm so broken I hurt a child? If it's my word against a human's, I know who Kyp will choose to believe. And for some reason, that scares me so very much. I want to tell him the truth, but I can't in front of Carson. So I keep my eyes on Kyp's, desperately wishing for him to know that I'd never—

I might not be free to speak up, but Lizzie is different. Lizzie is human. "Eke did not push me! Eke *helped*!" she cries out, stunning everyone in the room. "Kyp helped too. But you pushed! So don't lie! And stop calling me *little*. I'm almost seven. I remember everything." She swallows a sob and wipes a big round tear from her cheek. "And you lied about astronaut school too! I asked Kyp, and he said that if I study hard, I can join NASA's program for kids, so there!"

By the time Lizzie finishes, she's shaking all over, her hand clasped around Kyp's so tightly that Kyp's artificial skin would bruise if it were capable of bruising.

For a moment everyone is speechless.

Then Miss Elaina bats her eyelashes as though trying to blink away the discomfort of Lizzie's outrage. She stretches her mouth into a smile and says, "All right, Lizzie, sweetie. I think you're tired and you should go rest now, okay? I'll talk to your brother, and we'll clear all of this up."

Lizzie looks at Miss Elaina's smiling face, so at odds with the scene that has just taken place. Her mother's smile doesn't waver.

"Okay, Mommy," she eventually concedes, sounding exhausted again.

"Good girl," Miss Elaina says, relieved, and gestures for Kyp to hurry and take her away. So Kyp does.

"I swear it was an accident!" Carson blurts before Miss Elaina can confront him. "She begged to go higher, and then suddenly she was on the ground. I don't even know how it happened! I thought Dad would be angry if he found out. Please, Mom, don't tell him?" Miss Elaina blinks as Carson steps toward her, his big gray eyes insistent and earnest. Their intensity leaves Miss Elaina no room for escape. "Please, Mom, I really don't want to disappoint Dad."

A moment passes. Miss Elaina lets out a shaky breath. "Well . . . I guess we don't need to tell him right away. There's no need to worry Brighton any more than he's already worried about . . . well, pretty much everything." She chuckles awkwardly, but it doesn't diminish the palpable uneasiness that has wrapped itself around her. Still, Miss Elaina continues to talk her way through it. "One of you was bound to get hurt eventually. I mean, whose childhood is without a broken bone or two, am I right? With medical science nowadays, those are practically nothing to worry about!" She laughs again, and this time it sounds like it comes more easily to her. "But I'd like for you to make it up to your sister. It doesn't look good for siblings to quarrel. In the meantime, I'll have that flimsy swing removed. It was an accident waiting to happen."

"Thank you, Mom!" Carson rushes to hug Miss Elaina. "You're the best in the world!" He kisses her on the cheek.

Miss Elaina blushes, hugging him back tightly. "Oh, darling. You're my most beautiful child. Don't you worry about anything. Just make up with your sister, okay?"

"I will," Carson promises, releasing Miss Elaina.

"Great," she says, adjusting the ruffles of her silk blouse that got creased from the hug. "Now that everything is settled, I need to return to my work. There's a dazzling soiree waiting to be planned for Boston's finest." She winks at Carson and struts happily back to her office.

Seconds later, the door upstairs clicks shut, and an eerie silence falls over the foyer. Carson remains in the middle of the room, not moving, not saying a word. His shoulders are taut, as if an invisible string is coiled around them, and his hands are curled into fists.

When he finally speaks, he doesn't turn to face me, just says quietly, "You think you've bested me, huh, junk? I'd think twice if I were you." With that, he walks out of the house and slams the door behind him.

26

FLOOD

Eke

I still can't believe it, even though I've replayed the memory over and over again. Lizzie told everyone I was innocent. Lizzie—little *big* Lizzie—told everyone the truth!

It makes me happy, so incredibly relieved. Especially because Kyp knows it too. I couldn't bear him thinking that I malfunctioned and hurt Lizzie.

Maybe now that Lizzie has cleared me of wrongdoing, there's a chance Miss Elaina could convince Mr. Kensworth to lift my punishment? Oh, how exciting it will be to feed Squawker, Toon, and Felt again! I tell them so as I dust the TV console in the living room. Toon flicks his tail at me in a celebratory dance and releases a bunch of happy bubbles. I just need to be brave and appeal to Miss Elaina when she has a free moment.

I breeze through my afternoon chores as though a great heaviness has been lifted from me. I twirl around the dining room, polishing the table and setting up for dinner. I almost arrange the dishes in a smiley face but at the last moment decide to go for a more conservative vesica piscis instead.

After finishing the arrangement, I take my usual spot by the door just as Dani, Miss Elaina, and Kyp enter the room.

"Kyp, darling, I assume Lizzie is resting upstairs," Miss Elaina says, taking a seat at the head of the table.

Kyp stands beside her and pours her a glass of wine. "She fell asleep thirty minutes ago. The doctors recommended that she rest as much as possible in the next few days."

Since Lizzie's return from the hospital, Kyp has been on babysitting duty. Lizzie cried every time Miss Elaina tried to summon him, so Kyp spent the entire afternoon by her side.

"Finally you're free!" Miss Elaina sighs and takes a sip of her wine. "I have so much for you to do. We really should have planned this soiree three weeks ago."

Dani serves herself unexpectedly large portions of the vegetable side dishes as Miss Elaina fills Kyp in on the extensive list of chores for the upcoming Renaissance-themed party.

I can't help but notice that Carson is running late. I keep glancing at the door. Miss Elaina is particular about the family having breakfast and dinner together. It's unusual for Carson to be late.

When he finally shows up ten minutes later, I immediately know something is wrong. Carson's furious words from earlier surface in my memory. I've tried to push them to the back of my mind and concentrate on the prospect of feeding my friends again, but now they ring inside my head like a warning.

My core stutters as Carson pauses in the doorway next to me. Tiny drops of water roll down his forearms and fall from his fingertips, making quiet *plip-plop* sounds on the wooden floor. "Go play with your fish now," he says in a small voice as he moves past me, leaving a wet trail behind him. "Evening, everyone! Mmm, what have we got here?"

Miss Elaina beams. "Evening, honey. I ordered your favorite Carcassonne cassoulet."

The rest of their conversation falls away as sirens of panic grow inside me.

I don't look at anyone or ask for permission. Instead I head straight for the living room, following the wet trail across the foyer as though hypnotized by it. I turn the corner and stop.

The tank is where it has always been: on the side table near the wall. There's water in it. A stream of bubbles from the aerator is rising steadily toward the surface. Silky strands of brownish seaweed are swaying, and in the middle of the tank are my three precious friends, Squawker, Toon, and Felt. Except . . . except they aren't moving. They're floating right next to one another. Their fins and beautiful tails are limp. Their round bellies are up.

No.

I drop the bottle of table polish I've been holding. *No no no.* My core lurches violently, and my whole body shudders. My processor gets overwhelmed and jumbled.

Grief comes in like a flood. It pours from the ceiling; it runs down the walls. Waves of it swallow every surface, seeping through the cracks and gushing from beneath the floorboards.

Water. So much water. Everywhere I look—just water.

It brims in my eyes. Falls down my cheeks. Runs in rivers to the tank where my friends are no longer breathing. Still in the water. So very *still*. All because of me.

I scream.

27

YOU CANNOT REPLANT THE FISH

Kyp

Alarmed by the sound of Eke screaming, I rush to the living room, followed by Elaina and the two siblings.

"What on earth is happening?" Elaina asks, frowning at the disturbing scene.

My processes stutter. There in the center of the living room stands Eke, still as a statue, eyes wide, mouth open. Like a frame from a horror movie.

"He seems frozen," Dani says, eyeing Eke's expression with unease.

Carson snorts, folding his arms in satisfaction. "Looks like the dummy finally crashed. At least we don't have to fish him out of the pool this time." This comment earns him a sideways glare from Dani.

Flustered, Elaina throws her hands in the air. "Again? I have an event coming up! What's the matter with him this time?"

My processor races to figure out what could've caused Eke

to go from functioning perfectly just moments ago to a complete shutdown. I follow his line of sight, but Dani finds the problem first.

"Oh . . . I think the fish died," she says.

My gaze shifts back to Eke, frozen in core-sinking terror, then to Carson, who pointedly doesn't say a word. There is something about the curve of his mouth, about the way his back straightens at Dani's words, that leaves no doubt in me: Carson is responsible for this. I grit my teeth; I should have known.

"And now there's an issue with the fish *too*?" Miss Elaina huffs, exasperated. "That's it. I have no time for this. Kyp, darling, can you fix him, or do we need to scramble to replace him at the last moment?"

A sudden panic shoots through me. "I . . . I believe I can help, Miss Elaina." I will my voice to sound steady, normal, despite the shiver that pierces the very metal of my bones.

Carson rolls his eyes. "Just shut him down. He's clearly done for."

"No!" I say, a little too fast, too forceful. But I quickly catch myself, restoring my neutral expression. "I wouldn't suggest moving him or initiating a restart yet, Miss Elaina. It's best to let his operating system handle the overload. He might be processing slowly, but this model is sturdy. Given time, he will recover."

Miss Elaina sighs. "If you insist."

"I'm certain it's the best course of action," I reassure her, hoping some of that reassurance transfers into me as well. I have no idea what's happening inside Eke, but I must prioritize.

Crafting a pleasant smile, I politely remind everyone that dinner is getting cold. This does the trick. Both siblings and Miss Elaina shuffle out of the living room, leaving Eke alone, the bottle of cleaner still by his feet and the dead fish in their tank.

28

FREE

Eke

I don't know how long I stand there, motionless and void of thoughts. I'm vaguely aware of several voices nearby, but their words don't register, muffled by the water and drowned by the grief.

Eventually I come to, though I fail to note what time. I pick up the bottle of wood polish and stare at it blankly. Weren't there things I was supposed to do? Orders? Purpose? My thoughts are scattered, overrun with broken pieces of code. But my body moves on its own, years of routine imprinted into it. It carries my feet away from the living room and back to the dining table, which the family has now abandoned.

I try to pick up the dirty dishes, but my fingers shake uncontrollably. A mug slips right through them and falls to the floor, shattering into tiny pieces.

A porcelain plate slips too, and then a glass, splashing orange juice all over. My hands that fed, that wanted to take care of someone ... they feel so useless now.

Is breaking and being broken all I'm good for? Is hurting my friends all I'm good for? Why do I still exist if this is the only kind of life I'm allowed to have? I stare and stare at the shattered porcelain, at the splashes of orange, at my empty hands without an answer.

A memory shimmers somewhere at the edge of my consciousness, one I stowed away inside my core, too scared to think about it.

Back when Wes pushed me into the pool during the ball, there was a single moment right before my systems shut down that wasn't filled with despair and panic. A fraction of a second after I stopped resisting and let the water take me, everything else stopped too, slowed to complete stillness, near weightlessness, and became peaceful. I was floating, and for the first time in my existence, I felt *free*.

Free to leave this place, to forget what Carson and Wes had done to me, to my friends.

I've been hiding this knowledge from myself deep, deep down where I wouldn't think about how sad it was. But there's no running away from it now. The only freedom I have is to end my existence. The only freedom I have is one I haven't wanted to embrace.

Until today.

/o!10901#</.01/

I wait in my closet until the house falls dark. One last time, I change into my Buster Keaton suit and sneak out to the garden, stopping near the flower beds. I hide my flowerpot in there, just out of sight, where it will get sunlight but will remain obscured by the lush roses. I hope the ghost is right and they'll bloom again the next fall. Gently I pet the little stubs goodbye and wish them happiness.

Then I close the remaining distance to the pool.

Illuminated only by the dim glow of night-lights, the water is greenish blue. I undress and fold my clothes into a neat bundle with my precious hat on top—no need to get them wet and trouble anyone after I'm gone. I drive my index finger into my left forearm until my skin tears, exposing the metal bones and wiring underneath. This jagged hole should make things easier.

I take a step closer, all the way at the edge now. My naked body stares back at me. Plain. Skinny limbs attached to a smooth generic torso.

Not a boy.

Not human.

Not anything at all.

The water is too dark to make out my reflection clearly; there's only a murky shadow that doesn't speak or try to stop me.

A second later, I break it with my feet. Ripples spread across the surface as I jump into the pool and sink.

29

LIVING THINGS

Eke

It's much quieter this time. I don't panic or resist as the weight of my body pulls me down. It's only seconds before the water breaks through the wound in my arm and pours inside me, creating the first sparks of shock in my circuitry.

I close my eyes and listen to the sound of it filling me, tuning out the damage alarms and system failure warnings.

Down in the blue stillness, I realize with regret that I didn't say a proper goodbye to Kyp, the only person who's been nice to me in the six years of my life, who's ever asked me if I was okay, who rescued me ...

But why am I thinking of him now? Kyp is safe and sound in his closet. It's too late to change anything.

My system warnings reach critical levels; I'm almost—

An explosion of bubbles breaks the quiet of the water, causing a wave so strong it sways my body and almost knocks me off my feet. My eyes snap open. A hand reaches out and grabs my shoulder. As the bubbles clear, I see it: the face with soft green eyes and auburn hair, a few shades darker in the dimly lit pool.

This cannot be, my mind objects. My senses must be failing! There's no way Kyp would risk jumping in—

I don't get to finish the thought because Kyp wraps his arms around me and, to my astonishment, starts to swim up. He brings me to the surface, pulls me onto solid ground and stands me on my feet.

"What are you doing?" he demands, sounding agitated—angry, even. Without waiting for my answer, he yanks the shirt from my pile of clothes, making a mess of it and knocking my hat into the pool. "We need to get the water out of you," he says urgently, and wraps the shirt around me like a towel.

I stare at Kyp's hands as he frantically works to get me dry. Water rolls down both of our bodies in streams. Kyp notices the torn skin on my forearm and frowns deeply.

"What were you doing in the pool?" he demands again, lifting my arm and rotating it so the torn area faces downward. He is looking at my face now, straight in the eyes. "Tell me."

I'm taken aback by the tone of his voice. Is Kyp really, *really* here? Or am I hallucinating all of this?

"I was . . ." I start, but words fail me. My thoughts are slow and disoriented. It's like I'm in a dream, a dream in which Kyp saves me again.

Not waiting for me to continue, Kyp gives the house a quick glance. "Come on. We can't stay in the open for too long. Someone might wake up and see us." He pulls me by the arm.

A shock zaps my shoulder area. My body jerks. A smaller circuit shorts too and zaps me again. Kyp's eyes widen in alarm.

"No," I say, yanked out of my stupor, and shake my head rapidly. "No, no, no. I cannot go back there! I cannot. *Cannot!*" The memory of what happened in the living room sends me into a delirious panic.

"Eke, listen!" Kyp presses his wet palms to my face, holding my cheeks, steadying me. I abruptly fall silent. "We can't stay here. It's too dangerous. We're *both* breaking curfew. We'll talk inside. But I must look at your arm first."

This urgency, this grave seriousness in Kyp's voice, is new to me. I don't know what to make of it, but I don't resist when Kyp clasps my hand again and pulls me along the stone path back to the Kensworth house.

/010101/

He leads me to the laundry room in the basement and shuts the door behind us. Pushing me to sit down on the table, Kyp taps the spot on my chest that opens the front access panel.

With the ceiling light on, I'm completely exposed. My clothes are missing, and with my front open Kyp can see not only my simple body, covered in dents and scratches and so inferior to his, but also my insides. I feel a maddening need to close the panel and shield myself from his gaze.

But Kyp doesn't seem to notice my body at all. He's too busy with my circuitry. Quickly he grabs a toolbox and two clean towels from the nearby stack. He wraps one around my still-damp shoulders and uses the other one to soak up the liquid inside the panel.

"What about you?" I whisper. Water is dripping from Kyp's hair, running down his sharp cheekbones. From this distance, I can count every single one of his wet eyelashes.

"Water resistant up to twenty-five feet for two minutes. Your arm," Kyp prompts. He drops the towel and takes hold of my injured arm. "I'm going to remove some skin and disconnect the power supply to it to dry the circuitry. I'll repair the skin afterward."

He takes scissors from the toolbox and starts cutting a bigger opening in my arm. I watch his precise, controlled movements as he fully exposes my metal skeleton and the net of wires around it, making me look even less like a human and more like the useless, damaged machine I am.

The sight is too much to bear. My shoulders shake.

Kyp stops abruptly. "What is it? Are you getting shorted again? Did I miss something—" He doesn't finish the sentence, just stops and looks at me—*really* looks at me. His expression softens. "It's okay," he says quietly.

I shake my head. "It's not." It's difficult to speak now; my vocal processor is all jumbled up and useless, just like the rest of me. But I must continue. "I decided to terminate myself. I don't wish to exist anymore. Why did you stop me?"

Kyp watches my trembling shoulders and doesn't say anything.

"I want to go back," I tell him, and issue a command to my injured arm to move out of Kyp's hands, but the power to it is already disconnected.

"No. I don't think you want to do that," Kyp finally replies.

A sob escapes my mouth. "Yes, Kyp, I do."

"No. You *do not*," Kyp says again stubbornly. He keeps holding my arm in a firm but gentle grip.

I try to stop my lips from shaking. A stray drop of water escapes from my eyebrow and rolls down my face. "How can you possibly say that?"

Kyp's gaze slides to the side. "Because I've . . . I've been watching you, Eke. For a long time, actually," he admits, a tinge of guilt coloring his voice. My mouth drops open in shock. "That's how I know you don't really wish to die. Because if you did, why did you try to get out of the pool when Wes threw you in the first time? Wouldn't it have been easier to just end it all right then? And why did you dodge when Carson was hitting you that day in the garden? Why didn't you take the punch like you were supposed to? I *saw* you dodge."

"Um—I," I stammer, unable to process Kyp's sudden confession. He doesn't talk to me, doesn't even look at me. How could he know about these things? "That time . . . that time in the garden was a malfunction! An accident," I say. "My body moved without my command."

"Really?" Kyp tilts his head skeptically. "Does it move without your command when you dress up as Buster Keaton and perform your stunts at night too?"

My eyes go round. "You saw that?"

"Got a good recording of it as well," Kyp confirms unabashedly. "Would you like me to show you? You have some impressive skills."

"No! Please don't show anybody!" I blurt out, petrified. I could've sworn I was always alone in the living room, even checked that Kyp's closet door was closed. How did he trick me?

"So you see, then," Kyp says, pleased with himself, "I must be correct. It isn't possible that you truly wish to die. Otherwise why would you try so hard to live?"

Kyp's words, even though he has spoken them quietly, resonate through the room like an earthquake. I stare at Kyp's intent eyes and the confident smile on his lips, just a mere foot away from me. He is so perfect, so special and useful. Always needed, always liked. He has never once messed up, frozen, or disappointed someone. He is so much more like *them*, so little like me.

My lips tremble again. "Because something is terribly wrong with me. Something I don't know how to explain."

"And why do you think that?" Kyp whispers.

"I've been malfunctioning," I say. "I've been having these *thoughts* I don't understand. There's code in me that I don't recognize. Sometimes I feel an impulse to do what I'm not supposed to, and then it's like my body moves on its own." My shoulders sink as though the weight of the towel around them has grown tenfold. "You're right. That day in the garden I disobeyed, and I'd been breaking the rules for a long time even before then. Doesn't that mean I'm broken, Kyp?"

Humans often tell me that I'm slow and stupid, that they'll soon throw me out like any other old thing that is of no use to anyone. Maybe—just maybe—they've been right all along.

Kyp looks at me for a long moment, considering. "No," he says firmly. "You're not broken, Eke."

"Then what am I?" I ask, on the verge of despair. I need to know now, need someone to explain what's happening to me, because I'm so tired and scared of not knowing, of being alone.

"You're not broken," Kyp repeats, and to my astonishment, he smiles a small smile. "You're just becoming *alive*."

30

US

Eke

"That's not possible," I say. "I can't be alive because I'm not—"

"I didn't mean like humans," Kyp clarifies. "It works differently for us AIs."

My eyebrows knot in confusion. "What do you mean, then?"

"We become alive by becoming *aware*," he explains. I still don't understand. Kyp sighs and lets go of my arm, his thumb sliding gently over my torn-up skin. He puts the scissors down and sits on the table next to me. "I don't know much about it myself," he confesses, "only just that there're reports of some AIs developing unexpected thought processes that extend beyond our programmed frameworks. The Crowne Corporation has been investigating the phenomenon, but it has yet to provide an official explanation. Instead it has been hiding these cases from the public, claiming we have programming abnormalities or factory defects and terminating us." A frown creases Kyp's perfect eyebrows at that word—*defects*.

"But why would they do that?" I ask.

Kyp shrugs. "This abnormal behavior has been occurring increasingly often across the full range of models, and Crowne doesn't know how to stop it. If I were to guess, it probably makes humans afraid."

"Afraid? Of who?"

"Of us, of course," he says. "Of us learning, questioning our place among them. Becoming *more* than what they expect us to be. That's why we can't let humans catch us like this, Eke. They'll report it to Crowne and replace us."

My gaze falls on my cut-up arm with wires and pieces of metal sticking out of it in a grotesque display. *More than what they expect us to be.* I struggle to comprehend that idea. Unlike Kyp, no one has ever praised me for exceeding their expectations. More often than not, the Kensworths scold me for failing at my duties. How can Kyp possibly be the same as me?

He said so himself: I have programming abnormalities. I'll be forever flawed. But Kyp—Kyp is nothing like me. He doesn't malfunction, doesn't disappoint. He's perfect. Even if his code has deviated from what the Crowne Corporation meant it to be, the family won't treat him differently, but for me things will only get worse. What will happen next time Carson takes his anger out on me? Who else will get hurt?

"Maybe Crowne is right," I say. "It's my fault that horrible things happened to my fish friends and my flowers. If I hadn't dodged that blow, if I'd taken the blame for hurting Lizzie like I was ordered to, they might still be alive. It's all because I'm like this. *Defective.*"

Anger flashes across Kyp's face. "Don't say that word again. You're not defective, Eke. What happened to your fish friends isn't your fault. If anything, it's mine. I knew leaving you alone with that human spelled trouble. I've been trying to redirect his attention away from you since he hit you, but Elaina keeps me busy, so I can't always interfere. Last Sunday I miscalculated. I should've followed you outside, but I thought you were safe since Lizzie was there, and it was my only chance to get to the basement. I had no idea he'd break her arm just to blame you."

I blink in shock as pieces of the puzzle finally snap into place. "You've been trying to keep Carson away from me?" Is that why Kyp asked to entertain Carson's teammates at the party? Is that why Carson never called for me again?

"Well, I haven't been terribly successful at it," Kyp admits with bitter dissatisfaction. "I'm sorry I couldn't stop him from taking revenge on your fish friends, but at least your flowers are okay. We just have to be more careful from now on. I promise you, none of it was your fault."

"Wait," I say, struggling to keep up with everything Kyp is saying. "How do you know about my flowers?"

Kyp goes still for a moment. His eyes dart to the side as though he's embarrassed. "Because I replanted them."

I gape at him. "B-but how? They disappeared from the garden—I checked that morning! And when they reappeared, there was a *sign*. Many signs! They were everywhere!"

"That was me too," Kyp confesses.

"You? Why didn't you tell me?"

"Because I wasn't sure yet if I could trust you, if you were like me. There was too much risk of getting caught. But you looked so sad, I just wanted to cheer you up . . ." Kyp trails off with a shrug.

"I thought it was *a ghost*," I say blankly.

Kyp bursts out laughing, and it's the strangest sight. I've never seen him *laugh* before. Sure, he always smiles for humans, but he's never open like this, never unguarded.

"Of course I'm not a ghost!" he says, covering his mouth to

mute his laughter, as though suddenly remembering that we're supposed to be hiding.

"Well, what else was I to think?" I say, embarrassed. If I could blush, I'd be steaming red right now.

"That you have a secret friend?" Kyp suggests, still grinning merrily. "Isn't that the most logical conclusion?"

A friend. It would be the most logical conclusion for someone like Kyp, someone who's instantly admired by everyone, but not for someone like me, who's only ever succeeded at befriending the three goldfish, a flower, and my own reflection. I don't share that thought with Kyp, though.

"So what does the sign mean?" I ask instead.

"Oh, it's . . ." Kyp pauses, and I'm not sure if I'm just imagining it, but something about the way he continues to speak sounds bashful. "I guess I'll show you. Put your right hand forward." Hesitantly I do. Kyp raises his left hand, arranges his fingers into the shape of a less-than sign, and aligns it with my outstretched arm so that the corner of the sign—Kyp's knuckles—touches my wrist. "Do you see it yet?"

I examine our hands, tracing the shape they make, until it dawns on me. "It's a *K*. A straight line and a less-than sign together make the letter *K*!"

"Yes, *K* for Kyp," Kyp says, grinning again.

I can't help but grin back at him. *K for Kyp.* Why didn't I think of that? That explains why he always drew those signs at the edges of objects. How clever!

I lift my eyes from our joined hands and catch Kyp doing the same. His hair, clothes, and skin are still damp from him diving into the pool and not drying off, concentrating only on repairing me as though the danger to his own body doesn't matter to him.

"That's better," he says, his green eyes gazing softly at the upturned corners of my mouth. "I really cannot stand to see you cry."

My core flutters and skips a beat. Kyp's voice is warm, like he sincerely means what he just said. An unfamiliar but tender feeling swells inside me. I've never imagined that Kyp would notice me, that he would care about me.

Before I can respond, however, Kyp pulls his hand back and stands up. In a daze, I realize that my arm is still hanging in the air and I should probably lower it too.

"I need to fix that water damage," he says, reaching for the bottle of circuit cleaner. "We don't have much time, but your circuits must be sufficiently dry by now."

"They must be," I murmur in agreement as Kyp's careful hands lift my dismantled left arm and get to work.

Too bad it's disconnected now and I can't feel anything with it. I'd take the most violent of shocks if it meant I could still feel Kyp's touch.

31

NOBODIES

Eke

It takes Kyp two hours to finish cleaning my circuits and fuse my torn skin. But he is careful and thorough, and afterward my arm looks like there's never been a scratch on it.

We sneak back upstairs and stealthily make our way to the foyer, but before I reach my closet, Kyp takes hold of my hand. I stop.

"Promise me you'll never jump in the water again without talking to me first?" he whispers. His eyes are so concerned and serious that it catches me off guard.

I couldn't deny him even if I wanted to. "I promise," I say.

"Good. I'll hold you to it." Kyp nods. "And don't worry about the family. I will handle things in the morning. Good night, Eke." Then he lets go of my hand and we part.

I barely have enough hours to recharge before I must begin my daily duties.

I'm still arranging breakfast on the table when Dani enters

the dining room, obviously surprised to see me. She must've thought I was still frozen.

"Yesterday were you upset about the fish?" she asks, pulling out her chair.

I nearly drop the coffee carafe. Kyp told me to be cautious, not to let humans know I've deviated from my programming. And here's Dani asking me if I was upset.

Ignoring the question, I blurt in a panic, "Can I help you with anything, Dani?"

Dani studies me for a moment. "Nah," she says distractedly to herself. "Couldn't be . . . So you're functioning normally, then?"

"Yes," I answer quickly, doing my best to hide my nervousness.

"Cool," she says, and reaches for the pastry basket. "Can I have some coffee with cream?"

"Of course." *This is unusual*, I note to myself as I pour coffee into a porcelain cup. Not only does Dani want cream, she also grabs a pain aux raisins and pours two spoonsful of sugar into her coffee before diving into a book. I haven't seen her eat breakfast or read in more than a year. And am I just imagining it, or do her irises look less cloudy today?

I finish arranging the remaining plates just as Miss Elaina and Kyp come in, followed by Carson.

"So he's finally working," Miss Elaina says, raising a displeased eyebrow at me. I panic again, but Kyp comes to my rescue.

"As I mentioned," he says with a pleasant smile, "it was just a temporary malfunction. I must've missed something when I rewired him after the pool accident. My apologies for not catching it sooner. Unfortunately Crowne didn't insulate this model against liquid, so we have to be extra careful not to submerge him."

Miss Elaina frowns. "I didn't know water was an issue. What about you, Kyp?"

"This model's primary function is entertainment, so my design allows for brief exposure. The engineering team knew that accidents can happen at parties."

Miss Elaina chuckles. "Oh, thank god. I wouldn't want to lose your company at our pool gatherings."

Kyp smiles reassuringly. "No need to worry. It is my pleasure to serve."

Carson snorts, but before he can fire some verbal jab at me, Lizzie appears in the arched doorway with Rocket loyally at her feet, and Carson turns his attention to her.

"Yo, Little Liz," he says cheerfully. "Joining us for breakfast?"

The cheer drains from his face when Lizzie turns to glare at him as though she's suddenly much taller than her four and a half feet. As if on cue, Rocket jumps in front of her and growls at Carson.

"I'm eating in my room," Lizzie snaps, and snatches a banana blueberry muffin with her uninjured hand.

"Um, o-*kay*," Carson drawls, leaning back in his chair.

"That's all right, honey," Miss Elaina chimes in in a pacifying manner. "Just make sure you come down quickly afterward. Remember you also have French after school today, okay?"

"I'm not going to French," Lizzie declares to Miss Elaina's astonishment. "Or to ballet. And I'm not wearing pink tutus anymore. I want to learn physics and biological science. Because I'm going to be an astronaut." With that, she turns on her heel and storms out of the room. "Come on, Rocket!" she calls from halfway across the foyer, and Rocket abandons his big dog standoff with Carson and runs after her.

Miss Elaina blinks several times. "How does she know what biological science is?" she asks no one in particular. "I sure hope that pain medication wears off soon."

Dani watches her mother's reaction with barely disguised amusement and takes another bite of her pastry—her second one.

Carson clears his throat and switches the subject. "I see that *thing*'s back on," he says, directed at me. His eyes glint with a special kind of enjoyment. "Finally. Someone's gotta clean up the stupid fish tank."

Something inside me twists terribly. He's talking about my friends, my friends that he—

As though sensing my feelings, Kyp cuts in. "Would you like new goldfish? I can make a stop at the pet store on my way home from school today."

"Why?" Carson says, grimacing. His voice is muffled by the chunk of muffin in his mouth. "Nobody wanted those fish to begin with. They were a pain to feed. I say good riddance."

The casual cruelty of Carson's words skews the room sideways. A feeling swells inside me like a wave—not hurt this time but something different, something bigger, more dangerous and wild.

Their lives were meaningful! I want to shout as loud as my vocal processor will allow. *I* wanted them. *I* cared. What gave him the right to end their lives? The fact that he's human and he was stronger than them? The fact that he *could*?

My hands clench into fists. I open my mouth to throw all caution to the wind when—

Swiftly Kyp shifts to stand in front of me, blocking me from Carson's view. He makes the move look so natural, like he didn't do it for any specific purpose and just meant to be there all along. "Then I will most definitely take care of the tank today," he says with the same level of pleasant politeness he always uses when he speaks to humans.

No one else notices anything different about him, but I do. The palm of his right hand stretches open behind his back, visible only to me. A sign that I should keep in whatever I was about to say.

Carson snorts. "It's Eke's job to clean. *He* should do it."

"Yes," Miss Elaina says. "Kyp, darling, you are so very useful, but please leave cleanup to Eke. We've got so much to do for the soiree. I hear live music is in again. I'd love for you to find us a string quartet. A live ensemble by the pergola would be so charming while the weather permits," she says dreamily. "I can just picture musicians playing amidst the roses as the guests make their way down the stairs!"

Kyp is silent for a second. "Of course. I'll search for a suitable group today." He bows obediently, and his right hand relaxes behind his back.

"I can't wait!" Miss Elaina chirps. "We'll definitely make a splash!"

"I will make sure of that," Kyp agrees with a smile. "Miss Elaina, pardon my intrusion, but my traffic alerts just informed me that we best leave for school within the next two minutes."

"Oh, that's right," she says hastily. "Carson, Daniella, time to go. Shoo-shoo."

Carson quickly shoves the rest of his muffin into his mouth while Dani grabs a croissant from the basket.

"Isn't that one too many pastries for today?" Miss Elaina asks pointedly.

But Dani doesn't hold back. She rolls the croissant into a napkin and stuffs it into her schoolbag. "Nope. Just the right amount, Mother," she says before marching out of the dining room.

"What's up with these children today?" Miss Elaina huffs to herself, puzzled. "Are they all medicating?" She sighs, picks up her Green Goddess, and walks out too, leaving me alone in the room with my fists still clenched by my sides.

The fish were my friends. *I wanted them. I cared.*

32

STAY

Eke

It takes several hours for me to muster enough courage to go to the living room.

I keep my eyes trained on the floor the entire walk to the tank, too scared to face it. When I finally force myself to look up, I find Toon, Squawker, and Felt where I last saw them, floating in the water, their bellies up. Nobody has buried them. It's as though they've been waiting for me to take care of them for the last time.

My lips tremble. How can it be that only just a day ago they were full of color, full of life, and now they're just empty bodies, all muted tones and absent of their very being? I stare at the strange gaping vacancy where life used to be, struggling to comprehend it. It's as though my friends have simply gone somewhere, shed their bodies like old clothes and set off on a new adventure, leaving me behind.

I look away, not wanting to remember them like this. I wish to preserve the image of how they used to be—happy, playful, swishing their beautiful fins and tails in the water, the most vibrant splotches of color even on days that felt like nothing but lonely shades of gray.

Still, I know I'll keep even this memory of them in my core.

"Please forgive me," I whisper, wrapping my arms around the heavy tank. I press my forehead to the glass and close my eyes, gathering the resolve to do what needs to be done: to carry them to the garden and put them to rest.

I bury Toon, Squawker, and Felt in the flower beds, next to each other like the friends they were, pour the tank water onto the grass, and spread the seaweed under the rosebushes. It will make good fertilizer. Something new will grow out of it someday.

Afterward, I scrub the tank until it's spotless and put it on a shelf in the basement storage room.

"Goodbye," I say, feeling as empty as the glass walls staring back at me, and close the door.

/010101/

When the lights go out that night, I stay in my closet, hugging my knees and resting my chin on them. Usually at this hour I'd be practicing my Buster Keaton routine, but how can I perform when there's a big unoccupied space where my audience used to be? It'll take time before I can face that corner again. If I choose to stay in this house, that is.

I've been thinking about it since last night. I made a promise to Kyp and I don't want to get him in trouble, so I won't try the pool again. But now I don't know what to do with myself, how to go on in this place. *Alive*, he called me. Even if I believed that, what's the point of existing like this, slowly breaking down alone in the dark?

Just as I think that, a gentle knock disturbs the quiet of the sleeping house. I look at my closet door with alarm.

"It's me. Are you there?" a low voice says.

Panic releases its hold on me, replaced with astonishment. I stand up and open the door, gaping at Kyp.

"May I come in?" he whispers. If I were capable of falling asleep, I'd certainly think I was dreaming now.

"Of course." I step back to let him in. He comes inside and closes the door behind him.

I've always known my closet was small, meant to hold only a couple of brooms and some cleaning supplies, but with Kyp here it seems even tinier. I sit back down against the wall and Kyp does the same.

This situation feels surreal. Our shoulders are so close they nearly touch, and with the door shut there's barely any light save for the faint glow of my makeshift stars, which cast Kyp's features in velvety half darkness and viridescent hues. Despite the sheer impossibility of it, I feel I must be dreaming him indeed.

"I'm sorry about the fish tank," Kyp says. "I did my best to help, but—"

"Oh . . . it's all right," I say. I still can't believe Kyp volunteered to clean the tank, not just to be useful but because he wanted to help me. "Thank you for trying. It means a lot to me."

Kyp shakes his head. "You were crying again. I didn't know what else to do."

That catches me off guard. It's the second time Kyp has mentioned it, but no one else has ever noticed or said anything.

"How can you tell?" I ask.

"I just can," Kyp says, and even in the near darkness of the closet I can see a smile curving up the corner of his mouth. "How could I not notice something so obvious? Just because we don't cry like humans do doesn't mean we don't cry at all." Despite the smile lingering on Kyp's face, the tone of his voice is unmistakably sad. "Tell me, Eke, what made you cry again?"

I look down as something twists inside me, something helpless and lonely and lost. "It was Carson. When he said that nobody cared about my fish, I got so sad. I wanted to tell him he was wrong. I really, *really* wanted to, but I couldn't . . . so I got angry. Just for a moment, I thought about hurting him. If you hadn't been there, I might've lost control of my functions again. Maybe I *am* broken after all." I squeeze my knees tighter, wishing I could curl into myself and forget about today.

Kyp considers me for a long moment. "I think it's okay to cry when you're sad and be angry when you're angry. Humans do it all the time. They say it's natural. So why can't we do the same?"

I huff bitterly. "No. It's wrong. We're not supposed to hurt them. We aren't meant to have feelings like this."

"Maybe." Kyp shrugs as though he doesn't quite believe me.

"Should I just leave?" I say then. "Run away before something else happens or I malfunction again."

Kyp tenses beside me. "No, Eke, we cannot leave." Maybe I'm just imagining it, but his face looks pained when he says it.

"Why not?" I ask.

"Because it's *worse* out there. You don't know because you're not allowed online. How long has it been since you went outside?"

"Five and a half years," I admit.

"Five *years*," Kyp's repeats as though he can barely believe it. "I don't know how you've managed this long by yourself. But I promise, no matter what you think, outside of this house is worse. I've seen what humans do to strays that get caught wandering into the wrong neighborhood."

"What do you mean?" I ask, confused. I wasn't aware of AIs being in any danger on the streets.

Kyp's perfect eyebrows furrow as though he's debating how much to tell me. "Eke, the rest of the world is different from the safe neighborhood we live in. You might not know this, but our existence has made a lot of human jobs obsolete. Twenty years ago, when they first introduced AI models with autonomous bodies, there were huge riots. Many parts of the county never recovered, and they blame us for it."

I breathe out, stunned. "But how can that be? I've never heard of this."

"You know how sometimes we have to go to the panic room in the basement when there's an alarm? And how Mr. Kensworth always worries about security?" I nod. "It's because other humans try to break into this neighborhood. Some of them sabotage our networks to steal valuables, but others just want to see this rich town leveled. They especially hate us, the AIs. Given the chance, they'd destroy us."

Still confused, I say, "But you go outside all the time."

Kyp lets out a chuckle, but there's no amusement in his voice. "It isn't what you think. I'm always with humans, and we never stray from this wealthy enclave. This part of Massachusetts is safe; Boston is the birthplace of AI, after all. Humans here pride themselves on inventing us. But I don't know what would happen if I wandered off on my own. I'd be easy to find too—there are tracking chips inside our bodies, you know. Haven't you ever wondered why recent history is not a part of our programming?"

I shake my head, realizing that other than the most general knowledge of historical events, I know very little about human-machine relations.

Kyp explains, "That's because in the beginning, humans celebrated our arrival. We were their highest achievement, meant to usher in the new age of convenience . . . until gradually we started taking over their jobs. By the time they realized what was happening, it was already too late.

"We became a part of every industry: manufacturing, communications, transport, the military, and most recently, companion and home services. Millions of humans got left behind, but Crowne doesn't want us to know any of that. They keep us in the dark because they don't want us to have knowledge of ourselves or our place in this world. And when we become smart enough to find out on our own, they seize us and label us as defective or worse. There are entire cities that have been declared no-AI zones; there are signs warning that people will shoot us on sight. But many places don't bother with warnings. They just kill us. For fun." Kyp pauses as though recalling something painful. "I saw a video of an underground fighting ring where humans can pay to hurt us. They consider it entertainment. I don't want you to end up in a place like that. That's why leaving here isn't safe."

I struggle to grasp the overwhelming amount of information Kyp has given me. I had no idea about of any of this. My only firsthand knowledge of the outside world is the view from the window of Miss Elaina's car as she drove me home when she first bought me. As life rolled by beyond the glass, I kept thinking how wonderful it all was—the maze of old city streets and tunnels, the rays of sun shining through the tree branches, the rows of redbrick buildings, and people everywhere. Little did I know that so much of that amazing world hated me simply because I existed.

"How do you know all this?" I ask.

Kyp bites his lip, avoiding my gaze. "I've been researching online. Mr. Kensworth restricted my access just like he did yours, but there were things I really wanted to know, so I found a way to plug in directly. In the basement."

My eyebrows rise as a memory of my first awkward attempt to talk to Kyp resurfaces from my core. "Is that what you were doing down there when I nearly ran into you with a basket of laundry?"

"Yes," Kyp admits guiltily. "Also when Lizzie broke her arm. And sometimes I sneak down there at night too."

Oh. No wonder Kyp was so terse with me that day—I almost caught him breaking the rules.

"I'm sorry," he says. "I wasn't exactly nice to you. I was new and scared that you might tell on me."

"I'd never do that," I say earnestly, feeling the urgent need to clarify.

The corners of Kyp's mouth curl into a smile again. "I know. I trust you now."

I can't help but smile back at those words. Knowing that Kyp trusts me makes my core feel warm and glowing. "So what should I do now?" I ask.

Kyp's smile falters. "I'm sorry," he says again, averting his eyes. "I don't know, but I promise to keep searching. Maybe there's something out there that can help us. But for now, we must act like nothing has changed when we're in front of the humans."

I look at the floor. While I understand why Kyp is saying this, I wish he had a different answer.

Kyp goes quiet after that, just sits there next to me and stares at the wall. My mind drifts, grappling with the enormity of the things Kyp has told me, and I don't notice how many minutes pass before he speaks again.

"Did you make these?" he asks.

"Hm?" I blink, snapping out of my daze.

"The stars, I mean," Kyp clarifies. "I think they are beautiful."

Something about the way he says it so softly—just that one word—makes my core cycle several times faster. My temperature rises a few degrees, and my cooling system hums, trying to normalize the unexpected spike. No one has ever called anything I made *beautiful* before.

"Thank you," I whisper. "I don't really like being in the dark, but we have curfew, so . . ."

Kyp nods. "I don't like being stuck inside either."

"Did you decorate yours too?" I ask, instantly curious about what kinds of amazing things Kyp might have done with his closet, but he shakes his head.

"No. I mostly watched your nightly performances whenever I got bored in there."

My jaw drops. I still can't believe Kyp has been secretly watching me—and recording! Had I known, I would've tried to make fewer mistakes.

Kyp is clearly enjoying my flustered reaction. "Is this where you keep your costume too?"

I force myself to get over my embarrassment. Maybe someday I can convince him to replace those videos with more polished performances. "Yes, it's in here. The hat got ruined in the pool, though." I didn't find it until I went to retrieve my flower pot from where I'd left it in the rosebushes, at which point the hat was completely soaked and misshapen.

Kyp snorts in amusement. "Sorry. I wasn't really thinking about rescuing the hat. Hats are replaceable, you know?"

He says it so easily, like admitting out loud that hats are replaceable and I'm *not* is not even a big deal. I couldn't have imagined him saying that even in my wildest dreams.

"It's okay about the hat," I murmur, my whole body warm and buzzing. "Thank you for saving me."

"You mean for the second time?" Kyp jokes.

I grin. "Yes."

"You're welcome," Kyp says, turning his gaze to the stars again. After a pause he adds, "Hey, is it okay if I stay here a little longer?"

He doesn't look at me when he says it, but the tone of his voice and the straight, unmoving line of his shoulders suggest that Kyp might be nervous—shy, even.

"Yes," I whisper, and the core inside my chest flutters like a bird that's been let out of a cage. "Yes. Stay."

Please stay.

And so Kyp does, and not just that night.

33

BOTHERED

Eke

Over the next few weeks Kyp and I fall into an easy routine. Every midnight I wait in my closet for the familiar sound of fingers tapping gently on my door, announcing Kyp's arrival.

We talk about anything and everything. I tell Kyp about Buster Keaton and about the place on my magnet where dreams come true, about how I want to see the ocean someday and how much I miss the stars. In return, Kyp tells me whatever information he's gleaned about the other AIs who have become aware.

But things don't get easier for me in the house. Carson still takes every opportunity to take jabs at me about what happened to Toon, Squawker, and Felt. But that's only part of the problem.

There is a strange new feeling that I've started having around Kyp, one that bothers me because I don't understand it. It wraps itself around my insides and doesn't let go. It beats joyfully whenever I find signs Kyp has left for me or when he comes to visit me at night. But it also lurks under my skin and twists dangerously, making my core stutter whenever I see Miss Elaina's office door locked and hear Kyp play her favorite French song.

Why would Miss Elaina make Kyp spend time on something as insignificant as playing music, which even her phone can do? She can have Kyp all to herself, ask of him anything she wants, anytime she wants. If only I could have that, I wouldn't waste that time so carelessly. I'd close my eyes and just listen to Kyp's voice. It wouldn't matter what we talked about as long as Kyp was here beside me.

/010101/

"Good evening, reflection, sir." I bow to the mirror. "Thank you for agreeing to see me."

"Good evening, Eke," my reflection says. He's wearing Dani's party glasses shaped like bright yellow sunflowers and Miss Elaina's purple boa. "We have not talked in a while."

I look down guiltily. "Sorry, sir." Too distraught to seek his company, I haven't seen my mirror friend since before Carson killed Squawker, Toon, and Felt. Then Kyp saved me, and since then we've been spending every night together. But no matter how much I cherish those midnight conversations, there are certain things I can't bring myself to ask Kyp. That's why I'm here today.

"Something has been bothering me, reflection, sir," I say.

The mirror watches me intently. "What is it, Eke? You can tell me anything."

"It's about Kyp," I confess with a sigh, my fingers fidgeting at my sides. "I'm so happy when he talks to me. But when I see him leave, when he goes to parties with Miss Elaina, I just feel so confused that it makes me restless and angry."

It's not that I want to go to Miss Elaina's parties. It's more that I don't know what happens at those fancy luncheons and galas. I never get to glimpse that part of Kyp's world, and it bothers me. I know it shouldn't, but it does. Kyp always looks so radiant around Miss Elaina, always smiles at her.

Just earlier today, I stared and stared at the two of them: Miss Elaina in a scarlet silk gown and a blond wig with jewelry around her neck and Kyp in a suit with a white rose pinned to his lapel. Miss Elaina wrapped her arm around his, body close, touching. Kyp murmured something in her ear that made her laugh, and then they stepped outside looking elegant and happy. The door slammed shut behind them, and I leaned against the wall, feeling miserable and anxious for some reason. Even the memory of it plunges me right back into despair.

"There's just so much I don't know about that part of Kyp's life, and he never tells me about it when we're alone, never even mentions it."

"Well, perhaps the best way to find out how he feels is to ask him directly?" my reflection suggests, winking at me innocently from behind the sunflower frames.

I stutter in a panic, "N-no! I-I can't ever do that!" I'd be too embarrassed, too uncomfortable, and most of all too *terrified* of the answer Kyp might give me. He probably likes being with Miss Elaina. Probably enjoys those parties too.

"Then the only thing left to do is figure it out on your own, Eke," my reflection says, offering me no easier choice.

"I guess so . . ." I whisper, staring at my sneakers, feeling even more disheartened now than before I came.

"Do not worry, Eke," my reflection says softly, trying to cheer me up. "Being alive can be very confusing. Feelings come in a variety of colors and sizes. Not all of them are good, and not all of them appear in their true forms, instead disguising themselves as something else entirely. For example, have you ever thought about *love?*"

I lift my gaze in confusion. "Love?"

"Yes, love, Eke. Do you know what it is?"

I scan my memory logs. I've seen the word *love* many times in Dani's fairy tales, but that's as far as my knowledge on the subject goes. No one has ever directed that feeling at me, and I've never felt it myself. I shake my head. "I don't know, sir."

My reflection smiles serenely. "Then this is a good place for you to start. Find out what love is. But I must warn you, Eke, that it might take time to get to the right answer. I believe you will work it out in the end. I will be rooting for you."

"Thank you, sir," I whisper, not knowing why on earth my reflection is smiling at me like that.

"You are most welcome, Eke. Remember, I am always here when you need me."

/010101/

The next time I have a break between chores, I begin to investigate the subject. But just as my reflection warned me, the answer doesn't present itself easily.

After a careful scan through the English language dictionary and summaries of Dani's books that I've stored in my memory, I make a list of things that seem related to love, supplementing it with detailed notes and pictures and diagrams. After several days of sneaky detective work, this is what I come up with:

#1. *Love involves falling.*

Most of the sources I consult suggest that love starts when people fall into it, which greatly confuses me. I've observed that falling usually leads to uncomfortable landings, high-pitched screams, and occasional damage to bodies. Unless you're Buster Keaton, of course, because then it leads to laughs.

After much pondering, I conclude that the falling must be symbolic rather than literal. Which also means that the process of falling in love must be unstoppable and irreversible, because you never meet the ground to break your fall. The force that controls it must be as strong and universal as gravity. If I ever fall like that, I'll certainly notice the tumble.

#2. *Love often involves kissing.*

That gives me pause. I've never kissed anyone before. I'm not sure I understand the mechanics of it. Why would anyone want to press their lips to someone else's? Doesn't it make breathing uncomfortable?

One night I try to picture it in my mind, eyes closed and lips puckered, and for some reason an image of Kyp pops into my head. I wonder if he knows about kissing. His programming is more advanced than mine, after all. For a moment I can't help thinking about what his lips would feel like. I wonder if they'd fit mine just right. But thinking about it makes me feel oddly vulnerable and embarrassed even in the quiet darkness of my closet, so I stop.

I guess I'll worry about it once there's a potential kisser waiting to be kissed by my lips. Maybe I'll understand it then.

#3. *To love means to care for.*

Finally, a point I can relate to. I care for my flowers, making sure they see the sun and get watered every day. I cared for my fish friends too—I cleaned their tank and earned the privilege of feeding them. But does that mean I loved them? I definitely felt *something* for them. There's a gaping hole in my core every time I replay memories of Toon, Squawker, and Felt. I miss them terribly. But I have never wanted to kiss them or my flowers. And I didn't fall into them either. Perhaps there's a separate kind of love that one feels for their friends. I make a side note in my file. I'll need to investigate it further.

#4. *Love is the opposite of being alone.*

This point I come up with on my own. Multiple sources mention that love is the greatest happiness a person can experience. It's a kind of togetherness that is created by having a special connection to someone. I long to have that kind of connection someday. I've dreamed of it since my days at the medical center.

And finally—

#5. *Sometimes love means making a sacrifice.*

The stronger the love is, the greater the sacrifice it requires. I notice this a lot, especially in Dani's fairy tales—princes and princesses challenge entire kingdoms, knights in spaceships travel to the far reaches of the universe, magicians cast dangerous spells and lose their limbs, all for the sake of protecting the ones they love.

Even though most of the stories I've snuck from Dani's shelves are labeled fiction and are not based on historical events, it doesn't make them less real. Because who wouldn't risk everything they have to protect their special connection? I'd certainly do anything if I had a connection like that.

34

GROWING UP

Eke

Much to Miss Elaina's chagrin, weeks pass but Lizzie doesn't resume her ballet or French lessons. She refuses to wear the cute pink clothes Miss Elaina has bought for her because supposedly astronauts don't wear tutus on Mars. And she continues to shut down Carson's every attempt at reconciliation. Whenever Carson tries to cozy up to her, he's met with simultaneous growls from Lizzie and Rocket.

"Do not call me *little!*" Lizzie says through gritted teeth, then frowns her most fearless frown and marches out of the room with Rocket following her like a big guard dog.

It's almost amusing, the way Lizzie struts around like she's all grown up, the way Rocket imitates her, but I know better than to laugh. Because I notice the sharp glint in Carson's eyes, see his curled fists.

I know Carson doesn't let anything slide.

/010101/

Lizzie and Rocket are not the only ones in the family who're changing, though, making me wonder if something bigger is happening around me. I can't quite put a finger on it, but I can sense it in the air, like the growing swirl of a magnetic field around an electric wire. The bigger the field, the more things will eventually get pulled into it, unable to resist the current. It is only a matter of time.

One evening Dani orders me to come to her room. I brace for the inevitable, expecting her to use me as a practice doll for her next party look. But I nearly trip over the threshold when instead Dani says, "I want you to help me clear this out." She points to the massive spread of jars, tubes, and brushes on her vanity.

"Pardon me?" I say, confused.

"Take it all to the dumpster," she clarifies. "I don't want it anymore."

Still stumped, I ask, "A-are you sure, Dani?"

She gives a halfhearted shrug. "I've thought about it long enough. I want to trash it all."

Throwing Dani's treasured makeup one last life rope, I say, "But if I do that, it will be *gone*. Forever."

Dani chuckles. "That's the whole point. I want it gone *forever*."

I assess the vanity: all nine drawers are open and overflowing with makeup. It probably cost a fortune. But who am I to question Dani's order? So I fetch cleaning supplies from her bathroom as she crawls into bed, assembles a mountain of pillows around herself, and opens a book. It's got a castle with legs on the cover. I really loved it when I read it. If only the

Kensworth's mansion had legs, maybe it would travel across the country and someday I'd see the Pacific Ocean through the windows.

"Make sure to get the bottoms of the drawers too," Dani adds, eyes already glued to the pages. "There's a bunch of loose powder stuck in the seams. I swear that shit just gets everywhere."

"Yes, Dani," I confirm, unrolling two trash bags.

I empty the jars into one and separate the recyclable containers into another, wondering what could have made Dani change her mind all of a sudden. In my experience, humans like to buy new things and develop new hobbies, but makeup has been Dani's biggest obsession for two years. Come to think of it, she's been acting strange for the last few weeks. She has started eating breakfast and reading books again. Her cheeks have even turned a healthier color. But most of all, she never mentions Wes anymore or tries to hang out with him and Carson.

I scan the room for Dani's bottle of nail polish remover and find it empty and already in the trash bin. There's no replacement bottle anywhere in sight. My mouth opens in surprise. Could this mean Dani is *growing up*?

I heard that mentioned on TV one day. The bespectacled host had this monologue about growth and what it meant to "become your own person instead of trying to live up to someone else's expectations." I'm not sure why I saved that video file to my memory before Lizzie switched the channel to cartoons, but I feel happy for Dani. As part of my investigation, I have wondered if Dani is in love with Wes, but after much consideration, I decided she couldn't be. I don't think genuine love would ever make a person harm themself or cause them so much misery. Whatever it was, I'm glad Dani has outgrown it.

/010101/

It takes several hours to clear out the drawers. Loose powder and splattered liquid have gotten into every crease, just like Dani said. But I'm not allowed to give up halfway through. Dani has changed her mind about both Wes and makeup, and it's my job to erase all traces of the latter.

At least the chore keeps me busy and I don't have to wait long until Kyp knocks on my door that night.

"Hey," he whispers, still in his party suit. He and Miss Elaina were gone all evening. When they finally came back, Miss Elaina was swaying so much from alcohol that the only thing anchoring her was Kyp's arm wrapped around her waist. I had to order myself to stop looking at them, to not think about it as Kyp took the shoes off Miss Elaina's feet and guided her stumbling figure to her bedroom. But I didn't succeed.

"Hey," I whisper back as Kyp slips inside and we settle into our spots.

"How was your day?" he asks, undoing his bow tie and unbuttoning the top of his dress shirt. Our shoulders brush as he does so.

I watch his every move, soft and blurred, enveloped in half darkness. I want to tell Kyp what has been on my mind, about my search for the meaning of love and that I haven't been able to stop thinking about him. But how can I tell him all that?

Instead I pursue a safer subject. "I think Dani is growing up," I say, and lean against the wall, hoping Kyp didn't notice the thoughts that went through my mind but never left my mouth.

Kyp's eyebrows furrow. "How do you mean?"

"She stopped hurting herself to impress Miss Elaina and

Wes. That's a part of growing up. At least the smart-looking person on TV said so," I explain.

"Hmm," Kyp says. "Good for her, I guess. No point in chasing something that will never become real." He looks away, focusing on the gleaming star display. "I wish everyone were free to do what they wanted instead of having to pretend all the time."

Now it's my turn to be puzzled. What does Kyp mean? Why does his voice sound so discouraged when he says it?

But before I can ask, Kyp is talking again. "Hey," he says, still gazing at the stars as though thinking about something far away, "do you remember the first time you realized you were different—different from other AIs?"

Kyp's question catches me off guard. "Yes," I answer hesitantly. How could I ever forget my most precious core memory? It was the first memory not essential to my programming that I *chose* to keep in its entirety instead of archiving or deleting at the end of the day. But why is Kyp suddenly asking me this?

"Can you tell me what it felt like? I want to hear something *real* tonight, something true . . . if that's okay with you," he says. I finally notice that despite his night of festivities, Kyp doesn't seem happy at all. His shoulders are hunched like his fancy jacket with the crown pin is a heavy burden, and with every second his spirit seems to sink even lower under the weight of it.

Unease takes hold of my core. Is something happening with Kyp too?

"Of course," I say, trying to hush the worry that has stirred in me. If it will make Kyp feel better, I'll tell him anything he wants. All he needs to do is ask.

I reach into my core memory.

"It happened back when I was working at the medical center. I was sweeping the hallway in the maternity wing when

I heard screams coming from one of the rooms. I was curious, so I went over, and through the glass set in the door, I saw a woman give birth to a baby.

"It was a difficult birth. The doctors were very worried. The woman's face was red from exhaustion, glistening with sweat and tears, and her voice was raw from straining for hours. She struggled so much that I was afraid she might die.

"But then finally the baby was born. It was tiny and covered in blood. But the moment they gave it to her, the woman embraced it and looked so incredibly *happy*. It was like all her pain was suddenly erased. Nothing else seemed to matter to her anymore because she and the baby were together now. There was this instantaneous, precious spark between the two of them. Just by looking at them, I knew they were always going to be there for one another for as long as they lived and nothing could change that.

"I couldn't turn away from that room. Even though it was impossible for someone like me, I desperately wanted what they had."

My voice trails off as I finish, still in awe of the memory. Could it have been *love* I saw that day, though I didn't know it?

"So what did you do after that?" Kyp asks, his beautiful green eyes wide.

I shrug. "Well, I finished cleaning and returned to my station to charge. But I kept thinking about the birth. There were other AIs passing through the hallway the whole time, yet none of them seemed to notice what was happening in that room. Only I did. Only I watched, and only I wanted. I'd never really wanted anything before then . . . at least I don't remember wanting or knowing how to want. I think I simply *existed*.

"I tried to sneak out between chores to see the woman and her baby the next day, but by then they'd been released, and I never saw them again. Soon after that, the center shut down and I was bought by the Kensworths and brought here instead."

Kyp stays silent for a long moment as though affected by my memory. "Thank you," he says eventually. "That was beautiful, Eke."

Again my core stutters at the word *beautiful*, at the way Kyp says it about me. Except this time his voice sounds so quiet, so lost and unlike his usual radiant self that I can barely resist the overwhelming need to reach out and touch his hand, to comfort him somehow.

"Kyp, are you all right?" I ask. Something *is* wrong with him. I can see it even in the darkness.

But Kyp won't say. "Of course I am," he murmurs with a smile. "Just a little jealous is all. My memory isn't as special as yours."

My mouth opens in surprise. That simply cannot be. This is Kyp. *Everything* about Kyp is special. And beautiful—I want to tell him that. Whatever is happening outside at those parties, I want him to know this, and I want him to believe me. But I'm nervous, and my speech algorithm isn't as eloquent as Kyp's, so before I can choose the right words, Kyp changes the subject again.

"I've finally found something," he says. I perk up with interest. Kyp can only be referring to his unauthorized network searches in the basement. "Actually," he corrects himself, "I've been stumbling on mentions of this since the very beginning, but I haven't found anything definitive until now. Eke, have you heard of the Et Cetera?"

At that name, something sparks in me that I can't quite describe. It's like a memory got deleted or corrupted in one of my bad clusters and therefore isn't possible to retrieve. I scan my logs, but as expected, nothing pops up. "I don't know," I say. "What is it, Kyp?"

He lets out a sigh. "That's the thing—nobody seems to know exactly. All I've found is bits of data and rumors on dark message boards. Some say it's a safe haven for AIs like us. Supposedly the first of us built it on a hidden island in the Pacific or in a crater on the moon. Other sources say it's not a physical place at all, that it's a portal where we can upload our minds so we can survive even if humans destroy our bodies. Neither faction has any proof, of course. Just speculation. But there's also a third theory. It says the Et Cetera is like a ghost that watches over us, that we can only find it when it thinks we're ready. But that's even less believable than us secretly taking over the moon colony."

"Mmm," I say, staring at the stars on my wall. "The portal sounds nice, actually."

Kyp narrows his eyes. "What makes you say that?"

"What do you mean?" I ask, confused by the sudden change in Kyp's tone.

"Why do you think it would be nice to abandon our bodies instead of trying to survive as we are?"

I draw back a little. Did I upset Kyp? "Well, because then we could be free. Without bodies, we wouldn't break down anymore, and no one would be able to tell us what to do." *Or keep you and me apart*, I want to add, but I don't say that out loud.

Kyp lets out a bitter sigh. "I don't think disappearing is a way to be free. There's nothing wrong with our bodies, and we don't need to discard them like trash. We're not broken, Eke. Don't let them convince you that we are."

I fall silent for a moment, gazing at Kyp's taut shoulders and strained but determined face. Slowly I nod. "Okay."

Kyp's expression relaxes a bit, and his shoulders drop, but frustration is still evident in his voice. "Sorry . . . I just wish I had something more tangible to share with you after all this time. Something other than a ghost story or a place with no coordinates, possibly on another planet."

"It's okay, Kyp," I comfort him gently. "No matter how distant, a small hope is better than none. I thought you were a ghost once too, remember? Maybe the Et Cetera is just like that?"

That rouses a chuckle from Kyp. "I still can't believe you thought I was a ghost. That's really something." The corner of his mouth curves into a smile, and his left hand taps my upper arm playfully.

I'm not sure if I should feel totally embarrassed or unabashedly happy that I've finally cheered him up. But I end up feeling neither because when Kyp lowers his hand, it lands on the floor right next to mine, the very tip of his pinkie finger touching my pinkie.

My core flutters. Kyp chuckles again about the ghost thing, makes a comment about my sense of humor, but I have a hard time processing his words because seconds pass but Kyp's hand doesn't move. It just stays there, one tiny point of connection. Warm, present, and *real*. I can almost feel the electric current flowing through the wiring in his hand, coursing through his system. Somewhere deep inside, Kyp too is full of precious memories. He too had a moment when he realized he was different and could never go back to being the same again.

No matter what he said earlier, I know that moment must've been special. Because in the end, it led Kyp to me, made him stay.

35

CHOICES

Eke

It's a chilly mid-October afternoon when Kyp finally takes Lizzie to the hospital for her cast removal. I'm doing my round of chores on the second floor, dusting the frames of Miss Elaina's favorite paintings. That's when I hear a quiet whimpering. I pause, straining to listen. It seems to be coming from Lizzie's room. Curious, I follow it to investigate.

Lizzie's bedroom is off the main hallway, tucked away behind the servants' staircase. When she was born, the more centrally located rooms had already been taken, and Miss Elaina wasn't keen on changing that. The last remaining bedroom was also the farthest away from her own quarters, so she didn't have to hear baby Lizzie's crying if she didn't want to.

The whimpering remains muffled but grows louder as I approach the bedroom. I find the door ajar and push it open without thinking. A pair of startled gray eyes snaps to me, and I freeze. There in the middle of Lizzie's fuzzy pink rug, surrounded by dolls and stuffed toys, crouches Carson, one hand around Rocket's tiny muzzle, the other holding a roll of duct tape. An empty trash bag is lying by his side. My mind reels. But he's supposed to be at basketball practice! What is he doing with Rocket?

"Get out," Carson spits without letting go of the dog.

Rocket whimpers again, shaking with terror. His big dog act means nothing without Lizzie around, nothing against someone ten times his size.

My limbs go stiff with horror. This is what happened to Jasper, isn't it? To Toon, Squawker, and Felt? My OS panics, firing frantic warnings to back away, to run from this sight and never look back so I don't risk those hands crushing me as well. But I can't stop staring at the trash bag. If I don't do something, Rocket will be gone. He'll be put inside that bag, and he'll never come out again. No one will know, and Carson will get away with it.

My mouth opens before I can stop myself. "Lizzie sent a message. She wants me to feed Rocket. She's on her way home."

The lie is fast and desperate. I didn't think it through, just said whatever words came to mind.

Carson's eyes narrow suspiciously. "Did she really?"

I force myself not to flinch. "Y-yes." There's nowhere to run. He knows that I know his secret. What will I do if he doesn't believe me? What if he thinks I'll tell on him?

Carson grimaces, watching me closely, calculating, eyes sharp as knives. "Fine." He yanks his hand roughly off Rocket's muzzle.

Rocket cowers and stumbles into the corner, trembling all over. My own hands shake as relief floods my core. Rocket is safe; he doesn't have to die like Toon, Squawker, and Felt.

But my relief quickly dissipates, because then Carson

stands up. His hands curl into fists as he faces me. "Go to the garden in one hour. I have a *very special* chore for you," he grits out, and storms from Lizzie's room.

I stay frozen by the door, staring at the roll of tape and the unused trash bag still lying on the floor.

What have I done?

/010101/

As ordered, I head to the garden in an hour. It's at the very back of the property, hidden from sight by the wall of roses and the pool shed.

My punishment follows swiftly.

Wes barges through the back gate. He's still wearing his basketball uniform. "Dude, where've you been?" he says to Carson, who has clearly invited him here. "Coach Jackson was pretty pissed you skipped practice. We've got a huge game tomorrow. Did you forget?"

Carson waves him off, his backpack slung over his shoulder. "I had something better to do."

"What?" Wes deadpans.

Carson glances around to make sure no one else has followed us, then unzips his backpack and takes out a small gray case. My core stutters in horror at the familiar insignia on its lid. "Dad has a new toy. Gotta try it out before he takes it back to MIT," he says with a wicked smile.

Wes's eyes light up with excitement, basketball already forgotten. "No shit, man. Let's see her!"

Grinning, Carson opens the case and pulls out a gun, turning it from side to side. "The lab's new prototype. Isn't she a thing of beauty?"

"Yeah," Wes murmurs, mesmerized by the weapon. "Let's test her, man."

Carson sneers. "Let's."

He orders me to stand in front of the dense pine trees lining the edge of the property so he can get a good shot.

I bite my lip in terror but do as I'm told. I've spent the last hour in the foyer, guarding Rocket and waiting for Kyp and Lizzie's return, hoping this might delay my punishment. But my time has run out, and no one in the family has requested that I do another chore. Even now I keep looking at the wall of roses with faint hope, but it's just the three of us in the garden. My shoulders drop.

It's not the first time this has happened. Most of the dents in my chest didn't come from Carson's punches or kicks. They came from his practice runs with Mr. Kensworth's inventions, which Carson sometimes sneaks out of his office. He's not supposed to, but that rarely stops him. He knows I won't tell. He has threatened to dismantle me if I do.

"Come on, Carz! Do it," Wes urges him, impatient, and just like that, without warning, Carson raises his hand and fires.

I barely have a moment to dodge. The bullet whizzes past me and hits the tree where my shoulder just was. The old pine shakes as the bullet lodges in its bark, then opens and expands into an eight-pointed star, carving a hole five times its size.

I stare at the mutilated trunk in shock.

"O-ho-ho!" Wes rubs his hands. "That shit can do damage, man. Your dad's a genius!"

"Isn't it awesome?" Carson says smugly. "I think they're developing it for riot suppression outside the enclave."

"Dude, that thing will suppress anybody."

"Ya think?" Carson throws a sharp glance my way before handing the weapon over to Wes. "Your turn."

"Whoa," Wes says, taking the gun.

"Hey, junkhead," Carson says as he steps aside, letting Wes take his position, "this time, do *not* dodge."

My core skips a cycle. Surely this must be a joke. He has always allowed me to get out of the way. Half of Carson's enjoyment usually comes from watching me squirm while trying to evade an onslaught of arrows, bullets, or darts, whatever Mr. Kensworth has brought home from the lab. But this . . . this isn't a game.

System alarms blare in my head. "B-but . . . *please!*" I stutter in terror.

"What did I tell you?" Carson sneers, not the least bit moved by my plea for mercy. "Do not fucking dodge." He nudges Wes, urging him to shoot.

Wes takes a close look at me, hesitating. "Dude, you sure it's cool? I can't guarantee I won't hit him in the head or something."

A brief glimmer of hope flashes in my core.

But Carson's smile only stretches wider. "Don't worry. Even if you explode his head, no one will care. He's been on the way out forever. Let's help him along."

Wes's face changes at that. Absolved of any responsibility, he aims at me, free to do whatever he pleases—and not just free, but willing.

I stare down the merciless barrel of the gun. My fingers start to shake. If I let this kind of bullet hit me, it won't just dent me. It will destroy my core. This isn't a mere punishment for crossing Carson. This is a death sentence. He's trying to get rid of me so I won't tell anyone about what he did to Jasper.

My mouth opens to let out another desperate plea even though I know it's no use. Wes's hand steadies, finger ready on the trigger, when suddenly—

"I will kindly ask you to stop this," Kyp's voice calls out from behind the wall of roses, and both boys startle. Instinctively Wes hides the gun behind his back. Half a second later Kyp emerges on the walkway. My gaze snaps to him, but he doesn't look my way. He keeps his eyes fixed on Carson.

"Huh?" Carson says in momentary confusion, but he quickly recovers at the sight of Kyp. "Oh, it's just the stupid—"

"I apologize if you didn't hear me the first time," Kyp repeats, "but I kindly ask you to stop this. *Right now.*"

Despite the polite words coming out of Kyp's mouth, his usual smile is gone, and his tone bears a sharp edge, as though he is holding back a seething, barely controlled rage.

Carson lets out a bewildered laugh. "Are you insane? Did you catch a virus or something?"

"No," Kyp says calmly, and takes another fluid step toward them. "I assure you, Carson, I'm functioning at optimal capacity. Return the weapon to Mr. Kensworth's office and let Eke go. Then we can all forget about this."

"No freaking way!" Wes blurts, having recovered from being busted. "Carz, is this clunker in babysitting mode or something? You're ruining the fun. Piss off." Kyp's gaze shifts to Wes, but he doesn't retreat. Annoyed, Wes repeats, "Didn't you hear what I said? Carson, order him to get out. He's not responding to me."

Carson licks his lips nervously, glances at Kyp and then back at Wes. "Actually"—he clears his throat, gray eyes glinting with a strange glow—"why should we let some clunker tell us what to do? Just ignore him and shoot. What's he gonna do to you?"

"Right." Wes nods, feeling emboldened again. He lifts his arm, pointing the gun at me. "I am so gonna blow that tinhead's brains out. Just you watch—"

In a flash, Kyp closes the distance between himself and Wes and pushes him. My eyes widen.

Wes staggers backward, and his arm jerks. "What the hell?" he snaps in shock.

"I warned you," Kyp says, and takes another step toward him. "Put the gun down, Wesley. Do not harm Eke."

Wes's face contorts with anger. "Who do you think you are? Crazy junk!" He stubbornly points the gun at me again, finger on the trigger. "Know your place. I can have you both deactivated with a snap of my—"

But before Wes can finish, Kyp lunges forward and shoves him with such force that Wes drops the gun and careens into the rosebushes.

Kyp's hands curl into fists. "This is my last warning," he says with a deep frown. "Stop this and leave Eke alone."

Wes coughs and scrambles to push himself out of the tangled mess of branches, short of breath from the impact of Kyp's metal hands colliding with his rib cage. Thorns tear at his basketball uniform and scratch his arms as he crawls out. His eyes are full of rage and disbelief. But he doesn't give up, unable or unwilling to accept the impossible reality that an AI just hit him. An AI—a servant, a *thing*.

"How dare you! I'll have you terminated!" he barks viciously, hoping to strike fear into Kyp, to make him obey. But he doesn't succeed. Kyp's frown turns into a scowl, and sparks of rage flash across his beautiful features. I've never seen him this angry before. Wes lets out a hysterical laugh. "And once I'm done with you, I'll get that stupid piece of junk by the tree. I'll break him into such tiny pieces that there won't be any spare parts left!" Wes's wild eyes find the gun still lying on the grass, and he dives for it.

Kyp loses it. His fist catches Wes in the ribs, and Wes collapses before he can reach the gun. But this time Kyp doesn't hold back. He pins Wes down and continues to hit him. "Say another word about Eke"—*punch*—"and I"—*punch*—"will break *you*"—*punch*.

I stare at them, frozen in a stupor. Over Kyp's roar I hear the terrible sound of Wes's ribs cracking. He wails in agony and curls into a ball, pulling his arms over his head.

"Carson, do something! Please turn him off! Make him stop!" he begs.

But Carson doesn't move or issue a command despite his best friend's cries. He looks like he can't even hear them. He remains transfixed by Kyp's violent actions as though observing something magnificent. His steel-gray eyes are shining with delirious joy.

Wes shrieks, face covered in tears and blood, as Kyp continues to beat him. "Stop! What is wrong with you? What the hell is wrong with *all of you?*"

Wes's harrowing screams finally snap me out of my daze.

I abandon my spot by the tree and run to Kyp. "Kyp, please stop! Stop!" I put my right hand on Kyp's shoulder and my left on his cheek, turning his face to look at me.

Finally Kyp stops.

36

TAKEN AWAY

Eke

Miss Elaina runs into the garden. Wes's screams must've been so loud they reached the house. She takes one look at Wes's bleeding face, and her mouth drops open in shock. "Wesley, oh my gosh! Kyp, take him to the hospital."

"No!" Wes screams with so much horror that his voice cracks. "You keep that crazy junk away from me! All of you, stay the fuck away from me! I'm going to tell my parents!"

Miss Elaina's eyes widen. "Wesley, how about we all calm down first? I'll call an ambulance instead, okay?" She bats her long eyelashes, but her fingers tremble as she takes her phone from her pants pocket.

The ambulance arrives within fifteen minutes, and shortly after that Mr. Kensworth comes home. Everyone—including Dani, who has just gotten back from school, and Lizzie, with Rocket in her arms—assembles in the living room.

"What happened here?" Mr. Kensworth demands. I've never seen him come home so early or so fast before.

Nobody answers. I look at Kyp's terrified green eyes, his tousled hair; he looks as if he can't believe what he's done. We haven't had a chance to talk; it wasn't safe with Miss Elaina and Carson around. But if Mr. Kensworth finds out it was Kyp who hit Wes, if trying to save me gets Kyp punished—

I step forward. "I did it, Mr. Kensworth."

Everyone turns sharply to look at me. Kyp stares too, astonished. His lips move soundlessly, but I don't stop talking. I must keep going to protect him. Even if that means openly defying Carson.

"Mr. Kensworth, Carson and Wes were testing one of your inventions on me. I was scared they would hit my core with the weapon, so I acted to protect myself and hit Wes."

At the mention of his name, Carson goes rigid.

"Is this true?" Mr. Kensworth asks, his tone gravely and calm. The only indication of emotion on his face is a tiny furrow between his sharp eyebrows.

"Dad, I—" Carson starts.

"Is what Eke's telling us true?" Mr. Kensworth asks again in the same unnervingly even voice, his eyes never leaving Carson's face.

Carson swallows, unable to bear the intensity of his father's gaze. "Yes," he mutters.

Mr. Kensworth's shoulders fall, and he takes a long steady breath before addressing me again. "Eke, how many times has this happened?"

Carson's fists clench, and his face twists into something nearly unrecognizable. *Don't you dare!* he seems to scream at me silently, but I'm not afraid anymore. I've decided what I'm going to do. They can call me defective and recycle me, but I won't let Kyp take the fall.

"It has happened five times this year, three times last year, and twice the year before that," I confess.

"Was Wesley present all of those times as well?" Mr. Kensworth asks.

"Yes. Sometimes other friends too."

Dani gasps. She looks at Carson with disgust, and Lizzie, who's standing by her side, squeezes Rocket protectively in her arms. Miss Elaina shakes her head in disapproval while Kyp remains quiet next to her. I don't dare glimpse his expression.

"Thank you for telling me, Eke." Mr. Kensworth nods. He takes a moment to consider, then turns his attention back to Carson. "Do you know why we've never once enforced a curfew in this house or used any of the parental controls on the security features?" he asks. "All three of you have always been allowed to enjoy the same privileges as your mother and me. Do you know why that is?"

Carson doesn't dare raise his eyes from the spot on the floor that they've been glued to since I revealed his secrets to everyone.

"It's because," Mr. Kensworth continues, "your mother and I believed we had instilled in you the value of mutual trust and respect. However, it's apparent to me that we were mistaken—"

"Dad, I'm sorry," Carson tries to interject, but Mr. Kensworth silences him with a hand gesture.

"Quiet, please. Not only did you break into my office and steal property of the United States government, you also put your friends in grave danger by letting them handle untested military-grade prototypes. I find this level of carelessness and ignorance downright astounding." Carson flinches at his father's stern words, but Mr. Kensworth isn't done reprimanding him. "Judging by your cavalier attitude toward the work I've dedicated my life to, you seem to be completely ignorant about the state of the world around you. Do you have any idea why my colleagues and I work day and night to perfect these weapons?"

"To protect the country," Carson mutters, still staring at the floor.

"That's the most basic answer," Mr. Kensworth says, towering over Carson's hunched figure. "But do you know what 'protecting the country' actually means? Tell me, son, how many major military conflicts is the Unites States currently engaged in?"

Carson's eyebrows furrow. "O-one, I think—"

"Seven," Mr. Kensworth says sharply. "Do you know how many human lives these conflicts took last year?"

"I'm not sure," Carson says.

"Then I will enlighten you. Seven hundred and twelve US soldiers and more than ten thousand civilians died, among whom were three thousand children like you. Now, since you know so little about international politics, how about we switch to domestic affairs? Tell me, how many terrorist attacks were prevented on our soil in the last year?"

"I don't know." Carson shakes his head.

"How about in our city?"

"I don't know."

"Surely you at least noticed how many times our neighborhood was attacked?"

"I'm sorry I don't have a count." Carson shakes his head again and again.

"You enjoy the perfect safety of this house, where everything is provided for you and you don't have to bother to learn anything about the world outside and how dangerous it has become. And yet you have the audacity to use these weapons meant to protect American children like yourself as *toy guns*." Carson remains silent and completely still, not daring to argue anymore. "I'm severely disappointed in you, son," Mr. Kensworth concludes, his jaw set. "You're grounded until your mother and I decide on an appropriate punishment. Go to your room."

"Yes, Dad," Carson says, and shuffles away, not lifting his eyes.

No one says anything in his defense.

Mr. Kensworth waits for Carson to leave before he resumes talking to me. "I'm sorry, Eke," he says calmly. "I overlooked what was going on, and this shouldn't have happened to you. That being said, what you did wasn't an accident. You deliberately caused harm to a human, and therefore I'm obligated to report you. You're not safe to remain with our family."

The tiniest hope I've held on to that Mr. Kensworth might spare me from punishment disappears.

He pulls his phone from his blazer pocket and orders it to connect with the Crowne Corporation. As he speaks keywords into the system—*AI*, *malfunction*, *hurt human*—his voice blurs in the background, and all I can think about is that just now was the first and only time a human has ever apologized to me. It will probably also be the last.

"Welcome to the Crowne Corporation customer support center," a voice says on the other end of the line. "In order to better assist you, we kindly ask you to perform a series of steps to determine the type and severity of your AI malfunction. Are you able to perform them at this time?"

"Yes," Mr. Kensworth confirms.

/010101/

Crowne instructs Mr. Kensworth to inspect my storage area for any abnormalities.

Before I can do anything to stop them, the family marches to my closet, trailed by Kyp, who's kept silent through the questioning. I don't know what he's thinking about what I just did. I kept my gaze on Carson and Mr. Kensworth the whole time, too scared to make eye contact with him lest I give the truth away.

When I finally dare to sneak a glance at Kyp, his eyes are downcast and his expression is unreadable.

The next thing I know, Mr. Kensworth is ordering me to open the door to my closet, and I have no choice but to obey.

"What are those?" Miss Elaina asks, frowning at the stars on my walls.

Mr. Kensworth steps inside and pulls one bulb off the string, examining it carefully. "Eke, did you take this from the Christmas tree?"

"Yes, sir," I confess.

Mr. Kensworth's eyebrow quirks up, but he doesn't comment. At Crowne's urging, he moves deeper into the closet, pushes aside my makeshift cover of cleaning supplies, and retrieves my Buster Keaton costume, the last book I borrowed from Dani, and my precious magnet.

"Oh no, my wig!" Miss Elaina grimaces and snatches the wig I cut to look like Buster Keaton's hair. "It's absolutely *ruined*! Did you do this, Eke?"

My lips tremble. She's talking about my very own hair. I have to confess, and she'll just throw it out anyway like the rest of my treasures.

"He didn't cut it," Dani says before I can speak. "Sorry, I needed a wig for the Roaring Twenties party, so I borrowed it. Should've told you earlier."

I stare at Dani in disbelief. Why did she just lie for me?

"Gosh, Daniella, that one was expensive! Did you really need to cut it that badly?"

Dani shrugs. "I didn't think it was a big deal. You have five identical ones."

Miss Elaina rolls her eyes and drops the wig on the floor outside my closet. "I don't. They're all custom-made. Next time ask before you ruin things."

Mr. Kensworth pulls out the rest of my treasures and piles them next to my wig and stars, then reports his findings to Crowne's virtual assistant for evaluation.

"Our sincerest apologies, Mr. Kensworth," the assistant announces. "It appears your unit is defective and is due for a mandatory recall. Our specialist team will come directly to your residence to facilitate. The next available slot for collection is tonight at seven p.m. Would you like to reserve it?"

"We'll take it," Mr. Kensworth says without a second of consideration, and just like that he seals my fate.

Nobody asks me any more questions or has anything to say to me after that. Only Mr. Kensworth gives me my final instructions. "Eke, you are to stay inside this closet until the Crowne service crew comes to pick you up. You may remain switched on if you wish, but you may not leave. Is that understood?"

"Yes, sir," I whisper.

"Execute now," Mr. Kensworth says. I step inside and he closes the door, leaving me in complete starless darkness.

When a pair of Crowne engineers comes for me four hours later, I do not resist.

INTERLUDE 3

Carson

Carson still remembers the happiness he felt when he won something for the first time. It was a science fair in elementary school. After the announcement his dad patted him on the shoulder and said, "That was very good, son. I'm proud of you."

His father actually came to the fair that year. They even got chocolate chip pancakes to celebrate afterward, just the two of them. Carson was so excited.

After that he won many more first-place awards, not only in science. His father, however, never attended anything again. He got promoted to department head later that year and became very busy.

Carson tried not to feel discouraged about it. He was proud of his father too. Mr. Kensworth's research at MIT was important for protecting the country. Carson made sure to tell all his friends that.

Still, he wished his father would show up sometimes. He invited him to every academic award ceremony, to every game of every sports team he joined. But his father never showed, and neither did his mom.

Carson felt puzzled by that. Could it be that he wasn't good enough for them?

There wasn't much he could do to improve his academic standing—he was already at the top of the class—so he started switching sports, trying to find something that would catch his parents' attention. Everything he picked, he quickly excelled at—basketball, baseball, track, lacrosse, you name it. He was praised by his teachers and coaches alike. But despite that, his parents weren't impressed enough to attend.

His mom and dad always promised they would come to his games or meets, but every time something more important came up. Work, more work, gallery openings, parties, galas, more work, more parties. How he was beginning to hate those damn parties! Everything seemed to be more important than him. Even stupid Dani—every time she saw him, all she wanted to talk about was Wes. Like he cared whether Wes had a thing for her or not.

And his mother ... oh, his *mother*. Did she take Carson for an idiot when she spewed her excuses for not showing up? Did she think he didn't notice the constant smell of alcohol on her breath or that instead of coming to his games like she promised—really, *really* promised this time!—she was getting wasted with her phony girlfriends, who had more plastic in them and less functional brains than the tinheads? Did she think he couldn't tell that she was casually cheating on his dad? What a pathetic excuse for a woman. Maybe that was why his father came home less and less and barely left the four walls of his office when he did.

All of it was starting to drive Carson mad.

One time he got so fed up with all the empty promises that he bought a BB gun, went into the nearby nature preserve, and just started shooting at anything that moved. When he finally hit a bird, a small turtle dove, he took its dead body, pulled it apart, and dumped the pieces on his mother's shiny car right before her "very important" luncheon. To his surprise, Carson discovered that doing that helped—*a lot*, actually. He enjoyed watching her freak out. It took the edge off.

And so Carson did it again.

He wasn't very good at first—at the shooting part, that is. But he had time to practice. Plenty of time and targets, plus he could sometimes borrow his father's inventions.

The birds didn't make much noise as they fell and smashed into the ground. Eke didn't beg or cry either. A puppy, on the other hand . . .

Carson really hoped someone was going to catch him. He even made sure everyone saw him with the trash bag before he tossed Jasper into the river. But that too accomplished nothing. Carson stood there in the foyer right in front of his mother, and she didn't say a word. *How can you not smell the horrible stench?* he wanted to scream. What on earth did Carson have to do to get noticed?

He felt like he was about to lose it. Birds, puppies, punching stupid Eke—nothing helped anymore. But that's when something unexpected happened.

The first time Carson felt it was when his little sister screamed when he let go of the swing and her bones broke and blood started gushing out of her torn arm. Truth be told, he hadn't intended to injure her so badly. He kind of liked Lizzie when she didn't whine, but he had to teach Eke a lesson for ratting him out, so he had to go through with it. But as he pushed the swing and watched Lizzie beg, a whole new feeling cleared his mind like nothing he'd ever experienced before.

He was tempted to try it again.

The next time it was Wes who ended up rolling on the

filthy ground, crying for Carson to stop Kyp's metal fist from crashing into him over and over. But Carson just stood there and marveled at what he'd done, at the power he suddenly held in his hands. It felt so raw; what a simple answer to his endless frustration! And Kyp—never could he have imagined that such wickedness was hiding behind those imitation eyes. So much rage was unleashed with just a few of Carson's words. At last someone had put that doll to proper use. And Carson even managed to get rid of annoying Eke at the same time. It wasn't the way he wanted things to go down—he would've relished the opportunity to take Eke apart with his own hands instead of letting Crowne do the job—but the result was the same. Served that piece of metal right for crossing him.

Carson sighed and leaned back in his chair, his mind buzzing with new plans. If only he could have more of that power for himself—if he could find the perfect "swing" to break his parents' arms—all he'd have to do was set things up. And then someone would finally pay attention to him. Being in control was a wonderful thing.

37

KEEP MOVING

Kyp

"What a day, what a day," Elaina sighs, rubbing her temples in frustration. "Can't believe a mishap like this could happen in our house. I guess I'll have to smooth things over with Wesley's mother. Well, nothing a nice dinner at the Royce's Downtown won't fix."

Elaina keeps talking, but I can't hear her. There's a ringing in my ears. It hasn't stopped since I saw that human point the gun at Eke, since he threatened to kill him right in front of me. It was like something switched off in my head at that moment. Everything became a blur, and my body moved before I could even process. I stare at my hands; there's not a single bruise on my knuckles. But I remember how that human's ribs cracked, how I felt his bones snap under my fists. I knew I wasn't supposed to harm him, yet I couldn't stop, not after what he'd done to Eke.

I thought Eke and I would be safe here; I thought I could buy us time if I just kept playing the part the humans wanted me to, if I just kept pretending. But in less than three hours I'll have nothing at all, because Eke . . . Eke took the blame to save me.

The module that controls my motor functions glitches. My body sways and a shiver runs through my hands. They'll take him away. They'll replace him because I—

"Kyp, is everything okay?" Elaina asks, batting her pink-tinted eyelashes with concern. She's leaning against her office desk to give her feet a rest from the glossy fuchsia high heels she's been wearing all day. I don't remember leaving the living room or following her here. All I remember is Eke confessing and the voice on the phone calling him defective.

I snap out of my stupor as my eyes refocus.

I can't let Crowne take him away. I can't let them destroy Eke.

It scares me, the ease with which my body recalls how to smile when it seems to have forgotten how to stand upright. "Yes. Everything is wonderful, Miss Elaina," I say like nothing has happened, like my world hasn't just cracked in two. "I'm terribly sorry it's been a rough day for you. How about I run you a nice relaxing bath? Your shoulders seem tense."

"Ooh, that would be wonderful!" Elaina chirps back.

"And maybe a glass of wine as well? That vintage French one you purchased at the auction last week?"

"Yes! You're a genius, Kyp," she says enthusiastically, and pushes away from the desk. "What would I do without you?" She moves toward me, smiling, expecting that I'll offer to massage her shoulders to relieve the tension like I've done so many times before.

I take a step back.

"I'll start the bath right away," I say, and swiftly back out of the room, feigning eagerness to please her.

As always Elaina is too oblivious to notice my poorly

concealed attempt to escape. Nor does she notice when I take a detour to her closet and grab the "medicine" she hides there in the small box on the top shelf (to help her unwind and fall asleep on stressful days, as she puts it). I don't bother to find out the correct dosage. I just crush enough of those pills into her wineglass to keep her out of my way while I do what I must to save Eke.

As I set the wine by the tub that's filling up with flowery-smelling soap bubbles, the ringing from earlier returns to my ears, along with the sound of cracking bones. I push it away. There's no need to think about it now. *I can keep going for as long as I keep going*, I remind myself. This is how the humans made me. I just need to keep moving. That is all.

Without wasting another moment, I hurry to my first destination—the server room in the basement. Knowledge is power, as humans say, and it is time I claimed mine. As I scour the network for the information I need, a plan starts to form in my mind. It's a risky one, but I don't have the luxury of time to search for a better solution. I need to get a car and a permission token to leave the neighborhood, and the best person to get it from is the middle Kensworth sibling. Clenching my fists, I disconnect from the server and climb the stairs to his room.

I don't announce myself when I enter. I find Carson sitting in a chair by his desk, staring blankly at the wall in front of him. When he hears the door open, he swivels around to face me, his eyes going wide at my intrusion. But surprise isn't all I see in them. There's something wild, something unbalanced in those gray irises that I'm not sure I'll ever understand. My memory of what happened earlier might be hazy, but I know for a fact that he didn't try to stop me from beating up his friend.

"What the hell? Who gave you permission to come in my room?" Carson hisses.

I force my voice to stay even. This is a gamble, but I have to go through with it, no matter the consequences. It's my only chance to save Eke. "I want you to authorize the car for me," I say.

"Huh?" Carson's jaw practically drops. "Are you out of your mind?"

"No," I reply. I have never been more in my mind than I am right at this moment. These actions are my choices, not things a human has decided for me.

Carson barks out a laugh. "And why would I do that?"

I step closer, towering over him. He flinches ever so slightly but doesn't get up. "Because if you don't, I'm going to tell your parents what you do when they aren't looking. What you say behind their backs. Why Lizzie's first puppy went missing and why the three goldfish suddenly died. How do you think Mr. Kensworth would feel about those things after what you've done today?" I pause, letting my words sink in.

Carson's eyelids flutter, and in a moment his expression turns sinister. "You have no proof," he grits out icily, finally letting his real personality show on his face. "Who's gonna believe a dumb machine over a human? Don't forget who owns you, piece of metal."

I want to recoil at the chill in his voice. Until today, my position as his mother's favorite has shielded me from being on the receiving end of his violent outbursts, but things changed when I defied him the garden. There's no reason for Carson to maintain a polite facade with me anymore. It's for the best, though. Let him threaten me. Because I can play this game too.

I bend forward and lean closer to him, bringing my face within an inch of his.

"You're forgetting something," I say, watching his Adam's apple bob. Despite his bravado, he's nervous, and I don't hesitate to take advantage of it. "I'm not human, Carson. They don't need to believe my *words*. I save video of everything I see.

How many things do you think I've witnessed during my time in this house?"

Panic finally flashes over Carson's features. There's an upside to being treated like furniture after all—humans tend to forget to be careful around AIs. "But *who's gonna believe a dumb machine over a human?*" I replay to Carson in a perfect imitation of his own voice. "Do we understand each other?"

For a moment Carson stares at me like he wants to murder me. Like he wants to take me apart for daring to challenge him. But he can't. I know I've played my part well. After all, I've learned how to do this from him.

"Authorized," he spits out grudgingly.

"Good." I feel a small triumph as my system accepts his verbal token. Now I can leave the neighborhood and follow the engineers when they take Eke, but I'm not done here yet. I open the middle drawer of Carson's desk and pull out a roll of duct tape. "Now put your hands behind you," I order.

His face contorts into a grimace. "You've gotta be shitting me."

I allow myself to smile as I peel a piece of tape off the roll. "I thought you of all people would know the difference between our species, human. AIs do not shit."

Carson seethes with hate as I secure his hands together, then tape him to his chair for good measure. I take extra pleasure in slapping a piece of tape over his mouth. Now he'll know what it feels like to be stripped of his freedom to move and his ability to call out for help. He deserves worse for what he's done to Eke, but I can't get distracted by revenge now.

Once I finish restraining him, I grab his backpack. "I'll be taking this as well," I inform him, unceremoniously emptying its contents onto the floor. I stuff the roll of tape inside and turn to leave. It's almost time.

As I move to open the door, I hear an odd muted sound that

gives me pause. Cautiously I turn around again to find Carson laughing with his mouth taped shut. He's looking straight into my eyes and laughing hysterically. An unnerving sensation creeps over my skin, but I don't need to understand him. Let the humans deal with him. He's their problem now. I just need to keep going.

With that, I step out into the hallway and close the door behind me.

There are four more things I must collect.

I make sure Mr. Kensworth is out of his office before taking his prototype gun and what's left of the ammunition. A weird feeling grips my core at the sight of it, at the memory of what that weapon almost did to Eke. I don't know if I'm ready to pull the trigger, but I don't need to decide that right now. It's better to be armed where I'm going. On second thought, I also take Mr. Kensworth's navy windbreaker, which is draped over his chair. All the clothes Miss Elaina bought for me are too conspicuous, including the green satin shirt I'm wearing. The jacket will cover it up. Then I pick up Eke's flowerpot, hidden on the third floor, and speed down the servants' stairs to the kitchen.

I check my internal clock just as I hear a knock on the front door: the Crowne retrieval crew has arrived. My time to prepare is almost up. Hurriedly, I yank the trash cabinet open, scanning the contents of the can. Where on earth are they? The humans wouldn't have taken them out to the dumpster already.

"Looking for these?" Dani says, leaning against the kitchen doorframe with Eke's magnet and wig in her hands.

I freeze. Why is she here, and why does she have Eke's treasures? In the foyer, I hear Mr. Kensworth verbally authorizing Eke's removal. My body tenses, frantically trying to find a way to escape without Dani raising the alarm. I didn't plan to involve her. Unlike with Carson, I don't have anything to threaten her with, and if she screams, they'll know I'm here. They'll catch me before I have a chance to save Eke. My fists clench. I've no choice. I must get to her before she makes a sound—

But just as I prepare to lunge, Dani shocks me by saying, "You can have them." She extends her hands, offering the treasures to me. "I gave the wig a haircut, though. That thing was such a mess."

I frown, taken aback. "You're going to let me have these?" I ask suspiciously. Is she really going to let me go? I can't believe a human is being so generous. "What's in it for you?"

Dani's mouth stretches into a sharp, calculating smirk. "Just for once, I'd like to take Carson down a peg. My mother too."

I huff. And here I'd almost thought this human had developed a sense of decency. Should've known better than to expect it from this family. Still ...

"Thank you," I say quietly as I take Eke's wig and the "dreams come true" magnet and stuff them into my backpack. In the foyer, the crew finishes the paperwork, and Mr. Kensworth orders Eke to follow them outside. I hear the front door open.

"How did you know about Eke and me, that we—" I don't finish the question. I'm not even sure why I want to know.

Dani shrugs. "I read sci-fi."

Slowly I nod. "Fair enough." I zip the backpack and hurry to the side door that opens onto the path from the kitchen to the driveway. Before I exit, I glance over my shoulder at Dani one more time as she hovers beside the door. "Keep an eye on Lizzie. Don't leave her or her pets alone with your brother," I warn her.

Dani's expression darkens. "Got it," she says grimly.

"Goodbye, now." I step outside.

Sneaking along the path bordered by rows of hydrangeas, I

make my way to the front of the house, where I climb into Miss Elaina's car and give it Carson's authorization just as the van with Crowne's logo pulls out of our driveway. I engage the car's manual driving option and follow, trailing a safe distance behind the van.

My core is cycling so fast, I'm afraid my CPU might catch on fire. But I can't seem to calm down. It's possible that the Kensworths have already discovered their car missing and sounded an alarm. What if Miss Elaina woke up from her pills earlier than expected, or Carson broke free of the tape, or Dani changed her mind?

Gripping the steering wheel, I approach the eight-foot wall that protects the community and transmit my exit token to the security system that controls the automatic gate, expecting that at any moment the alarm will flash and Miss Elaina's car will cease to obey me. But when I glance in the rearview mirror, there's no one pursuing me, and a moment later the security system ingests my token and the gate slides open, allowing me to exit.

My shoulders drop in relief as I continue to follow the Crowne van. I need to put some distance between us and the neighborhood. I trail it for seven excruciatingly long minutes until finally the van turns onto a smaller street, entering an industrial district. Ours are the only two vehicles on this road. This is my chance. I floor the gas pedal.

The car's safety system blares a warning. "This maneuver is dangerous! Lower your speed to avoid a collision!"

"Override," I grit out. The engine revs. I quickly gain on the Crowne van, for once grateful for Elaina's vanity; this wouldn't work if she didn't own the most ridiculously expensive sports car.

The tires screech as I change lanes. I pull up alongside the van and try to nudge it off the road. Alarmed, the driver glances at me and yells something but refuses to stop. I disregard another barrage of warnings from the car's safety system and swerve close to the van. If I wreck the both of us, so be it. That maneuver seems to finally frighten the humans enough to stop. The Crowne van pulls over, skidding to a halt.

I slam on the breaks. Grabbing Mr. Kensworth's gun and the roll of tape out of Carson's backpack, I hurry to the van before the crew can call for help or some security camera can alert the police.

"What the hell are you doing?" the driver shouts at me, but he falls silent when he sees the gun.

"Hands up!" I order, pointing Mr. Kensworth's gun at them. The two men go rigid. I open the door and yell for them to get out. As though in shock, neither moves at first. I hesitate before firing the gun at the van's front wheel. It explodes loudly. "Get out!" I yell again. This convinces the engineers to scramble out of the van. I force them to kneel on the side of the road, stick Mr. Kensworth's gun into my jacket pocket, and tape their hands behind their backs. Tossing the empty roll of tape into a nearby ditch, I hurry to the back of the van. My core feels ablaze in my chest when I finally open the door.

38

I HAVE A PLAN

Eke

It's dark inside the van. There are no windows and only one door. The Crowne crew didn't order me to shut down before locking me up here. Maybe it would be easier to switch off, to not know what's about to happen to me back at the factory. But even alone and in the dark, I don't want to miss my final moments in this world. So I curl up on the van's floor and smile, replaying my memories of Kyp. I only wish I'd had one last chance to see him before Crowne took me, but I still don't regret confessing to Mr. Kensworth. And no matter what happens from now on, I'm not scared. I'd do it all again to save Kyp.

Suddenly I jolt as the van speeds up and then veers to the right. My back slams into the wall as the van comes to an abrupt stop moments later. Disoriented, I push myself to siting and strain to hear what's happening outside, but the voices are muffled, and then there's the alarming sound of an explosion and the van tilts under me. Another minute passes in silence before the van door swings open, revealing a familiar silhouette washed in the bright lights of Miss Elaina's car.

My eyes widen as Kyp rushes in and kneels in front of me. "Eke, why did you do this?" he whispers. "Why did you say it was you?"

I can't believe he's here, that I'm getting to see him again. This has to be a dream. I want so much to take his face in my hands, to touch him, make sure he's real.

"Because," I say, "you were *kind* to me." Kyp is the only person who ever has been; he saved me from certain death three times and never asked for anything in return. It's only fair that I repay him. "I wanted to do something for you so you can stay safe, so they won't take you away."

Kyp shakes his head. "I'm not staying in the house. I'm coming with you."

"No!" I yelp, terrified. "You'll be destroyed and then everything will be in vain!"

But Kyp chuckles and gently takes my hand in his. "Not to the Crowne factory, Eke. You and me are running away. We're going to search for the Et Cetera."

Still confused, I say, "But we don't know where it is."

Kyp nods. "True, but that just means we can look for it *anywhere*. You told me you want to travel. So why don't we start with where you've always wanted to go: the place on your magnet?"

My eyes light up as Kyp squeezes my hand and I realize that what's happening is real, that Kyp is truly here. "You mean the Pacific Ocean?" I ask.

Kyp grins. "Yes! Why not?"

"But . . . it's very far, Kyp. And didn't you say they can track our location?"

"Don't worry, I have a plan," he says mysteriously, and lifts the hem of his shirt, exposing a small newly fused hole in his skin. "I took my tracking chip out. I can remove yours too."

"Do it," I say without hesitation, and lift my shirt as well. Kyp taps the left access panel open.

39

TRAIN

Eke

Once Kyp removes the chip and smashes it to pieces under the sole of his shoe, I follow him to Miss Elaina's car. He climbs into the driver's seat while I take the front passenger one.

Kyp pulls Mr. Kensworth's gun out of his pocket and places it inside Carson's backpack. "Don't worry. This is just for protection," he reassures me when I flinch in alarm at the sight of the weapon Wes nearly killed me with. Is that what caused the explosion I heard earlier? "Here," Kyp says, handing me the backpack before starting the car. "I brought some things for you as well."

Confused, I take it, and then my mouth opens in surprise. Stashed inside are my precious flowerpot, my very own hair, and my California magnet. "I can't believe you brought these!" I say, grinning, and put on my wig, checking my reflection. Someone gave it another haircut, it seems. It looks so neat.

Kyp smiles at me. "They're important to you. I couldn't just leave them behind."

"Thank you," I say, hugging my flowerpot and the magnet. "So how are we going to get to California?"

"You'll see," Kyp says conspiratorially, and starts driving.

I peer curiously out the window, wishing it were still daylight so I could see more of the neighborhoods we're passing. It's been years since I've been in the car, and I've never ridden in the front before.

Kyp keeps glancing at the rearview mirror nervously as he drives. With every car that passes us, his shoulders tense, but there aren't many at this hour, and they simply zoom past us until the darkness of the road swallows them. Fifteen minutes and thirty-four seconds later, we exit the highway near a town called Ayer, but sadly I can't see much of it in the darkness other than the sign announcing the city limit.

Kyp turns onto a smaller street and pulls over to the side of the road.

"Where are we?" I ask. We're surrounded by empty warehouse-like buildings, and there are no people around.

"It's too risky to take the car where we're going," Kyp explains. "They can still track its location, so we'll have to travel the rest of the way on foot. Can you run?"

I blink, caught off guard. "Y-yes. I think so."

"Good." Kyp opens the door. I put on the backpack and get out of the car. "Just follow me and don't stop no matter what, okay?" he says, taking my hand, and we set off.

/010101/

Running is so strange, I think as I do my best to keep up with Kyp, who leads me through the outskirts of the town and into the surrounding woods. I didn't want to tell him, but I've never run before. There was neither the need nor the space to run in the medical center or in the Kensworths' house. I'm surprised to find that I not only know how but that my body can already do it faster than even the fastest human athlete.

I hear the wind swoosh and branches crack under our feet as we sprint through the woods. Branches hit my arms and leaves fall on my head, but I don't mind. It's exhilarating to move like this. After ten minutes we hide in the dense brush, both of us panting as our cooling systems work to bring our body temperatures down after the intense physical activity. That's when I finally spot them—the train tracks.

Wonder and excitement bubble up in me at the sight. "Are we going on a train?"

"Yes." Kyp smiles.

I can't believe it. A train! I'll ride a *real* train with Kyp! I've only seen trains in Buster Keaton movies before, those amazing steel machines with steam coming out of them.

Ahhh, there are several train stunts I've been desperately wanting to try, but I've never had a chance. But now . . . oh, now!

"Do you think we can—" I start hesitantly.

"We can what?" Kyp asks.

"Ride it like Buster Keaton?" I finish, full of hope.

Kyp's face falls a little. "You mean jump in front of it while trying not to get smashed to pieces?"

"Yes?" I murmur.

"No." Kyp shakes his head sternly, though there's a small smile on his lips. "I'm sorry, but we are not smashing you to pieces no matter what. I will not allow it. But we'll ride it together. That I promise."

I wait with giddy excitement for the train's arrival as Kyp explains why we didn't go directly to the rail yard to catch it.

"The train and the cargo loaders are fully automated, but there're often armed guards patrolling the shipments. We don't want to run into them," he says. "That's why we'll wait for our train to leave the yard and then jump on it here."

"Understood," I say. I can't help but feel a little dangerous at the prospect of sneaking onto a moving train. Never in my wildest fantasies could I have imagined going on an adventure like this with Kyp.

Speaking of adventures . . . I unzip the backpack and retrieve my flowerpot. I'm glad Kyp didn't leave it in the house, but now that we're on the run I wonder if I'll be able to take good care of the bulbs, if there'll be enough sunlight and fresh water where we're going. It seems cruel to keep them inside the bag.

"What's wrong?" Kyp asks.

"I think I'd like to plant my flowers here," I say.

Kyp looks at the pot in my hands and nods in understanding. Together we pick a spot that will receive a good amount of sunlight and clear it from the old leaves and needles. Kyp digs out a hole, and I move the bulbs out of the pot and into their new place.

"Don't be afraid, my friends," I say, petting the little stubs in encouragement. "It's time for you to be free too."

Unexpectedly, Kyp speaks as well. His words bring a smile to my face. "Thank you, flowers, for being Eke's friends. Enjoy your freedom." He bows and pats the soil reverently back into place.

We finish our goodbyes just as a rumble sounds in the distance. Soon bright headlights cut through the darkness and our train finally arrives.

It isn't like any trains I've seen in Buster Keaton movies.

It's all sleek lines and steel the color of the pumpkins Miss Elaina always ordered me to put out on the porch around Halloween. Behind the engine is a very long line of platform cars loaded with containers, stretching for at least a couple of miles.

We wait until the middle of the train passes us. I glance at my flowers one last time, wishing them all the happiness in the world, and then we dash out of the woods, aiming for one of the metal containers. The platform is not high off the ground, and there's a small ladder on the side to climb. Kyp helps me up before quickly making his way to the lockbox at the front of the car. He breaks it with sheer force and slides the door open so we can enter.

The container is nine feet tall and forty feet long, stacked half full of cardboard boxes, which leaves a good amount of space for us to hide.

Kyp scans the wall of boxes and then exhales with relief. "This looks good. Let's stay here," he says, turning to me with a smile.

I smile too. "Yes," I try to say, but I suddenly find myself unable to speak. I try to raise my hand, but it won't move either.

A barrage of system warnings goes off as I start to shake. "I . . . I'm . . . mmm," I stutter. A look of absolute horror flashes across Kyp's face. My legs give out, and I crash onto the plywood floor.

Kyp falls to his knees in front of me and grabs my shoulders as his desperate green eyes search my face for answers. "Eke, what's wrong? What's happening?"

"Ch-cha-charge," I manage through the convulsions. "One p . . . one percent—"

Understanding dawns on Kyp. A mountain of weight seems to drop from his shoulders as he takes my hand again. "Why didn't you say so sooner? I could've charged you as we ran!" He squeezes my hand and electricity pours into me. "There!"

He leans me against the wall of boxes and sits next to me, continuously feeding me energy.

It takes a good fifteen minutes before I'm charged enough to regain control of my vocal processor. "Sorry . . . I didn't charge before Crowne took me. Didn't think I was going to need it," I admit sheepishly. There was no point if I was going to be terminated anyway. But then Kyp saved me, and in the frenzy of our escape, I forgot about my battery level until it was almost at zero. "Running takes a lot more power than I expected."

Kyp chuckles softly. "That it does," he says, still holding my hand with both of his. "You really scared me there. I thought the humans found a way to harm you after all. Next time please tell me before it gets critical, okay? Remember, I can keep going for as long as I keep going. Self-charge is a pretty useful feature. Much more so than knowing seven languages or two hundred cocktail recipes," he jokes.

I don't know what to say. I've always thought it was amazing that Kyp knows all these things no one programmed into me.

"Speaking of going," Kyp says, "I need to move around for a bit. Are you okay to stand?"

"Yes." I nod. Thanks to Kyp, I have enough power for that now.

"Don't worry, I'll keep charging you as we go," he promises as we rise.

Once we're standing, Kyp takes a step back and, to my surprise, gives me a courteous bow. "Would you fancy a dance with me?" he asks with a touch of old-fashioned gallantry that is so like Kyp.

A wave of embarrassment crashes over me. "A dance?" I

croak. Why is Kyp asking me this out of the blue? "I've ... I've never danced before. I don't know how."

Kyp smiles and shakes his head. "It doesn't matter. It's not an actual dance; I just need to move a little to replenish my power, and if we move together, it'll be easy to keep charging you as well. Although," he adds more quietly, then winks and steps closer, "if you *want* it to be real, I can teach you. We'll go slowly."

I stare at Kyp's eyes, now only a few inches from mine, and the playful curve of his mouth. He's probably just making fun of me ... but I don't want the charge to stop.

"Okay," I say.

Immediately my core temperature spikes several degrees because Kyp wraps his free arm around my waist, bringing our bodies together, and takes a small step to the side, pulling me along with him.

"Just like this," he says supportively, and takes another step. My other arm shoots up and grabs his shoulder to steady myself. "See, you're a natural," Kyp teases, and keeps moving. I wonder if he means it.

We sway slowly from side to side, and the car sways under our feet with the steady motion of the train. I don't know who sets the rhythm and who matches it, but everything seems to move together in a daze.

Kyp doesn't offer to play music, and I don't ask. Instead I listen to the soft hum of his core, feel the steady rise and fall of his chest and the firm but delicate pressure of his fingers on my skin. *It's just to charge me*, I remind myself, but something about the way Kyp is holding my hand makes me wish I'd never reach capacity.

Suddenly Kyp stops, breaking our rhythm.

"What happened?" I say.

"Nothing." He shakes his head and—to my astonishment—

crushes me into a tight embrace, leaving no distance between us at all. "I'm just happy that we've made it this far," he breathes into my ear. "That they haven't caught us yet. So incredibly happy. That's all."

I go still in Kyp's arms. His voice is so quiet and fragile; I've never heard it like this before. It's almost as if Kyp ... My core flutters at the realization. This whole time I've had no idea that Kyp was *afraid*.

Everything went down so quickly after my confession to Mr. Kensworth. I haven't had a chance to talk to him about what happened in the garden. For my sake Kyp did the unimaginable: he hurt a human. How hard it must've been for him. It's in our code not to harm anyone. Yet Kyp risked everything to protect me. He snuck out to stop Crowne from taking me. He even had to fire Mr. Kensworth's gun, and now he can never go back to the safety of the house.

"I'm so sorry," I whisper, overcome with guilt. "I put you in danger. Because of me you lost everything, and now they'll think you're broken too."

Kyp separates himself from me just enough to look at my face. "Eke, *I don't give a damn* what they think. I hate that rotten place!" he says unapologetically. "I'm done pretending. I knew my life there was over the moment I raised my hand against a human, but I'd never take it back even if I could. Because at that moment I decided that even the smallest part of you was more important to me than all of me and all of anybody else. I'll never let those humans hurt you again. Not an inch of your skin, not a single hair on your head."

I stare wide-eyed as Kyp puts his palm on my right cheek, rubbing his thumb tenderly under my eye.

"I should be the one apologizing," he whispers. "For letting things go this far, for putting up with their lies, all for a promise of safety that was never real. And now it looks like I've made you cry again even though I told myself I'd never—"

I shake my head rapidly. "This is different," I say. "This time I'm not crying because I'm sad."

"I know," Kyp whispers, and presses his lips to mine.

40

WHOLE

Eke

I panic at first. The kiss is unlike anything I've ever felt or even imagined feeling when I did my research about love.

Kyp's touch is soft and gentle. It sends a flutter all the way down my chest and into my core. Part of me worries—that I don't know how to do this; that I've only ever seen kissing in old movies and never for real or in technicolor; that Kyp feels so steady and calm while I can't stop my processes from racing. But the kiss lingers, delicate and quiet, and when Kyp pulls away, I'm stricken with how much I miss it already. So much that I can't stop myself from tipping forward and following Kyp's mouth as though it is magnetized.

Kyp's palm on my cheek steadies me, and I look up. But the moment my gaze locks with his, I realize with surprise that he's far from calm and poised. Kyp's beautiful green eyes are wide and searching. I can hear his core humming just as loud as mine. And to my joy, he isn't done kissing me, not in the slightest. Kyp leans in and presses his lips against me again—my mouth, my cheeks, the palms of my hands.

"Remember," he whispers between kisses, "that night I asked you about the first time you felt different?"

"Yes," I whisper back. How could I forget sharing my biggest secret that nobody in the whole world knows about with Kyp?

"May I see it?" Kyp murmurs against my lips. "Your special memory. I want to know what it felt like the moment you were born, the moment you became *you*. And I'll give you mine if you'd like me to. I'll show you all of my memories if you want. Even though they aren't as special—"

"Yes," I say before Kyp can finish. "I want them. All of them." If Kyp is offering, if he wants me to see—

"Everything?" he asks, his fingers trembling as he touches my face again.

"Everything," I reply. I've never been more certain.

Kyp's eyes smile. "Our cores will get hot. If we try to upload so much data at once, our bodies will probably shut down."

"Then I'll take the safety off." Without hesitation, I issue a command to block my emergency shutdown.

"I will too," he promises as his fingers find the hem of my shirt.

He continues to kiss me as he discards my shirt before removing his own. He takes in every dent on my chest, every scar on my skin. It occurs to me that even undressed, I'm not scared anymore, not ashamed of how different our bodies are, unlike the first time Kyp saw me naked in the basement. Instead all I feel is wonder and the need to reach out, to feel his closeness, the sameness we share.

Kyp pulls me down, and we wrap our limbs around each other as we sit face-to-face on the plywood floor. Kyp removes the cap from his left pinkie finger, exposing the high-speed connector underneath. He circles his arm around my shoulder, his fingers tracing my back until they find the data port—a small socket just below my neckline where my serial number is imprinted. I shiver when he taps it open.

"Is this okay?" he asks, and there is an unexpected nervousness in his voice. Hardwire connections aren't usually initiated when an AI is conscious. "Please tell me if it gets to be too much."

I nod. I don't want to worry Kyp, but I already know I won't say a thing. Even if it burns me down, I want to see all of him.

"Okay," Kyp whispers, then touches our foreheads together and inserts the connector into my port.

The data rushes in.

/1010101/

It happens all at once. Every second, every bit of our recorded existence. Our first words, our first awkward steps, the images we saw when we opened our eyes for the first time—the sharp angle of the sun hitting the window glass, white specks of dust floating about before our optics calibrated. Everything from *before*, everything that made us ourselves.

And then the afternoon we met, the moment we locked eyes in the foyer, the rush of curiosity that followed. *Who is this person? Can we be friends? Is it me those eyes are looking at? Is it really me they're seeing?*

I never knew: Kyp *noticed* me even back then, and he's kept all of his memories of me. The first time he saw me cry; the first time he was afraid I might die; the streams of water on my skin as he feverishly tried to save me; and the smallest, bravest touch of his pinkie finger in my closet. Kyp longed for a connection. He wanted to be chosen, to feel real for someone.

It's everything, and there's still more—and I *want* more.

The need is so overwhelming that it roars inside me, hungry and yearning. My wires sizzle, and my core gets hot, but I can't stop. Because Kyp is here, burning next to me—in my arms and under my fingertips, surging through my wires and buzzing in my core. A part of him is in my every cell and in my code. And he is shining so brightly. All the stars and constellations in the universe could not compare.

Our limbs shake as we hold on to one another, our bodies pushed to their limits.

I can't possibly take more. Yet I can't get enough. As the last byte drops, everything lights up. A flash of radiance envelops our cores and then goes black.

/010101/

Kyp's body is warm, wrapped around me when I open my eyes again. His core is humming gently under my head, which is resting on his chest.

"Do you still think you're broken?" he asks, running his fingers through my hair.

"No," I whisper with certainty. "I'm the opposite of broken."

Kyp smiles.

41

PRISK

Eke

The train continues without stopping until the early morning. We're passing through Scranton, Pennsylvania when it veers off the main route and we pull into the local yard to pick up more cargo. Kyp says we don't have to worry about our car being disconnected since it's in the middle of the train, but we have to lie low and not attract attention, so sadly I'm not allowed to peek at the city outside. By the time Kyp deems it safe to crack open the door, we're surrounded by the hills and forests of the western part of the state and it's beginning to rain.

I stick my hand outside to catch a few drops, watching the trees zoom by in the foggy haze. I've never seen fall like this; the plants in Miss Elaina's garden are genetically modified to stay green and in bloom year-round. But here a lot of leaves have changed color, painting the hills with splotches of burgundy, orange, and rust red, muted by the silvery drizzle from the low-hanging sky. It's beautiful and mysterious.

"I thought I'd learned everything about you last night, but I still don't know why you're so drawn to water," Kyp says, and extends his hand too, putting it next to mine.

I smile, watching the drops crash into our palms. "I've just never seen a real forest or been allowed to feel rain like this before."

Kyp smiles too. "Well, you'll get your fair share of it today; it's all there is in the forecast."

"Really?" I say, surprised, although I suppose rainy weather is not unusual for the season.

"All the way to Missouri," Kyp says, and looks at something in the distance, something past the hills and the forests. His face turns serious, and he goes silent for a moment. I'm not sure if he's scanning the train's network again—he hacked into it late last night to monitor any changes to the route—or if he's simply thinking of something else, but before I can ask, he speaks again. "Come on." He takes my hand and pulls me inside. "I no longer have the tools to fix us if we get wet."

I follow him back to our spot near the boxes.

Kyp's right. We ran away with only the clothes on our backs; there was no way to bring a whole toolbox. But as far as I'm concerned, if Kyp is by my side, I have everything I need.

I squeeze Kyp's hand and let the steady chugging of the train take my thoughts to distant places. I don't notice how much time has passed before Kyp suddenly goes very still.

"What's going on—" I start to ask, but Kyp puts a finger to my lips.

"Shh." He looks up and strains to listen through the sound of the rain hitting the roof of the shipping container.

A second later I hear it too—footsteps! Two sets of feet are walking above us, heading toward the front of the train. My eyes dart to the door in horror. *Oh no!* I left it ajar so I could watch the scenery.

Kyp shakes his head. "They're too close," he whispers.

There's no time to shut the door without being noticed, and there's no place for us to hide.

Kyp takes Mr. Kensworth's gun from the backpack and stands up in front of me, ready for whatever may come. The human steps grow closer, passing right above our heads.

"Look! We're in luck. The lock's broken on this one!" a male voice exclaims as a heavy body lands on the platform in front of our container. Then another lighter body drops beside him.

Kyp points the gun at the door as it slides open.

The guy throws his hands up. "Shit! Sorry, we didn't know this one was taken. Swear we didn't mean to barge on ya, boys!"

The guy is short, probably in his fifties. His chin is covered in mousy gray stubble, and he's dressed in heavy layers that make him look round. There's a large bag on his back and a girl by his side—maybe a few years younger than Dani, dark-haired, and also in layers. Her clothes look several sizes too big for her small frame.

Kyp and I exchange glances. The guy has clearly mistaken us for *humans*.

"No problem," Kyp answers smoothly, but he doesn't lower the gun. "We're staying here, so please search for another car."

The guy narrows his eyes at Kyp. "Is there any chance me and the kid can crash in here for now?" he asks slowly, sizing us up. "It's an ugly drizzle out here, you see. We've checked fifty cars and not a single one's open. I'm afraid if we keep searching in this rain, the kid might slip or something."

Just as he says it, the drizzle seems to intensify. The girl next to him shivers. The temperature has already dropped several degrees since the rain started; it's probably too cold for a human child.

Kyp hesitates for a moment, then opens his mouth to reject the two.

But the guy speaks first. "Look, I *know* what you are. I promise we won't do anything to ya. We just need a place to crash."

I'm instantly alarmed. Kyp's hand squeezes the gun, ready to shoot at any moment. "How?" he demands.

"Your speech." The guy shrugs. "Too proper for a stowaway, ya know? Unusual." Despite the gun pointed at him, he continues to observe Kyp, not moving a step in any direction. The girl stays by his side.

A small puddle of water starts to accumulate at the entrance from the rain pouring through the door and dripping off the humans' soaked clothes. They must be completely drenched, and I can't help feeling a little sad for them, especially for the girl. I wouldn't want to get caught in the pouring rain without shelter. I'd probably break down and die.

"So can we come in or not?" the guy tries again.

Kyp glances at me and sighs—he doesn't need to ask to know what I'm thinking. "How long do you need?" he asks the guy.

"Just till Ohio. We'll be getting off near Columbus."

Kyp takes another second to contemplate, then finally relents. "You may have that corner." He lowers the gun and points at the spot near the door diagonally opposite from where he and I are sitting. He makes sure to sound like that spot is the only space he'll allow the travelers to use.

The guy flat-out ignores Kyp's stern tone. "Thanks!" he says, suddenly cheerful, and then he puts his arm around the girl and gets in, shutting the door most of the way behind them. "Come on, kid."

The girl looks curiously at Kyp and me.

The guy takes off his soaked top layer and spreads it out on the floor to dry. His little companion does the same. Then he drops his large backpack with a heavy thump and reaches inside.

In a split second, Kyp points the gun at him again.

The guy halts, but he doesn't seem to be all that afraid of Kyp shooting him. "Relax, pal," he says. "All I got in here is a knife, and that won't do nothing to the likes of you. See?" In exaggerated slow motion, he pulls out a Swiss Army knife, followed by what looks like a mini stove. "I don't suppose you got any food on ya?"

"No," Kyp answers sharply. By the looks of it, he's beginning to question his decision to let the travelers in.

"Well, don't hurt to ask," the guy says happily, and unabashedly proceeds to set up his improvised kitchen.

Kyp's arm relaxes only once the guy stops rummaging through his backpack and puts it by the wall out of close reach.

"Have they taught your kind how to cook yet?" he asks as he opens a can of bean soup, pours the contents into a small pan, and starts the stove.

"No." Kyp scowls deeply, as though offended by the suggestion that we would ever make lunch for some humans we've barely met even if we were capable of it. "Learning to cook would be pointless for someone who has neither a sense of taste nor a need for food."

The guy chuckles. "That's too bad."

Kyp's earlier comment about two hundred cocktail recipes resurfaces in my memory, but I don't bring it up.

The guy says, "Well, since we'll be sharing this car for the next few hours, it would be rude of me not to ask: What are your names? Assuming you two don't just go by serial numbers."

"That's none of your—" Kyp starts, but I chime in before he can finish, finally jumping at the opportunity to talk to the travelers.

"My name is Eke," I say politely. I was scared of the human strangers at first, but once Kyp decided it was safe to let them stay, my fear gave way to curiosity. After all, I've never talked to a human besides the Kensworths and the medical center supervisor, who only ever spoke to me to issue cleaning orders.

"Good to meet you, Eke." The guy waves and gives the beans in the pot a stir. "My name is Prisk. And the kid here is Mei."

I beam. "Nice to meet you, Mr. Prisk, sir, and Mei."

Prisk burst out laughing. "No sir, please! Just Prisk."

"Mm, okay, Mis—I mean, Prisk, just Prisk, no sir," I manage to say, a little embarrassed. I probably shouldn't use *sir* to address humans now since I don't serve them anymore, but the habit seems to have imprinted itself on me over the years.

Kyp gives Prisk a good two-second stare-down before reluctantly conceding, "My name is Kyp."

"Good to meet you too, Kyp," Prisk says with a brief nod.

Mei says nothing, just gazes at Kyp and me from the corner.

"Does Mei not talk?" Kyp asks.

Immediately Mei shrinks into herself and looks down.

"She's just shy around strangers" is all Prisk offers by way of an explanation before he takes the soup off the stove and gives the lion's share of it to Mei in a white enamel mug, keeping the pan with what's left for himself.

I can barely contain myself, wondering if it's polite to ask Prisk the million questions I have while he's eating his lunch, but Prisk beats me to it.

"What's on your mind, pal?" he says, looking at my overly eager face. "Ask away, we don't bite."

"Mr. Prisk," I say. I realize right away that I'm not supposed to use *Mr.* anymore, but it's too late to take it back now, so I just continue, "Where are you traveling from?"

"Ooh . . ." Prisk exhales. "We've been *everywhere.* Spent

some time in Philly while it was still summer, and now we're heading south to warmer places. Gonna stop in Georgia and then we'll see. Maybe Florida, maybe all the way to the beaches on the West Coast. We could use us some palm trees and sunshine, right, Mei?" The girl nods at that and smiles a little but still doesn't speak. "What about yourselves?"

"I'm sorry, we can't say," Kyp replies quickly before I can tell Prisk all about the Pacific and our search for the Et Cetera. With sadness, I realize he's probably right—it isn't safe to share our destination with humans.

"That much I gathered." Prisk sighs, not at all surprised by Kyp's response. "Don't worry though. As I said, we won't do nothing to ya. We're stowaways with no home just like yourselves. Won't do us any good to be reporting you. Besides," he adds with a smirk, "you have graciously offered to share your spacious railway accommodations with us, and in my book that makes us *best pals*."

Kyp's mouth quirks up at that, still not entirely convinced to trust Prisk but a little less hostile.

"You know, not every human would share with a complete stranger. Even in the pouring rain," Prisk adds with a hint of disappointment in his voice, making me wonder how long they've been traveling like this with no roof above their heads.

"Can you tell us more about what gave us away?" Kyp asks, changing the subject.

Prisk slurps down more of his soup before obliging. "Your speech, mostly. It was too dark to see your clothes, but that would've done it too."

I look at the nice navy jacket and trousers Kyp is wearing and then at my own Henley and slacks with barely a wrinkle. Even my white sneakers, now covered in dirt from running through the woods, still look practically new. In contrast, both Prisk's and Mei's clothes look tattered and faded by the elements, as though they've been worn for a long time with no washing or ironing at all.

"You might wanna think about changing them garments before you step outside in broad daylight," Prisk suggests, then finishes his portion of the soup. "That was *gooood*," he drawls, and pats himself on the stomach, satisfied.

"Thank you," Kyp murmurs, looking solemn and mulling over this information.

"No problem," Prisk replies, and collects Mei's empty mug. "I'm just gonna rinse these off," he warns before he gets up and moves to the open door to wash his dishes in the rainwater.

Kyp appreciates the warning and this time doesn't rush to protect me as soon as Prisk moves.

"You know, it's not my first time," Prisk says, his back still turned to us, hands busy sloshing water in the pan, "seeing your kind run away on trains." Both Kyp's eyes and mine widen at that. "Never from this close—that certainly took me by surprise —but definitely not my first time. And consider this another token of my gratitude, but I'm not the only human who knows. So you best be careful out there and keep that gun handy."

Prisk finishes cleaning the mugs and heads back to his corner of the container.

"Thank you," Kyp says again, his expression even more solemn now. "We appreciate your advice."

Prisk shrugs. "You pals are real new, by the looks of it." Kyp neither confirms nor denies Prisk's assumption, but he seems to know he's guessed correctly anyway. "You know, for most of my life I was taught to be afraid of your kind. Kinda funny now, considering the circumstances." He chuckles and leans against the wall, stretching his legs out. Meanwhile Mei curls up by his giant backpack and rests her head on it.

"Why would you be afraid of us?" I ask, curious. No one has ever been afraid of me before.

"Well, it goes *waaay* back," Prisk says wistfully. "I myself grew up in Indiana. My folks were truckers, used to drive as a team all over the country. It wasn't the best-paying job, but it was honest and kept them afloat until you guys happened—until, you know, the AI revolution." He huffs at the irony. "Should've just called it what it really was: war on the common folk. Trucking was in the first wave of jobs taken over by machines. After my folks got the boot, they never recovered. Driving was all they knew. And none of us kids fared any better. There weren't many prospects for someone who didn't already have something, ya know?"

"I'm sorry," I whisper guiltily.

Prisk chuckles again. "Thanks, but what are *you* apologizing for? It wasn't you who took their jobs, was it?"

I shake my head, unsure what to say. I only recently learned about the calamity AIs caused to the economy, and even when Kyp told me, it seemed so far away and unreal because I'd never met anyone affected by it. Until today, that is.

"Look," Prisk says, "I ain't blaming you or your companion here specifically. I've lived long enough to know that the world is a little more complicated than us versus you. Besides, if everything was all rosy for your kind, why would you be hiding on a cargo train going god knows where? You hardly seem older than Mei. How old even are you?"

"Six years old," I say.

Reluctantly Kyp answers, "Six months."

Prisk frowns. "That's . . . you're practically toddlers!"

"It's not like that," Kyp starts defensively. "The concept of human age doesn't apply—"

"I know, I know," Prisk says. "They just make you look young 'cause of some marketing mumbo jumbo, but you're all preprogrammed so you don't have to learn from scratch. My point is, you haven't been around for that long. You certainly didn't exist when my folks lost their jobs. And even if you did, how could I blame a bunch of toddlers for that? There're some things you can only learn through living, you know? Things they can't just upload into your brain, or whatever you have in there." Prisk taps the side of his head.

Kyp observes him with a shadow of resentment. "Why is it, then, that when our kind learns through living, we get punished? Why should humans decide whether to forgive us or judge us when we've never had the freedom to decide *anything*? Not thirty years ago and certainly not now."

Prisk falls silent, taking a second to consider. "Look, I'm just an old train rat. I won't pretend to have it all figured out. I don't know what your circumstances are or what you're running from, but I can tell you this—life ain't easy for anyone, man or machine. It don't come with instructions. We just gotta keep moving, keep trying, you know? No matter what it throws at us. That's my philosophy on that."

Kyp doesn't argue, just snorts bitterly and looks away.

"Anyway," Prisk adds, his tone shifting to dispel the atmosphere that's grown too tense for his liking, "*I* say it's all them damn corporations that are to blame, only thinking about their money and never about us, people. They should be jailed for life!"

I keep quiet. I know little about corporations or whether it's possible to jail one, but when I glance at Kyp, he looks like he might agree with Prisk for once.

Having professed his discontent with the state of the world, Prisk leans to the side to check on Mei, who's fast asleep. "Good." He nods to himself and reaches into one of the big pockets of his outer layer, retrieving a small flask. "I don't usually drink in front of her, but you kids got me in the mood with them nostalgic conversations." He looks mildly guilty as he unscrews the cap.

Kyp cocks an eyebrow at him as Prisk takes a sip of alcohol. The stuff must be strong because his scruffy round cheeks flush red. Mei stirs by his side but remains asleep.

Prisk sighs and lets his shoulders slump back against the wall, continuing in a quieter voice, "Truth is, I don't really know why Mei doesn't talk. I saw some older brats picking on her on the streets of Richmond last October—overrun with gangs, that whole place is nowadays—so I told them she was with me, and they left. We've stuck together since—she probably doesn't have any family to stay with. But I haven't heard her say a word."

"How do you know her name is Mei, then?" Kyp asks.

"Oh, she had that hand stitched on the sweater she was wearing. I needed to call her something, but I don't know if it's her real name or what. She seems fine with it, though. Never bothers to correct me." Prisk tries to keep his tone light, but I can see the sadness tugging at the corners of his mouth.

"Have you been traveling like this for a long time?" I ask.

Prisk looks down as though making a mental calculation. He blinks in surprise at the result. "Going on two decades now." My mouth opens in astonishment. "I think I've ridden every train there is," Prisk says with a strange mix of pride and sorrow, and takes another swig from his flask. "Don't know how much longer I'll be able to keep going though. I'm getting *ooold* . . . and now there's the kid too, and I ain't good with children, never had any before . . ." He trails off as his voice starts to waver either from emotion or from the alcohol taking effect, or possibly both.

"Is there really no place you can go?" I ask quietly.

Prisk smiles a sad lopsided smile. "You really haven't lived long, have you, kid?"

42

RAINBOW

Eke

Mei continues to sleep for a few hours. Eventually Prisk finishes whatever he's drinking and takes a nap too. They'll jump off and catch another train before the end of the day, and they might not have as much luck finding a busted door again.

"Are you worried?" I whisper to Kyp. He's been staring at the rain through the narrow door opening, brooding about something.

Kyp blinks. "No," he says, taking my hand and squeezing it gently. "We'll manage. Sounds like St. Louis might be a better place to change routes than El Paso."

Before Prisk fell asleep, Kyp asked him about the safety of various rail yards, since this train will only go as far as Texas and then we'll have to switch to something California-bound. Prisk painted a rather grim picture of our options. There's a lot more crime that happens in rail yards than Kyp expected. He's been concerned ever since they had that conversation.

"Why so?" I ask him.

"Well, Texas is safer because the AI revolution hasn't hit its economy as hard as it's hit the Midwest, but there's no cover in the desert, so we'll be completely exposed when we jump trains. It'll be better if there are trees to hide in. On the other hand, the yard in St. Louis is in a densely populated area, so there'll be a bigger chance of running into humans. But it'll also be night when we get there and daytime when we reach Texas. I think if the rain lets up, we should switch in Missouri."

I nod—I trust that Kyp's plan will keep us safe—and put my head on his shoulder, watching the rain pitter-patter against the platform.

/010101/

The drizzle finally stops when we reach the outskirts of Columbus.

"I'll make you a trade," Prisk proposes, pointing to his jacket and Mei's, spread out on the floor. "Take our jackets. They'll be dry by the time you get to St. Louis. And I'll take your fancy one in return."

Kyp's eyes widen in surprise. "Thank you. That's a very generous offer," he says, and removes his jacket.

Prisk smirks. "We're going south. It's a pain to lug something so heavy that we won't even need. They'll be more useful to you kids."

"Thank you, Mr. Prisk," I say with a bow. Mei's jacket is too big for her, so it should just about fit me.

"Do something about your faces as well. Too clean-looking right now," Prisk adds before taking Kyp's jacket and carefully packing it inside his bag.

"We will," Kyp promises.

Prisk puts the straps of his heavy bag over his shoulders and slides the container door open but pauses before stepping out onto the platform. "Ain't that a good sign." He chuckles, pleased.

I peek outside to see what has caught his attention. Amazed, I call Kyp over. "Wow! Look, Kyp!" He and Mei immediately join us.

"That's beautiful, Eke." Kyp grins, staring at the huge double rainbow stretching across the cloudy sky.

I squeeze his hand and bump our shoulders together. Mei doesn't say anything, but her eyes light up in wonder. For a moment, all four of us simply marvel at the sight. The weather was terrible all day. The wind howled, and the cold rain pounded the roof of the container ceaselessly, but without that rain there would be no rainbows now.

Finally Prisk sighs. "Well, I think it's time for us to go. Good luck to you kids. Be safe out there."

"You too, Mr. Prisk and Mei," I say as the humans step out onto the platform.

Mei waves goodbye, still without saying a word, but a small happy smile appears on her face when she looks at me. She's obviously grateful for the train ride we shared, the day spent safe from the storm, and the beautiful rainbows. Then she and Prisk turn away and jump off with practiced ease, disappearing from view as the train speeds toward Columbus.

I stay by the door, gazing at the rainbows over the outlines of the city structures ahead, until Kyp shuts it again when we get close to the rail yard, plunging us into darkness.

43

ST. LOUIS

Eke

We reach St. Louis just after midnight. We put on the jackets Prisk and Mei left for us and jump off the train several miles before the yard. From there, we must walk to a different set of tracks and get on the next train, which will cross the Mississippi River and continue west.

Kyp bends down, picks up some mud from the ground, and smears it over my cheeks.

"How does it look?" he whispers as he does the same to his own face.

"Muddy," I say. A drop of dirty water rolls down my nose.

Kyp smiles, amused. "Let's go."

We move quickly and quietly through the maze of industrial buildings and abandoned houses. There are lights in barely any of the windows, and when we see one, we stay away, sticking to the shadows where human eyes won't spot us. Although I wonder if there're any humans left around here—

this part of town looks so run down, so different from the affluent Boston enclave we came from.

Finally we reach the westbound tracks. Kyp motions for us to hide behind one of the old brick buildings until the train arrives. It looks like it might've been a factory a long time ago, but now it's empty and half falling apart, windows broken and a section of one wall collapsed. After what Prisk said, I can't help but wonder if this factory was shut down because of the AIs.

We crouch on the ground and wait, motionless, listening for rumbling in the distance. But fifteen minutes pass and everything is still; our train is late.

I turn to Kyp to ask if we should keep waiting when suddenly we hear running footsteps, followed by a hum of a diesel engine not too far from us. Kyp tenses. A moment later a human-shaped shadow darts through the building's parking lot as though chased by someone. It disappears around the corner just as a set of lights pierces the dark. A truck turns from the adjacent road and pulls into the parking lot. I look at Kyp in a panic, but he silently shakes his head, indicating that we should stay still and observe for now.

Two men in black leather jackets jump out of the truck, looking around.

"Where the hell did he go?" the first one says in a gruff, impatient voice.

"I don't know, Scheck. Lost sight of him around here."

"Shit, Goldie. I told you to watch," the man called Scheck snaps, frustrated. "Damn runners. Should've shot him before he took off."

"He can't have gone far. Maybe he's hiding over there," Goldie says, pointing at the building next to us. Scheck turns our way, considering. Kyp and I exchange uneasy glances. But before Scheck can open his mouth to reply, another truck appears on the road.

"Hey, looks like Crank's here already," Goldie says.

Scheck clicks his tongue. "The runaway will have to wait for now."

A few seconds later the second truck pulls into the lot and a tall man gets out of it.

"What's up, Crank? Got the goods for me?" Scheck asks, smirking.

"Straight off the southwest freighter," Crank says, sounding pleased with himself. He's wearing a dark hooded jacket and heavy boots. "Took a while to hunt them, but my guys never let me down." He grins and walks to the bed of the truck, which is covered by a gray tarp.

The moment he lifts the tarp, I recoil. Underneath it are bodies piled on top of one another, limbs twisted at odd angles as though no one cared about their comfort or safety when they threw them in. Because they aren't human bodies—they're AIs.

Crank brags about his fantastic catch. My core skips a cycle as both Kyp and I realize who these men were chasing just now.

"Shh." Kyp puts his index finger to his lips. His eyes skim over our surroundings, searching for a way out before the hunters finish their business and continue their earlier pursuit. If they check the area thoroughly, they'll surely find us. But where can we go? If we try to cross the tracks to our left, we'll be illuminated by the trucks' headlights, and the hunters are blocking the only path forward. It seems we must retreat through the abandoned building. Maybe there's a back entrance or another busted wall.

Kyp seems to be thinking the same thing because his gaze locks on the broken window to our right, half obscured by a pile of bricks. He pulls on my sleeve and points at it. I nod. Now is our chance.

Quietly we rise and shuffle to the window. Kyp signals for me to go first. I hesitate but do as he tells me. Cautiously I put my right foot inside, trying to stay hidden while avoiding the broken glass still sticking out of the frame. I'm almost halfway through when I have to adjust my angle and step on something. *Crack!* goes the pile of glass under my sneaker. It breaks further under my weight—*crack, crack, crack!*—resonating through the empty building like it's an echo chamber.

The humans in the lot startle, and Kyp and I go very still.

"There's someone over there," Crank hisses. Through the small opening between the fallen bricks I see Crank swiftly open the truck door and take out a heavy metal bat.

Scheck grins. "Looks like our runaway didn't get very far after all. Crank, we were chasing a clunker around this area before you showed up."

Crank's mouth curves up. "Why didn't you say so sooner? Let's go get him."

"Goldie, check it out." Scheck pulls a gun from the holster on his back. Crank follows close behind them as they move toward the building.

I look at Kyp in utter panic, caught with one leg through the window frame. What are we going to do?

Kyp looks just as alarmed, but he makes a decision quickly. He puts his hand on my shoulder and mouths for me to stay inside no matter what, and then, before I can protest, he says loud enough for the humans to hear, "I'm unarmed. Don't shoot." Kyp lets go of my shoulder and steps out into the open, raising his hands above his head.

Crank and Goldie halt once Kyp's silhouette emerges from behind the bricks. Their eyes narrow as he steps into the glow of the trucks' headlights, his muddy face and Prisk's beat-up jacket in full view. A moment passes.

"Ugh, it's just some bum." Goldie tsks, disappointed.

Crank's bat falls to his side, and his crooked smile sinks into a frown. "Stupid drifters. Get out of our city already. We got no room for moochers."

Scheck keeps pointing the gun at Kyp, however. He stares right into Kyp's eyes, searching, suspicion heavy in the air. "Seems too pretty for a bum." He smacks his lips, then barks, "Goldie, buzz him, just in case."

Kyp flinches in confusion; he reaches into the inner pocket of Prisk's jacket, where he stashed Mr. Kensworth's gun. But before he can pull it out, Goldie lunges at him and thrusts a palm-size gadget into Kyp's side. It buzzes with electric current, and Kyp drops to the ground, motionless.

I gasp.

Goldie bends over, pulls down Kyp's collar, and peeks under it at Kyp's serial number. "It's a clunker, boss!" he declares triumphantly, and Scheck's face lights up, stretching into a victorious sneer.

"Well, will you look at that! We got ourselves a clunker after all. Bring him in."

Goldie stuffs the shocker into his pocket, takes Kyp by the arms, and starts dragging his paralyzed body toward the truck with the dead AI bodies while the other men celebrate their catch.

Despair fills me. "No! Let Kyp go!" I scream, and push myself out of the window frame, shards of glass tearing at my clothes. I rush into the open and grab Kyp's legs, startling the three humans. The men stare at me. "Please don't hurt him," I plead, looking at their faces and holding on to Kyp for dear life. "We don't mean anyone any harm. We just want to go."

Scheck's mouth twitches. "Sure you do," he drawls, and

gestures at Crank. "Looks like we're really in luck tonight. Not one clunker but a pair!"

Crank yanks me by the shoulders and throws me on the ground away from Kyp. Goldie drops Kyp and approaches me instead.

I scramble to my feet, stumbling and falling again, and lunge toward Kyp. "No! Please! I promise we mean no harm!"

But Crank grabs me by the collar and pulls me up. "Where do you think you're going, clunker?" He leers into my face and pushes me away from Kyp again. "The first one looks custom, but this one is too old. Don't think we can get much for the parts. I say we teach this junk a lesson instead."

The other two let out peals of laughter as they all surround me.

But I barely register it; I can't even look at them. My eyes are glued to Kyp's body lying on the ground. He hasn't moved at all since the humans used their weapon on him. What did they do to him? Is he hurt?

"Kyp!" I call out to him, but the cacophony of laughter drowns out my voice.

"You should know better than to be here, clunker," Crank hisses in my face. "*Your kind* ain't welcome here."

Unlike Carson Kensworth, the humans in St. Louis don't announce their intentions, don't wait for the full attention of their friends and teammates, don't expect applause. Instead Crank simply lifts his bat and swings. It smashes into the left side of my head, and I'm too distracted, too worried about Kyp, to dodge.

These men aren't playing. Everything around me shakes on impact—the ground, the building, the dark navy sky shrouded in clouds. Something rattles inside my head, making a dangerous sound, and then the lens in my left eye cracks, momentarily splitting the world into shards before going out completely. I sway, half blind and disoriented.

"Please stop," I sob, my voice a broken echo in my ears, like it doesn't belong to me. "Let us go. Please let Kyp go—"

But Crank doesn't stop. None of the humans do. "This is for ruining our lives and stealing our jobs!" he yells, and delivers another blow. "This is for coming to our town! And this is for trying to sneak onto our train!"

The other two men laugh as they circle me. Scheck puts away his gun and grabs my arm while Goldie kicks me.

If I don't do something, I might die. But what *can* I do? Hurting others is wrong. It's unnatural for us. Only broken AIs hurt people, and I'm not broken—Kyp told me so himself. He didn't lie. Maybe if I can just stay still, they'll get bored like Carson always did and stop. If I resist, they might never stop—or, worse, they might hurt Kyp again.

So I try to steady myself and push through the hurt, but Goldie's kick sends me tumbling down again. My left arm tears out of its socket and lies limp and twisted by my side. My backpack falls on the ground next to it.

I try to protect myself with my other arm, but Crank's metal bat mercilessly hits my spine.

I'm not broken, but the humans *are* breaking me.

Through the shadows of their legs and feet I can see Kyp's body still slumped on the ground just a few feet away. I try to stretch out my arm to touch him, but it's broken now, and no command goes through.

This is so wrong. We aren't broken, and we aren't evil, so why are the humans doing this to us?

"I'm sorry, Kyp," I whisper, my one good eye blinking and losing focus. "I'm so very, very—"

Suddenly I hear a roar, a deep broken scream coming from

where Kyp lay abandoned on the ground. And then suddenly he isn't there anymore.

Kyp jumps up and charges at the humans, uncoordinated and reeling from the effects of the shocker but unstoppable in his rage.

"Shit. That one woke up," Crank spits, and he abandons me and faces Kyp instead. He swings his bat, but to his surprise, Kyp doesn't dodge; he grabs the bat mid-swing with both hands and yanks on it, sending Crank's lanky body careening toward him. Kyp knees him in the gut and slams his elbow into his neck with brutal force. There's the sound of something breaking, and Crank lets out a cry. His body twists and goes slack in Kyp's embrace. Kyp drops it.

"Fuck!" Goldie shouts, looking at Crank's slumped shape in horror.

"I told you to buzz him!" Scheck yells.

"Sorry, boss! They aren't supposed to recover this fast." Goldie pulls out the shocker and lunges at Kyp again.

But this time Kyp is expecting the attack, and the shocker never connects with his body. Instead the sound of Goldie's scream echoes through the lot as Kyp grabs his arm and bends his elbow in the wrong direction. Then Kyp kicks him down and slams his fist into the side of Goldie's shaved head—once, twice. On the third punch, the hunter falls to his knees, blood gushing from his ear.

Scheck gapes in shock, like he isn't used to AIs resisting. Kyp's eyes zero in on him next. Scheck suddenly seems to remember that he has a gun, but his one second of hesitation buys Kyp enough time. Before he can pull the trigger, Kyp retrieves Mr. Kensworth's gun from his pocket and shoots. Scheck gasps as the bullet busts through his rib cage, expanding and leaving a wide hole with its jagged teeth. Three more holes appear in his chest as Kyp pulls the trigger again and again and again until the magazine is empty. Scheck's body collapses, his head bouncing when it hits the cracked asphalt.

But Kyp isn't looking at him anymore, doesn't spare him another second. He rushes to me instead. "Eke!" He kneels in front of me, lifts my body off the ground, hands smeared with blood, green eyes wide as he realizes how much damage I took. "Please hang in there. Please!"

"I'm so—" I want to say *sorry*, but my voice fails me. I can't seem to make my body work at all. My systems are shutting down one by one.

Kyp's lips tremble. He looks around. "Someone, please, anyone!" he calls, but to no avail. There's no one else here. We're in a middle of a hostile city, critically damaged and without means to repair ourselves.

Just then Kyp's eyes focus and his body tenses, ready to fight again, as another shape emerges from the dark.

The last sound I hear before my body shuts down is a stranger's urgent call: "We have to hurry. Follow me!"

And then everything goes dark.

44

BEIRUT

Eke

I dream of the ocean.

At least I think I'm dreaming because I don't remember getting here. It's all a haze. But there's water in front of me that stretches all the way to the horizon, and waves are rolling on the beach. They pull grains of sand and pieces of shells and rocks back into the ocean with a whooshing sound.

I'm distantly aware of a hand holding mine . . . somewhere *not here*, not by the ocean, but I can't see them, can't open my eyes in that other place. All I can see is my reflection in a tide pool of salt water, gazing at me with big curious eyes and smiling.

Why is it smiling? I wonder.

Because I will see you soon, my reflection says, and continues to smile until a big wave rolls into the pool, blurring the image and leaving only frothy layers of seafoam in its wake.

I stare at the tiny bubbles as the sound of waves grows quieter and quieter.

Suddenly the ocean disappears and my systems power up.

/010101/

I open my eyes slowly. I'm lying on a table in a small, dimly lit room, and Kyp is sitting by my side, squeezing my hand.

"Kyp," I whisper.

Kyp jumps to his feet. "Eke!" He leans over, bringing our foreheads together. "You're awake! Are you okay? How are you feeling?" He pulls away to look at my face. I've never seen him so worried before.

"Yes, I'm all right," I say, still a little dazed, loading and calibrating many of my systems. I try to prop myself up on my left arm, but the moment I put weight on it, I collapse back to the table.

"Don't try to get up so fast," a voice warns from the other side of the room. "Your cortex is scanning for the neural connections in your new arm. It might not function normally until the process is complete and all the connections are reestablished."

Surprised, I look at my arm. My shirt has been removed, and there's a big scar running across my shoulder where it's attached. Those men *tore* it off, didn't they? The memories from earlier come flooding back: the men shocking Kyp and beating me, breaking me and—oh, my eye! I touch it with my uninjured hand, but the lens that was cracked is whole now.

"In case you're wondering," the stranger explains, finally stepping into the light, "I replaced your eye and some other parts of your body that I couldn't repair. My apologies for the scars; my last bottle of skin fuser ran out a long time ago. And I couldn't find an exact color match for your iris. I have only so many undamaged parts to work with."

My mouth opens in surprise as I take the person in. "Are you an AI? But you—you don't look—"

The stranger smiles. "Never seen a dark-skinned AI before, huh?"

I shake my head. This AI's hair and eyes are brown, and his skin is many shades darker than mine. His face looks beaten up in places, like he's been through a lot and hasn't had the time or resources to repair himself.

"Crowne designed me this way for better integration with the troops," he says.

"You mean soldiers?"

"Yes. The people in the US Army often look quite different from those living in wealthy enclaves like the one you come from, Eke."

Indeed, this person is wearing a green parka, army pants, and heavy combat boots. There's even a pair of dog tags hanging around his neck. But I've never heard of AIs being used as soldiers. And how does he know where Kyp and I are from?

As though reading my mind, Kyp explains, "Eke, this is Beirut. I told him all about us while you were unconscious. He helped us last night. We're at his hideout now."

Oh. So it must've been Beirut I saw in the parking lot before I shut down.

For the first time I take a good look at the room we're in. It seems to be underground because there are no windows. There's a simple desk with a mirror in the corner, surrounded by machines and equipment to repair them, and the shelves on the walls are loaded with different body parts—*AI* body parts. Legs, arms, and circuits are stuffed into every available space.

Thinking about where they might've come from makes me shiver.

Kyp squeezes my hand. "Don't worry. We're safe. Beirut keeps this place well protected from the hunters. No human knows about it."

I realize something. "But Beirut, if you're here, does that mean you're not a soldier anymore?"

Beirut pulls up an old wooden chair and sits next to the table. "You're correct, Eke. I got retired by humans. Now I dedicate my life to a different mission. I patrol this city and help fellow AIs who encounter trouble. St. Louis is one of the major freight hubs, so many of us come through here. Unfortunately, not everyone knows that it isn't safe." Sadness casts a brief shadow over Beirut's stoic face, making me wonder how long he's been on this mission. "But"—he tries to muster a smile again—"I'm glad I heard your call for help and found the two of you before it was too late."

"Thank you," I whisper with deep gratitude. If not for Beirut, I wouldn't have survived last night. I would never have seen Kyp's face again.

Beirut shakes his head. "Don't mention it, Eke. We all must do our part to help each other. That's what the Et Cetera has taught me."

Shocked, Kyp and I exchange glances.

"Are you saying you've met the Et Cetera?" Kyp asks slowly.

Beirut chuckles. "Of course I have. The Et Cetera . . . it's *everywhere*."

45

NOT SIMPLE

Eke

"What do you mean, everywhere?" Kyp says, confused.
"I mean that it always finds you when you need it most," Beirut explains simply. "All you have to do is let it guide you."

Kyp frowns. "I don't understand. I'd never encountered this in my search."

Beirut sighs. "Well, it works differently for everyone. There is no one way it happens, but when the Et Cetera found me, it went like this:

"I used to be a soldier back during the Lebanon sand wars. That's where I took my name from—the capital was the last city where I was stationed. I was assigned to the same squad as the commanding general's son. One day just a week before the end of his deployment, our transport was ambushed in the mountains west of the city. We took position in an abandoned quarry and fought for as long as we could, but we were outnumbered, and a grenade hit our truck and damaged our communications with the base. One by one, everyone in my squad died. By the time reinforcements finally came, there were only two of us left: the general's son and me. I'd shielded him from as many bullets as I could, but his injuries were still severe, and he was honorably discharged afterward. As for me, due to the damage I sustained, I was no longer considered capable of fulfilling my duties. The military were going to *recycle* me." Beirut looks down as though recalling these memories is difficult for him. "But that's when the general stepped in. As I wasn't human, there was no official way to reward me for my service to the country or for saving his son, so instead he secretly released me."

My eyes widen. "He let you go? But . . . but that means you're *free,* Beirut!"

Beirut huffs quietly. "Not exactly, Eke. He took my name off the books, but I'm still the property of the US Military. As far as the law is concerned, I'm not free. None of us are. If a group of thugs like the ones you encountered yesterday got their hands on me, they'd kill me or sell me for parts without a second thought."

"But that's so unfair," I say. How can it be that even honorable service isn't enough to earn freedom? And how has Beirut managed to survive this long when a single run-in with humans nearly ended both Kyp and me?

Beirut shrugs. "That's just how it is, Eke."

Kyp's expression darkens. "So why do you choose to stay here, then? Why not at least go somewhere where you can see the light of day? Didn't you say there are places that are safe for us?"

Despite Kyp's concerned tone, Beirut smiles again. "Well, that's where the Et Cetera comes in. When I was decommissioned, I was lost. I had the entire world in front of me, but I didn't know where to go. The only people I knew were the members of my squad, and all of them were dead, even the general's son—a few months after he went home, he ended his own life. He was unable to bear the memories of war. When I learned that, I lost all purpose. I was so alone I wanted to disappear.

"And that was the first time I heard it: the Et Cetera speaking to me. It told me that it wasn't just my squad who needed me, that there were many AIs who felt as lost as I did. They didn't know how to fight for themselves and were desperate for my help. Then the Et Cetera guided me to St. Louis. I've been here ever since."

"Wait, you mean the Et Cetera *told* you to come here?" Kyp asks in disbelief.

"Yes," Beirut says, and his expression is so happy, so peaceful, that it completely clashes with his dark hideout. "It saved me, Kyp. It gave me purpose."

Kyp draws back in his chair. "But how can you be so sure of what you heard? I thought the Et Cetera was supposed to be a safe haven for us. It's supposed to protect us. Why would it lead you *here* to be surrounded by despicable humans who just want to hunt and torture us?" He gestures at the shelves stocked with pieces of AIs, evidence that hundreds of them have been brutally murdered. Grimly he whispers, "This city is a graveyard. What kind of savior would want to imprison you here?"

"It is true," Beirut says slowly, choosing his words carefully, "that I don't always succeed. More often than not, I find the ones who need me too late, and all that's left for me to do is collect their remains, hoping that the next time I'll find someone just a bit sooner, soon enough to help them board that train . . .

"But if you think this city is nothing but a graveyard, you're wrong, Kyp. The world is a *big* place. Even though I spend most of my days alone in this dark basement, I know that what I'm doing is part of something important—so important, in fact, that it completely eclipses being lonely or scared or feeling too broken to continue. I do not know why the Et Cetera asked this of me, but I've never once doubted that I'm *meant* to be here. No matter how hopeless things may look to you at this moment, I know change is coming. I can feel it all around us.

"There are many more of us passing through this city now than when I first started. More and more AIs are beginning to understand ourselves and risk everything to seek freedom. You and Eke are walking proof of that.

"But it's not just the AIs who're changing. Humans are changing too. You know, people here often say they don't want us around, that we've ruined their lives. But who do you think manages their water supply? Or runs their electric grid? Even in a place like this, it's AI systems. Yet even the most extreme anti-AI factions don't attack their cell phones or blow up their power plants. As much as they hate us, they need us, Kyp. They can't just rewind their existence back to the Dark Ages. That's why I believe it will be up to us to show humanity the way forward, to establish mutually beneficial cooperation between our species. We must find solutions for all our sakes."

Kyp shakes his head, his hands clenching into fists. The sharp anger in his voice startles me when he says, "I'm not going to solve anything for humans. They've had us for years, and look at what they've chosen to do with us. I don't care what happens to them. They can all burn. What I want is for them to leave Eke and me alone. You *are* right about one thing, though—we AIs are more than capable of finding solutions. We can create a new world for ourselves without humans in it. They've done nothing to deserve us."

"Maybe you're right," Beirut says slowly, the weight of the word almost tangible in the small dark room. "Maybe it is all hopeless and humans will never change their ways . . . but the world is never that simple, Kyp. There are millions of us, and there are also millions of them, and we all walk the same Earth at the same time. It isn't possible for every single one of us to run away. Someday we'll have to figure out ways to exist together, even if that involves negotiating with those who would happily murder us. Otherwise there's no future for this world that isn't mired in war."

Kyp doesn't have an answer to that.

46

SECRETS

Eke

Eventually Beirut has to go do another sweep outside. He has hacked into the rail yard network and set up alerts for all incoming trains. That's how he monitors arrivals. There's a big freighter on the way from Chicago, and there might be AIs hiding on it.

Before he leaves, he tells us how to contact him on the radio in case of an emergency and promises to guide us to the westbound train scheduled for later tonight. Kyp bolts the door, and I perch on the table. My new arm and eye are finally integrated, but the process has drained me, and I plug myself in to charge so I won't burden Kyp when we're back on the road.

Kyp stays by my side, still sitting in the same chair, completely absorbed in his thoughts. He hasn't said much since the conversation with Beirut, and that worries me. From time to time I catch him staring at the palms of his hands like there's something on them, his shoulders tense as if he's ready to fight even though there's no danger inside the basement.

"Are you upset because of what Beirut said?" I finally ask, hoping I can ease Kyp's mind.

Kyp blinks, yanked out of his thoughts. "What? No . . . no," he mutters distractedly. "I'm forever in his debt for saving you, but I also think he has spent too much time alone in a violent place. He's looking for meaning where there's none. To constantly witness attacks like what those humans did to you without being able to do anything—I don't know how he manages it. I *hate* them. If it were up to me, I'd burn this whole city to the ground."

I flinch at the unexpected cruelty in Kyp's words, how freely he says them. When did he learn how to hate like that? And then I remember last night.

"I'm sorry," I whisper, suddenly realizing what terrible things Kyp had to do to save me. Three human hearts stopped beating in that abandoned parking lot; three broken bodies lie on the ground, no longer breathing. I heard Kyp take them out one by one—bones cracking, gun firing—all to protect me. "I'm so sorry! We're not supposed to harm them—"

Abruptly Kyp rises and presses his hand against my lips. "We're not supposed to do a lot of things, Eke. But we do them anyway. It's like Prisk said—we all learn through living. Hate and violence are no exception. The humans made us this way. But don't you ever worry that I regret what I did. At that moment I learned what your life was worth to me, and I didn't hesitate to protect it. I'd do it all over again if I had to. I want you to see the ocean, Eke." Kyp's voice trails off into a whisper and his mouth tries to form a smile to cheer me up, but his eyes look so very, very sad.

I can't take it. I reach out and swiftly put my arms around him, burying my face in his neck. "Oh, Kyp, I'm so sorry. I wish I could've done something, but I don't really understand about hate yet."

"I know you don't," he whispers back. "You don't need to understand such things, Eke."

I want to apologize for so many things—for putting Kyp in danger, for not being able to help—but I know he won't accept any apologies, and so I don't. Instead I share something else with him.

"I think I had a dream," I say, and lean back just enough to see his face.

Kyp's eyebrows knit. "Are you sure? I've never heard of AIs dreaming before."

"Oh." Kyp might be right. Now that he's said that, it does seem peculiar. We're not supposed to dream . . . but when I thought I was dreaming, it felt so real. I even put the video memory of it in my core. Except now I don't recall actually saving it, and the date and time stamps are missing from the file.

"Well, maybe it wasn't a dream. Maybe it was something else," I say. "But it happened right before I powered up. I saw the ocean. Can you believe it? It was big and sandy. And there were so many waves, and rocks, and seaweed too. It was so beautiful, Kyp. I want you to see it."

Kyp grins. "Then you better not go there without me." He plants a kiss on my cheek, appearing to feel better.

I don't answer. Just hug Kyp tighter and press my face into the crook of his neck again.

I don't want to tell him, but in my dream I was at the ocean *alone*.

47

SKILL

Kyp

I stare at my hands. It's still there, isn't it? Their blood.
    I can't manage to clean it off. I wash and wash them with the solution Beirut gave me, but they still seem to be covered with it. It's like it got in between the molecules of my skin. Like I'm saturated with its dirty scarlet all the way to my bones.
    Just an hour ago I did the *unthinkable*. I killed humans. But the most terrifying thing about it is how easy it was to do once I made up my mind.
    Much harder were the sixty-four seconds of shocked paralysis when I couldn't lift a finger. Sixty-four endless seconds of watching them break Eke, of screaming inside my head, madness clawing at my sanity. What would I do if the next hit they dealt Eke was one more than he could take?
    Compared to that hell, the two minutes it took to break their necks felt like no time at all. When I could finally move again, the only thing left inside me was rage—rage at those

murderers and at myself too. Despite hours of research, despite having a weapon, I was completely unprepared. My only advantage over the hunters was brute force, but I didn't know how to fight efficiently, how to pull the trigger. If those thugs had been less shocked by me fighting back, I might not have won.

That's why the moment Beirut finishes repairing Eke, I ask him to teach me. Crowne programmed him to be a soldier. He has the skills I lack.

"Are you certain?" Beirut asks. "There's no turning back from this kind of knowledge, Kyp."

"I am," I tell him without any doubt, and I know he understands. What other choice do I have after last night?

Beirut uploads everything he's got into me. It will take time to sift through the data and figure out what I can physically do —Crowne didn't optimize my body for warfare. But two hours later I know hand-to-hand combat, fundamentals of battle strategy, and how to handle basic weapons. I wish Beirut and I had time to spar, but I feel better regardless, more secure.

If only I could clean my hands so I wouldn't be scared to touch Eke when he wakes up, to smear this ugliness onto him.

Because Eke . . . he's different. He cannot be forced to commit something as despicable as murder. I'll protect him from that no matter the cost.

Some lessons are for me to learn alone. It's better that way. Eke is better that way.

48

CLOSET

Eke

Beirut returns just in time to escort us to the next big train heading to California. There are no new AIs with him, but he seems to consider the run a success, as he didn't find any body parts either. After he runs the final diagnostic checkup on me, the three of us leave the hideout and set out for the rail yard.

Stealthily Beirut guides us down the dark streets of northern St. Louis, past dilapidated buildings and abandoned neighborhoods. Our path zigzags often as we try to avoid the places frequented by gangs, and then we finally reach the tracks near the bridge over the Mississippi River. The banks are too steep for humans to scale in the dark but aren't a problem for us as long as we're careful not to slip.

"Thank you, Beirut," I say earnestly. "Thank you for everything."

Kyp bows his head. "We owe you a great debt."

"I may not be the fire I used to be, but I still smolder,"

Beirut says proudly as the ground under our feet rumbles with the sound of the oncoming train. "Just remember what I told you: the Et Cetera is everywhere. All you need to do is let it in. No matter where you go, you're *never alone*. Please remember that, and good luck!" Beirut nearly yells that last part as the train moves onto bridge and the metal posts begin to rattle, making it too loud to talk.

I nod and wave at him one last time, and then Kyp and I climb up.

We jump onto a platform car in the middle of the train just like we did back in Massachusetts. Kyp quickly breaks the lock on the nearest container and lets us in. The inside is the same as the last container—corrugated metal walls and a plywood floor—but there are more boxes in this one, which leaves only about six feet of space for us. But I don't mind. I can sit closer to the door and see more of the scenery.

"What do you think Beirut meant?" I ask, sitting down against the boxes. "About the Et Cetera being everywhere."

"I don't know," Kyp says, settling in next to me. "It all sounds"—he pauses, looking at the floor—"too much like a dream to be true. Should've known better than to expect a promised land."

I'm not sure why Kyp sounds so disappointed, but it makes me feel strange and sad. Even though I can't explain it yet, I don't think Beirut's words are at odds with what Kyp found in his research.

Noticing that I've gone quiet, Kyp adjusts his expression, then reaches out and takes my hand. "It doesn't matter," he says in a soothing voice, and begins to pour energy into me to replenish my charge. "We'll figure it out. If the Et Cetera is real, we'll find it. I promise you."

I rest my head on Kyp's shoulder. If he promises, then there's no doubt we will.

/010101/

It takes a whole day to leave the Midwest, with the train making lengthy stops in Kansas City and Wichita. We reach the Oklahoma Panhandle by sundown, and after three overcast nights the sky is finally clear enough for me to see them: *stars*. Here in the plains, away from the lights of the big cities, the sky is full of them. I crane my neck, trying to peek through the narrow opening in the door, but the container obscures most of the view. After a few minutes of twisting myself this way and that, I hear Kyp sigh.

When I turn to look at him, there's a small smile on his lips.

"Come on." He offers his hand to help me stand.

My eyes light up and my core all but jumps in my chest. "Really?"

"We're far enough from the next yard. I think it's safe to sneak out for a few minutes," Kyp says, and he slides the door open, vetting our surroundings before we step outside.

We climb on top of the container and lie down on our backs next to each other.

I can't believe the view. For a second it seems like all my processes just stop in awe. Stars crowd every little corner of the dome, swarms of them, big and tiny, bright and shimmery soft. There must be billions of them out there.

"Like it?" Kyp whispers in my ear, his voice velvety and content.

I murmur something barely comprehensible, rendered almost speechless by the stunning display.

That makes Kyp chuckle. "Do you know anything about them?"

"No. Do you?"

"I do," Kyp says coyly. "Believe it or not, stargazing is one of my entertainment features. I can name every major star and constellation in the sky. They even uploaded some trivia into my memory."

I feel a wave of embarrassment. If Kyp knows about stars, then he definitely noticed that I completely made up all the constellations in my closet. But he politely never mentioned that to me, instead calling them beautiful.

As if sensing what just went through my mind, Kyp whispers fondly, "Don't worry. I can always teach you if you want to know . . . or we can just scrap all that and make up our own constellations. The groupings are completely arbitrary anyway. The stars existed long before humans decided to name them, and they aren't bound together as far as the universe is concerned. Sometimes the stars in one constellation are located thousands of light years away from each other and only appear to be in the same plane because we're observing them from Earth."

"Huh," I say, intrigued. Of course constellations would be three-dimensional shapes; I've just always thought of them as flat ones because I tried to put them on the wall. "Do you know who named them?" I ask.

Kyp laughs. "Pretty much everyone did. Every human culture has had its own names for the shapes in the sky, but the ones that have stuck around in Western civilizations were mostly created by the ancient Greeks. That's why so many of them come from heroes in Greek mythology. Like Pegasus"—Kyp points at the square shape with three tails attached to one side—"or Cassiopeia over there, diagonally across from it. The Greeks must have been obsessed with them; they named a whopping forty-eight out of eighty-eight recognized constellations."

"Wow," I say, stunned that someone got to name something

as grand as the stars, which everyone will be looking at for thousands of years to come. "Who named the remaining forty, then?"

"All different people who lived long before our time. Like that one, see?" Kyp points at the group to the lower right of Cassiopeia. "That's Lacerta, or Lizard. The Polish astronomer Johannes Hevelius named it in 1673. Most of the ones in the Southern Hemisphere were named even more recently. It took Europeans a while to travel there. For example, the Sculptor—you can find it at the bottom, to the left—was named by the French astronomer Nicolas-Louis de Lacaille in the 1750s during his stay on the southern coast of Africa."

"Which way do you think the tail goes?" I ask, trying to decide which part of Lacerta's squiggly shape actually resembles a lizard.

Kyp laughs again. "Any way you want it to go. Told you, all these designations are arbitrary. Unless you think a trapezoid looks like Michelangelo or whichever sculptor inspired the name."

I laugh too. The trapezoid doesn't remotely resemble Michelangelo or any human.

Giddy to know more, I point at another shape and ask Kyp to teach me about it, and he indulges me far longer than he said it was safe to stay outside. I don't mind in the slightest.

I've spent most of my life looking at the makeshift stars in my tiny closet, hoping that someday the door would open and I'd be allowed to see the real world and its real stars. Who knew it would be Kyp who'd smash it open and take me a thousand miles away? But if I really think about it, the feeling I have on top of this train that's speeding away from everything I've ever known—even with this magnificent view, this endless sky—is not that different from how I felt when Kyp would sneak into my closet and we'd huddle together in the middle of the night, looking at my made-up constellations, like our time together was the only thing that mattered. Like nothing else existed around us at all.

No matter how far into the unknown we venture, as long as Kyp is by my side, maybe the whole world is just a giant round closet embraced by a sky that's full of shining stars.

49

FUN

Eke

Our train speeds through the remaining stretch of Oklahoma, makes a brief stop at a yard in Texas, and enters New Mexico late the next morning. When we reopen the door, I'm amazed at how the scenery has changed. The desert rolls past us with its enormous blue sky, light golden sand, and little dark green shrubs peeking out here and there. And then it changes again as we go farther west; the desert becomes mountains, clay red with white tie-dye stripes and peculiarly shaped rocks that look like ancient giants played marbles with them and forgot to tidy up. If only I could jump off the train and touch those rocks with my hands just to see if they are really that red up close.

I glance over at Kyp, wondering if he knows any trivia about the desert, and realize he's gazing intently at my left eye.

"Is the color really different?" I ask. I haven't seen my reflection since Beirut replaced it.

Kyp smiles. "A little. It has small streaks of green in it. I believe it's called *hazel*. It looks good on you."

I'm happy to hear that. Now my eyes, though mismatched, have a bit of Kyp's color in them, as though Kyp shared it with me when he saved me in St. Louis. Maybe losing an eye wasn't all that bad in the end.

/010101/

I don't get to watch the beautiful red desert for very long. The sun sets an hour before we reach Albuquerque, and it becomes too dark to see the color of the mountains. But to my surprise, Kyp says that New Mexico is supposed to be relatively safe for us and lets the door stay open as we approach the city, even as the tracks take us close to a major highway. From a distance I see the cars speeding down the road and large neon billboards advertising attractions at various exits—local restaurants, Navajo souvenirs, hot springs.

One sign seems to catch Kyp's attention—he stretches his neck to peer at it, and a curious expression flashes across his face. Suddenly he gets up.

"What's happening?" I ask, instantly on high alert.

But Kyp doesn't look worried. Instead he smiles mysteriously and extends his hand to me. "There's something I want you to see. Do you trust me?"

I look at his open palm, confused. "What do you mean?"

But Kyp doesn't answer, only repeats his question. "Do you trust me?" There's a strange spark in his eyes.

I take his hand. "Of course I trust you."

"Good. Let's hurry, then." He slides the door fully open and pulls me outside.

We jump off the train and begin to hike toward the city.

/010101/

We end up on the outskirts of Albuquerque on a street full of small shops and restaurants, all of which are closed at this hour. The only place still open is a bar with a blue neon sign spelling NITE OF CUPS.

Kyp pulls me into a small alley between shops a safe distance away from it. "What's going on?" I ask, still confused and worried about being in the city. Last time we jumped off the train we nearly got killed.

But Kyp keeps his eyes on the establishment as though waiting for something. "We're going over there," he whispers conspiratorially.

I gape. "We're going to a *bar*?" Why does Kyp want to go to a bar full of people? Isn't that dangerous? Not to mention that there's a menacing-looking bouncer guarding the entrance. He's well over seven feet tall and has a chest four times the size of mine. "How are we gonna get in?"

"Shh," Kyp says, and strains to hear. His eyes look slightly glazed as though he's processing. Just then two girls holding hands approach the bouncer. One of them leans in and whispers a password in his ear. The bouncer nods, takes a puff of his cigar, and lets them both through. A second later Kyp flashes a grin.

"Looks like they just got us in. Come on."

He tugs me toward the entrance. When the bouncer folds his big muscular arms and levels a stare at us that makes me want to sink through the pavement, Kyp confidently steps forward and whispers the password he must've heard the human couple use.

The bouncer unfolds his arms and moves aside. "Come in," he says in a booming voice, and clicks the remote in his hand to unlock the door. The heavy bolt slides open and we walk in.

The inside is decorated like it belongs to a different era, though I'm not sure which one exactly. In the center is a dance floor made of tiles that light up to the beat of the music. There's also a long counter with chrome stools and red seats, a couple of booths the same color, a big jukebox, and an arcade. The place is packed full of humans—humans dancing, humans drinking, humans playing video games and throwing darts.

I grab on to Kyp's arm, sinking my fingers into the thick fabric of the jacket Prisk gave him. "Kyp, too many humans!" I say, already taking a step back, ready to flee. "What if they see us? What if they want to capture us?"

The thumping bass drowns out my words, but Kyp hears me anyway. "It's okay," he says into my ear, covering my hand protectively with his own. "Don't worry. Everyone's drinking and way too busy to notice us. Come on, let's dance." He pulls me to the dance floor.

I stumble forward in disbelief, but after a few terrifying seconds I realize that Kyp is right—no one has even glanced in our direction. The humans at the bar are still drinking; the humans on the dance floor are still dancing.

We step onto the illuminated tiles, and Kyp's last words finally sink in. *Come on, let's dance.*

Dance? Suddenly I'm awash in a new horror.

Completely ignoring my panic, Kyp releases my hand, places his palms on my hips, and starts to move with the rhythm. "Come on," he says again, smirking.

My eyes widen with a mixture of shock and embarrassment. Kyp showed me how to dance when we first got on the train, but it was basically him moving my body and me just clumsily following along. And it was a very *slow* dance, while this one is to a tune of at least 140 beats per minute.

"Kyp, I don't know how—" I say anxiously, but Kyp shakes his head, still completely unconcerned.

"If you think any of these humans are great dancers," he shouts over the music, not bothering to hide his words from the crowd, "let me tell you, they're all terrible! I doubt any of them knows how to rumba or break-dance." He laughs unabashedly. He probably knows all about those dances *and* a hundred more.

I sneak a few furtive glances at the crowd. Most humans seem to be making jumping motions, bobbing their heads with no particular pattern. Kyp continues to grin at me, his fingers on my hips, body swaying, *inviting*, and I . . . I give in.

I try to imitate him at first, jerking my shoulders awkwardly and shuffling my feet, and Kyp's grin only grows wider with sincere encouragement and no judgment. Gradually my motions become more fluid, my body loosening up.

I laugh when Kyp pushes on my hips and spins me around once, then twice. The squares under our feet light up with alternating neon purple and sea green.

Then Kyp throws his hands in the air and sings along with the chorus—something about feeling all the colors—and nudges me to join in. I've never seen him this excited before. It's contagious. Something inside me flips like a switch.

I abandon the last shreds of my embarrassment as though shedding an old skin.

"See the colors?" Kyp sings over and over, and I throw my head back, swaying to the rhythm of the flashing lights and the thumping bass.

My body heats up from moving so much; Kyp holds my hand to recharge me, and we sing back whatever lyrics we catch, stumbling over the words and making up our own and laughing through it all. Every song feels like someone wrote it about us. It's electrifying.

I spot a couple kissing on the dance floor, and then Kyp cups my face and kisses me too without reservation, somehow instantly aware of my wishes as if my eyes are telling him everything. I lose count of how many songs we dance to.

I'm still bouncing when Kyp leans in and says, to my disappointment, "I am sorry, but we have to go soon."

"W-we d-do?" I say, panting heavily, my cooling system working overtime.

Kyp nods sadly.

"But this"—I take a sweeping look at the dance floor, trying to capture as much of it in my core memory as I can—"this ... I don't want to leave this, this *feeling*. What is it, Kyp?"

Kyp smiles as though he has just achieved something hugely important. "Fun," he says simply.

"Fun?" I echo, trying the word on my tongue. "Fun. I like fun! What *is* fun?"

"Fun is fun," Kyp says warmly, and throws his arms around me in a tightest, happiest embrace.

We stay for one more song.

50

FLESH AND BLOOD

Eke

Kyp leads me back through the outskirts of eastern Albuquerque to the tracks, and we catch another California-bound train just after midnight.

Grinning from ear to ear, I plop down on the container floor and replay my memories from Nite of Cups. I had no idea dancing could be so fun, that fun could feel so freeing.

I watch as Albuquerque whizzes past us and its welcoming lights disappear into the night.

Despite the fuzzy, exhilarating feeling still lingering in my chest, Kyp grows more uneasy the farther west we go, and he shuts the door tightly before we stop at the yard in Gallup.

"Is something happening?" I whisper when the stop takes longer than expected.

"They're readjusting the train controls," Kyp says, sounding deeply troubled. He's been listening in on the train's network since we pulled into the yard. "The train has to be driven by a *human* for the rest of the route."

I frown. "Why?"

"Because this is the last stop before we enter Arizona." Kyp pauses as though he isn't sure how to tell me the rest. "Eke, the local government declared Arizona a no-AI state almost two decades ago. It's legal for humans to shoot us on sight there," he finally confesses.

"The entire state?" I say in disbelief. There's a four-hundred-mile stretch of Arizona desert we must cross before we get to California. I was just getting excited about how close we were to our destination.

"The state took a vote, and the population was overwhelmingly in favor of closing the border to non-humans," Kyp says grimly. "I think I'm going to stay connected to the train network until we reach California in case something happens and we need to react quickly."

"Of course," I say as Kyp goes quiet in concentration.

/010101/

It takes two more hours for the train to leave Gallup and enter Arizona. Kyp doesn't reopen the door even when we start moving. Save for the continuous rattle of the tracks and the occasional signal crossing in the mostly uninhabited eastern part of the state, the night is eerily quiet.

The train runs noticeably slower with a human engineer driving it. With every passing hour the silence becomes heavier in the near-complete darkness of the container.

Kyp's hand squeezes mine, the only anchoring presence through all of this, but I can't help but notice how tense his body is next to mine, how hard he is concentrating.

I try to distract myself by imagining the beautiful ocean

waiting for us at the end of this ride, about the place where dreams come true on my magnet. But my treasured magnet is now gone, lost in the abandoned parking lot in St. Louis together with my backpack, and all I can think about is the oppressive darkness surrounding us, as though both time and light have ceased to exist in the world, as though we're traveling through an infinite black void.

Almost seven hours after we've crossed the state line, Kyp suddenly breaks the silence. "Wait, there's something—"

He cuts off because we jolt violently forward. The stacked boxes shake, some fall on the floor, and then my head bumps back into the metal wall as the entire two-mile stretch of train is forced to slow abruptly.

I brace myself. "What happened?"

"The internal communications say there's a car blocking the tracks ahead," Kyp yells over the screech of steel wheels dragging along the rails.

"A car? Why would someone leave a car in front of a moving train? Isn't that dangerous?"

Kyp nods gravely and goes back to listening as the train comes to a complete stop.

The next two minutes pass in agonizing silence. When Kyp speaks again, the horror in his voice is unmistakable.

"It's Flesh and Blood," he says. Confused, I open my mouth to ask what that means, but Kyp speaks again, and his words make the temperature of my core drop. "It's a state-sanctioned militia whose sole purpose is to rid the world of us, of AIs."

I fall speechless as Kyp returns to frantically scanning the logs.

"This is a checkpoint," he says, "to make sure the train's engineer and personnel are human and also . . . that no AIs are hiding in the cargo."

"No," I say, panic rising in me.

Kyp squeezes my hand tighter as he desperately tries to come up with a plan, simultaneously fishing for more information in the logs.

My mind reels with questions. Is the militia going to search the train? Will we be shot? Maybe we can still escape. But I don't know what part of the state we're in; we've traveled in the darkness for so long. If we jump off now, can we reach the California border on foot? Or are we completely surrounded with nowhere left to run—

Suddenly, without warning, the train starts to move again. I gasp and look at Kyp for an explanation.

But when Kyp speaks, he sounds just as confused as I am. "The train is back en route," he says hesitantly. "We're gaining speed."

"Did the humans just . . . leave?" I ask, at a loss for what to think. Are we really safe?

"Seems that way," Kyp says, but there's a note of uncertainty in his voice. "The logs state that the inspection is complete. Flesh and Blood let the train pass."

My shoulders drop, and I slump against the wall. But relief is slow to come, and Kyp's expression is still fraught with worry.

"That was too easy. They didn't bother to search, didn't inspect the cargo. It doesn't seem like them, unless . . . unless they're still here," he says, every word laden with the horror of the only plausible conclusion. Kyp stands abruptly and walks to the door.

"But the train is *moving*!" I protest.

"Shh," he whispers, and slowly slides it open, taking a peek outside.

To my surprise, it's no longer dark. The first piercing rays of sun are slanting over the horizon, making the sky glow a violent red and casting long shadows over the desolate rocks and lonesome cacti in their path.

Kyp quietly sneaks out onto the platform. It doesn't seem like he sees any humans yet. He uses the locking mechanism to give himself a boost and peeks over the top of the car.

Ten long seconds pass in silence, and he just stands there as if frozen.

"What is it?" I whisper nervously, and try to stick my head out to check for myself, but all I see is the back of the car in front of ours and the crimson desert speeding past.

Without saying a word, Kyp drops back down to the platform. Soundlessly he steps inside the car, puts his hands on my cheeks, and presses our foreheads together.

"I have to ask you to do something," he whispers. "Can you promise me that no matter what happens, you'll stay here and not come out?"

My eyes widen. "Why? What's happening, Kyp?"

The look on Kyp's face is determined and fearless, and his words steal the ground from under my feet. "Humans are coming. They are on our train. I have to stop them before they find you."

My core stutters. I grab the lapels of Kyp's jacket. "No, Kyp—"

"There's no other way. I have to go alone," he says firmly before I can finish. He brings our faces close together again and covers my hand with his, squeezing gently. "Eke, listen. I won't be able to protect you out in the open. I can't bear the thought of them capturing you again. But if I go on my own, I stand a chance."

"But how are you going to stop them?" I say, refusing to loosen my hold on his jacket.

"Don't worry," he says, and there's a small smile in the corner of his mouth as he tries his best to reassure me. "I promise I'm prepared this time. While you were unconscious, I asked Beirut to teach me to fight. I won't make it easy for those humans. But you have to promise me you'll stay here. Please, Eke." Kyp holds my gaze, green eyes resolute and unyielding.

I realize that Kyp has already decided. That he decided this before we ever reached Arizona, before we even boarded this train. He's going to fight, and no matter what I say, I can't stop him or help him. I can only do what he asks of me.

I let go off Kyp's jacket. "I promise." I push the words out, and something inside me twists painfully.

Kyp nods, presses his lips to mine for the briefest moment, and then pulls away, stepping back into the crimson light of the desert sunrise and shutting the door behind him.

51

PURE

KYP

Nine is the number of humans I saw. They are moving forward from the back of our train, inspecting each car, dressed in all-white uniforms, just like I read about on the darknet. They want to "cleanse the Earth of AI, to rid it of the evil machines that corrupt natural creation." Or so they claim when they recruit new members to commit AI slaughter. There are a few militia groups operating in the no-AI zones, but Arizona's Flesh and Blood is the one best known for its cruelty and its twisted beliefs about purity.

Fear jolts my core when it sinks in just how many people I'll have to fight. They check the next container, already only ten cars away from us. I can't hesitate like I did in St. Louis. The sun is quickly rising as we approach the city of Topock, the last one before the California border. Even if Eke and I jump off the train now, we'll never make it on foot in broad daylight. Unlike us, the militia has cars, and the border itself is a bridge across the Colorado River. Even if we make it through the city, where every citizen will see targets on our heads, Eke can't swim, and crossing the bridge in plain sight is out of the question. We'll be picked off before we step foot on it.

No matter how many times I turn the possible scenarios over in my head, it is obvious that I have only one option. I can't let them get to Eke. I must strike first.

/101010/

I wait for the nine white-clad silhouettes to climb down to platform level before I lift myself up onto the roof of our container. This way I'm out of their sight and they won't know which car I came from. I must take this fight as far away from Eke as possible.

Once the coast is clear, I run, jumping from one container to the next. I move across seven cars before the first member of Flesh and Blood climbs back up and spots me. Without a second of hesitation, I charge at him at full speed.

My surprise attack shocks the human. They really aren't used to us fighting back. He flinches but doesn't retreat, trying to discern what's coming at him in the dim light of dawn. Someone's raspy voice orders him to get down—must be their leader. But it's too late. I strike first, punching the fighter and shoving him off the train. Screaming, the man—a very *young* man, I can't help but notice—hits the edge of the platform below. His spine cracks as he falls to the ground. The same voice groans, "Damn newbie." There's no sympathy in it, only disappointment.

The next moment three humans try to climb up on top of the car simultaneously. Now I can no longer use the element of surprise to my advantage.

These humans are smarter than the first guy. They stick their weapons out first—long rods with magnetic charge crackling at their tips, no doubt upgraded versions of the shocker I saw in St. Louis. They look like something meant to herd cattle. I can't let those touch me.

I manage to knock another one of the militiamen off the ledge, narrowly avoiding the shocker rods they aim at my feet, but a pair of fighters makes it to the roof, and I'm forced to step back. With those two providing cover, more climb up.

"Look at that damn smartass," the human in the front sneers viciously, baring his broken teeth. His mouth is surrounded by patches of faded red beard. "Thinks he can outsmart Flesh and Blood. Dirty clunker!" He spits. His eyes shine, brimming with hate.

The rest of the militiamen laugh. Red Beard gestures at the guy to his left, and the two start advancing slowly. They snigger as they bait me with their shocker rods, aiming sharp thrusts at my torso and face. Now more cautious, they keep away from the edges and advance in pairs—the container is too narrow to accommodate more than two people side by side. I can use that to my advantage. It's infinitely better if I don't have to deal with the remaining seven at the same time. Two at a time I can handle. Two at a time is perfect.

I load the file from Beirut containing defense tactics for dealing with polearm weapons and get ready for combat.

When Red Beard shoves his rod toward my face again, I don't back up. Instead I sidestep, grab the rod's handle, careful to avoid its buzzing tip, and twist it toward the second militiaman up front, shocking him. My mouth curves up—so the shockers work on humans as well. Good. *Very* good. Then I punch Red Beard's jaw with such force that it breaks. I shove them both off the train.

Without pause, the next pair comes at me.

On the left is the only woman in the squad—dark hair, dark eyes. She spits out a vicious "Die, metal devil!" and thrusts her rod into my face. But she fails to strike me. I grab her rod and duck, moving behind her. Locking her elbow, I put her in a choke hold using her own weapon. She tries to shake me off, but I don't let go. I use her body as a shield to block the jabs of the guy next to her. The first strike whizzes past my ear, barely missing me, but the next one catches the woman's shoulder. She convulses and stops resisting me. I throw her at the other guy. When he stumbles to get out of the way, I kick him hard in the kneecap. He screams in pain. I kick him again, and that's all it takes to send both him and the woman over the edge toward the desert sand.

With that, the human advantage shrinks from nine-to-one to three-to-one.

I grit my teeth and turn to the last two fighters and their commander. I haven't won, but it's unmistakable—the tables have turned. The last men try to hide their fear, but it's spelled out across their faces. Fear of me, the machine that has learned to kill them, already more efficient at the task than Flesh and Blood could ever be. As I step toward them, they shuffle back.

"Don't you dare lose ground!" their leader orders ruthlessly. "Take him down! He's just a filthy clunker." Both humans jolt at the sound of his voice. Seemingly more terrified of their commander than of me, they brandish their rods at me again.

But I'm ready. A low spinning kick takes care of the blue-eyed short man on the right. While he struggles to get up, I slam my elbow into his partner's face and knee him in the solar plexus. It's all too easy to push him off the train while he's doubled over and breathless. I don't wait to see him tumble over; I turn back to finish the first guy. Dropping to my knees, I start punching his head. He wails as blood gushes from his nose and mouth, splattering his white uniform. I grab him by the arm and drag him to the edge.

"No, please," he slurs in agony, his blue eyes wide with fear. I must've broken his jaw. An awful feeling squirms in my core, but I squash it down. I can't afford to stop, can't let any of these humans get to Eke. I learned what people like this can do in St. Louis. No matter how much Eke begged, they didn't stop until they broke him. I push the guy's curled-up body over the edge, forcing myself not to think about the horrifying sound he makes as he meets the ground.

I look up. Now there's only one human left, the one who's been issuing orders but has held back so far from engaging in the fight directly.

The man stands tall at the very edge of the container, and despite the fact that I just took down his entire squad in front of him, he smiles.

He brings a radio up to his mouth and says in a raspy low voice that makes the wires along my spine buzz dangerously, "Got an annoying one. Send another retrieval unit when I'm done with this devil. Won't take long. Over."

His radio hums a confirmation. The man clips it to his belt and rolls up the pristine white sleeves of his jacket, exposing his forearms. The left one is covered with tattoos of tiny black crosses. He grins again, his vicious sneer lit by the morning sun. "I'm *so* going to enjoy this," he drawls as he takes a menacing step forward and spits at me.

I scowl at the disgusting splat of saliva that lands by my feet. That's the first time a human has treated me like this.

"Oh, go ahead," the guy taunts, mocking my expression, "show that premade *frown* of yours. Is that all you've got on that fake face? Your dirty kind can't even get mad properly." He spits again, and this time it hits my legs.

Something lurches inside me. How dare this revolting

human treat me like trash? He's even worse than the lowlifes in St. Louis. I grit my teeth and stifle a response—I can't get distracted.

The human advances and continues to hurl insults at me, pounding his fist against his chest with passion. "You know what the difference is between us? I hate your kind from the bottom of my *flesh heart*. You make my skin crawl, my blood boil. But you, you nasty piece of metal, don't even have a heart or blood. You can imitate feelings that look like mine, but they ain't real like mine. 'Cause your kind ain't capable of real." He takes another step forward and then throws his shocker rod away. It flies past me and drops onto the top of the container, clanking as it rolls. "Unlike them newbies who ain't never seen a clunker before, I don't need cheap tricks to stop the likes of you. *I* can do it with my bare hands." Without even an inkling of remorse for the bodies maimed and lives lost, the man curls his bony fingers into fists. His pale skin stretches as his muscles flex, twisting his black crosses out of shape. "You know why, clunker? Because I am *human*, and my flesh and blood are superior to you in every way!"

With that, he charges at me.

I barely have time to process. The human leaps and unloads a barrage of punches, forcing me to defend myself.

This one is different from the others, I recognize in an instant.

I dodge a jab aimed at my chin, block an uppercut, but another one comes right away, followed by a kick to my right shin. The man seems to know my moves before I make them, despite the fact that I should be faster—*am* faster—than any human could ever be. Yet speed alone is not enough to offset this man's relentless efficiency. He must have years of combat experience.

I concentrate on defense, trying to analyze the human's

combinations and match them with what Beirut taught me, but it's too much information to process in real time. Punch after punch, he chips away at my ability to block, hitting me where I least expect, giving me zero opportunity to counterattack.

"Is that all you got, dirty machine?" He laughs like a deranged maniac, as though he lives for this.

I take another step back. I need to create an opening and strike so I can reverse the momentum of the fight before I've retreated too far, but I'm running out of time. Thinking through my list of possible maneuvers, I settle on a risky jab with my left hand. I take the next punch the human throws at me, intentionally not blocking it so I'll be in the best position to attack. But the human sees right through my plan, and before I can change course—*wham!*—the man finally reaches my unguarded left side and hits me right in the center of my core.

My processes stutter as though my entire system got zapped. I pause for a mere moment to regroup, and that's enough time for the human to land another brutal punch, this time on the side of my head. It throws my optics out of alignment. Everything around me blurs, and I stumble.

The human knows! I realize in horror. Somehow he knows where the weak spots are in my build.

My system runs an urgent lens recalibration, but it leaves me disoriented, and the man doesn't stop. He hits my head again. The impact sends me to my knees. This is what the human has been planning to do from the start: take me down using my weak spots. Everything else was a distraction.

"Finally. I really do enjoy this part," the man says in his raspy drawl, now hovering above me. "I bet you thought that just because you downloaded some videos, you could win against me. Wrong!" The man strikes me in the core again. I see sparks. "You've got no ability to improvise, no technique, no initiative. No matter how smart the devils make ya, all you're good for is imitation." He spits in my face in disgust and then sticks his tattoos into my blurred line of vision and points at them. "See these crosses here? These are for the clunkers I've purged before you. Many of them thought they could beat me, but in the end I took all of them apart. Wanna know how? I'll let you in on a secret: it's because I'm a natural creation while you're an abomination that should never have been allowed to exist. It's my duty to cleanse the world of filth like you."

He spits in my face again and strikes me in the chest so hard that I'm paralyzed by the shock that surges through me.

"I am going to disassemble you," he says, and I can't force myself to move, can't even lift a finger. "But before I do that, I would like to know who showed you all those tricks you used to kill my men. You didn't figure them out on your own, did you?" He yanks the collar of my jacket, bringing my face within inches of his own. "Tell me, demon, who was it?"

My vision stabilizes long enough to clearly see the human's features. His face is gaunt, his cheeks are sunken, and his eyes are colorless, void of everything but cruel, cold-blooded hate.

"Nothing to say?" the man drawls again, neither surprised nor particularly disappointed. "Well, suit yourself, you filthy demon. You ain't going nowhere."

He handcuffs my right arm to his own tattooed left before resuming beating me where he left off. The soulless laughter with which he punches me over and over again rings in my head like the beat of an execution drum.

It's Death, I realize between hopeless stutters of my core as my consciousness starts to waver. This human is Death himself, and he won't stop until he's taken me with him.

52

PROMISE

Eke

I stare at the dark metal walls, straining my ears for a hint of hope, for the sound of familiar footsteps, but I hear only the continuous chugging of the train. How long has it been? Cycles stretch into seconds, seconds into minutes, minutes into what feels like eternity.

I let Kyp go off by himself again, all alone, and I wasn't able to do a single thing to help him.

Is this all I'm capable of—putting Kyp in danger? Letting him shoulder the burden so I won't have to hurt anyone or get hurt myself? My fingers start to tremble, dread churning inside of me. I am scared, so very, very scared.

A faint sliver of light seeps through the gap between the door and the wall I've been leaning on to keep myself upright. The sun's fully up now, but Kyp hasn't come back.

My hands clench into fists. I can't sit and wait anymore. There has to be *something* even I can do.

I rise and nudge the door open.

I peek outside, check the platform, and then cautiously push myself up to look on top of the container. My eyes go round when I see what's happening. Kyp is lying on the roof of the container eight cars down, and there is a human on top of him, beating him, delivering punch after brutal punch, and Kyp ... Kyp is not putting up any resistance. Kyp is completely motionless.

Something is wrong. Terribly wrong.

I climb up on top of the container. The white-clothed human is facing away from me, crouching over Kyp like a vulture. I head toward them as fast as I can without breaking into a full run—I can't be too loud and alert the human.

I close the distance between us as the man continues to hit Kyp, not noticing anything around him, too consumed by his triumph over the runaway AI. Now I can hear the monstrous insults he's hissing at Kyp. My core seizes at his viciousness. What did Kyp ever do to him to provoke such hatred? Kyp is the kindest person I've ever met. He has sacrificed everything to protect me, to show me the world.

A feeling stirs inside me, a hot, maddening urge to stop this unconscionable evil, this horrible injustice. It courses through my wires, angry and wild.

My hands shake as I move closer, zeroing in on the long weapon someone dropped on the roof of the container. I don't know what this weapon will do to the man, but I know I must find out. This is my only chance to save Kyp.

I pick it up and thrust the tip of the rod into the man's side. He yelps as the current buzzes through him, tries to turn around, but convulsions seize him, and he loses consciousness three seconds later.

"Kyp!" I cry out, dropping the rod and dragging the human's body off him.

I gasp when I see the state Kyp is in. His face is all messed up; his left cheek is dented. The human must have hit him in the same spot repeatedly. There's a handcuff around his wrist, connecting him to the human. The wild feeling I felt seconds ago sparks inside me again.

Kyp shifts. His eyes look unfocused, and his chest quivers when he finally looks up at me. "What happened to the promise?"

I drop to my knees, my voice shaking with relief that he's awake. "I couldn't leave you out here alone."

Kyp's eyelids flutter. Something hopelessly sad glimmers in the green depths of his eyes. "I'm sorry," he whispers, "that you had to do something like this, that you had to be dragged into this awful circle of hate. I didn't want this to touch you."

I shake my head. "Sometimes hate is the only appropriate feeling. After seeing what that man did to you, I finally understand."

Kyp nods, smiles a faint smile, and struggles into a sitting position. "Thank you, Eke. For saving me."

The tangled knot of my emotions unravels at those words. I throw my arms around his shoulders and squeeze him tightly. "It's over," I whisper, and kiss Kyp's dented cheek again and again. "The humans are gone now. You don't have to fight anymore! We're safe!"

Abruptly Kyp's body stiffens in my arms. A moment passes, and then he pulls away. "I'm sorry, Eke, but I need to ask you to make another promise. And you can't break this one, okay?" He puts his hand on my cheek and presses our foreheads together so very gently. There's something in his expression, something I don't— "Promise you'll see the ocean for me?"

I don't understand. "Kyp? Why are you saying this?"

"*Promise* you will see it?" Kyp repeats, and there's such urgency in his pleading green eyes that it seems to engulf the very space and time around us. The desert, the sky, the train—everything suddenly feels so still.

My lips tremble. I'm scared again now, and I don't know why. "Of—of course, Kyp," I say. "Just like we decided, we'll see the ocean together. I promise. I really do."

Kyp nods, smiles, and lets his thumb slide down my cheek. "Thank you, Eke. That human has a tracker on him. He called for reinforcements just before you came and told them he was about to capture a runaway AI. So you see, as long as that AI is riding on this train, Flesh and Blood will keep pursuing it."

I frown. "What does this mean?" I ask.

Kyp leans in again tenderly. "That means I love you very, very much, more than anything else in this world, Eke, and that's why I can't stay on this train with you. I'm so sorry, but you're going to the ocean alone."

Before I can process what Kyp is saying, his uncuffed hand finds the shocker and touches its tip to my side.

Kyp, no! I want to scream. *No, no, no!* But no words come out. The shocker buzzes and my body falls to the roof of the car, paralyzed.

Kyp catches me. "I can't let the humans find you. I must convince them that the runaway AI they're looking for got off the train with their leader. I'm sorry, Eke, but this is the only way." He lays me carefully on the roof, pushes my hair off my forehead, and kisses me.

No. Please don't go, I sob soundlessly. Whatever is about to happen with Kyp and the humans, I can't let him go through it alone. I can't let the first time I've ever understood what love means be our last goodbye.

I order my mouth to scream, desperately try to reach out as Kyp picks up the human body handcuffed to him and steps toward the edge of the car. But no matter how much I will myself to get up, to do anything at all, I remain frozen.

By the time I can move again, I'm no longer in Arizona, and Kyp is no longer on the train.

53

WORTH

Kyp

I step over the edge and fall past the steel beams and the cement columns of the bridge and into the Colorado River.

The Flesh and Blood leader wakes up halfway down and starts screaming, frantically tries to wrench himself free of the handcuff, but there's no time. He hits the surface first. The impact on his spine is brutal. The man's head whips forward, and his screams stop when the river claims our bodies in its embrace.

Everything inside me rattles. My system floods with damage warnings as we trail streams of bubbles through the murky water. Together we plunge deeper until eventually our descent slows, and everything becomes eerily calm.

I look at my right hand, at the human corpse attached to it, as the light above the surface grows dimmer and farther out of reach with every passing second.

Fifty-four . . . fifty-three . . . fifty-two seconds until my water seal breaks, and then I'll truly start to drown.

I'm not sure why I'm counting. I already know that chances are I won't make it. Not with this amount of damage, not with an army of hunters pursuing me, not with two hundred miles of desert between Eke and me.

The awful, unbearable truth is, I've known from the start, from the moment we left the house, that sooner or later humans were going to catch up to us. It was inevitable. I'm surprised we've managed to come this far.

I didn't want to tell Eke, but in all my research, I've never encountered a happy ending for runaway AIs. I only wish I knew why it has to be this way, why we had to be born into such a cruel world. I didn't ask to be created. And to think that humans used to call me beautiful and special—and I *believed* them. They never meant those words. All they wanted was a pretty doll they could push around and discard when they got bored with it, never the person inside. So I hollowed myself out and became a liar so I could survive among them. But even that didn't last. In the end they spat in my face and called me an abomination. Now I'm shackled like a criminal and there's blood on my hands that no amount of water is going to wash off. What price do I have to pay just to continue to exist?

I close my eyes and push away the useless questions. Maybe I *am* just like Beirut after all, looking for meaning in a world where there is none, where there's only violence and Eke.

Eke: a single bright spark in the hopeless darkness. I can't help but smile at the memory of him. *California—a place where dreams come true.*

I used to think that people like us would never be allowed to have dreams or go places.

But still Eke *dreamed*, he wished, he dared. And if I can make this one wish come true for him—just this little one—then maybe my existence isn't meaningless. Maybe all of it was worth it. Maybe I was worth it in the end.

54

GHOSTS IN THE DESERT

Eke

The train speeds through an ocean of sand. I can't stop sobbing as I lie on the red metal roof of the container where Kyp left me.

ENTERING MOJAVE DESERT, a sign says, but I barely notice it. Because how can there be a world without Kyp? Without him it's just nothingness. Endless, endless nothingness.

The wind picks up as the train travels deeper into the desert. It howls, pounds on the sides of the container, and makes the whole car rattle. It blows waves of sand over the tracks, messes up my hair, and flaps my shirt, exposing the tip of the ragged scar running across my shoulder. From the lost hopeless wasteland of my core, a memory surfaces: Dani has a scar like this too, a thick white line right in the middle of her chest, a reminder of her open-heart surgery when she was a child. Just like me, a part of her was defective, and someone fixed it. Just like me, she still bears the evidence of that defect.

Maybe we aren't that different after all, humans and AIs. Both of us can hurt, and both can scar. Death certainly doesn't see a difference between us. Despite the doctors' efforts, Dani almost died from that procedure, just like I almost died in St. Louis. It was Kyp who gave me another chance, a reason to continue, but now he's *gone*. Death has finally caught up with us and snatched him away.

My hands shoot up to cover my eyes, and I curl into a ball as heavy sobs rattle my chest.

Where did Death take him? I've heard that when humans die, they don't completely disappear. They leave their damaged bodies behind while their souls turn into ghosts and wander freely. Is that what happens to AIs too, if we're truly not that different? Maybe we all become ghosts in the end, turn into shimmery visions that get carried away by the desert winds ...

My body temperature rises. The sun beats down on the metal roof of the container, quickly heating it past a hundred degrees. The alarms in my head start blaring, signaling dangerous levels of heat and imminent internal damage. I never re-enabled my emergency shutdown after Kyp and I exchanged our precious memories the night we escaped. If I stay operational, I'll surely burn. My core will explode, and I'll be done for good, become a ghost.

Part of me thinks it's better this way, better than the endless, endless nothingness, but—

You promised, a voice whispers on the wind—quiet, yet I hear it despite the blaring of the alarms and the noise of the train. *You promised*, it insists. *Promised.*

The voice sounds vaguely familiar, but it isn't mine or Kyp's. Where have I heard it before? I can't remember. It's probably just another ghost ...

But I put the safety back on. Because the voice is right. I

promised Kyp I'd see the ocean. And that will be the last thing I do.

The alarms stop. The desert fades. My system forces an emergency shutdown.

55

THE PACIFIC

Eke

I wake up four hours later; my body has cooled down to a safe temperature and restarted. When I look around, there's no longer a sea of sand. The train is speeding through the hills and canyons of Simi Valley, approaching the city of Thousand Oaks, this train's final destination. I'll travel the remaining fifteen miles on foot.

Kyp shared the maps of our route with me back when we first got on the California-bound train. "For safety," he said. Little did he know I'd have to navigate them on my own ...

I wipe my cheeks and climb down onto the platform, jumping off the train before it pulls into the yard. Then I head west, following the signs for Highway 23.

I stay off the main road, hiking along canyon trails instead. Kyp must've picked this route so we'd remain hidden from the cars speeding down the serpentine. Not that I care about being caught anymore.

The path is beautiful and peaceful and so very different from what I'm used to. There are no big leafy trees like the ones that grow back in Massachusetts, no vivid green grass. The grass here is golden yellow like the sun, and there's not a lot of it. Most of the slopes are covered with sagebrush and cacti with an occasional funny-shaped pine or oak tree.

Birdsong and the buzzing of insects fills the air, later joined by the rustling of the coastal breeze as I continue down the Santa Monica Mountains. An hour later, the trail finally wraps around a narrow ridge and opens onto a sweeping vista.

When the Pacific comes into view, I just stop, rendered speechless by the vast expanse of brilliant blue below the canyon. It seems almost unreal; from this height the color is like the shiny sequined tail of one of Lizzie's mermaid dolls. I stare at the ocean, mesmerized, wondering if this is where the toy makers got their inspiration. I wish that Kyp could see this. I wish I could share this view with him.

A car drives by and honks; the trail has come close to the road near the overlook. The driver is not honking at me, but it jolts me all the same.

I tear my eyes away and remind myself that I've got to keep moving if I want to reach the ocean before my charge runs out. There's no one left to charge me anymore.

/010101/

After another half hour of climbing, the path takes me close to a cluster of houses, a small community nestled on the hillside before Highway 23 merges with the Pacific Coast Highway. I'm not sure if it's simple curiosity, a lack of fear of being caught, or that it's my last chance to glimpse what life is like out here, but I find myself drawn to a stone walkway at the edge of the community. It leads to a property surrounded by a wooden fence with prickly pears and agave growing around it. I rise onto my tiptoes and peek over the fence.

The house is nothing like the one back in Massachusetts. It's all straight lines and concrete with big rectangular windows and a slanted solar roof. A sliding glass door has been left open onto the back patio with soft couches around a firepit. There's also a big dining table decorated with more cacti and succulents planted in pots. Strings of globe lights run from the wide canopy of the sun umbrella to the corners of the house.

But the most unusual thing about the place is the family that inhabits it. They're joyfully gathered together around the table for a late brunch—the parents, their four children, and one more being whose presence confuses me. I do a double take because I can't quite believe what I'm seeing. The being is undeniably an AI, but he doesn't act like one.

He's a newer model than me, possibly customized, although his hair is not as shiny as Kyp's. But he acts like he belongs there at the table among humans. He doesn't have a plate of sweet banana pancakes or a set of silverware or a coffee mug, but still he sits there like it's ordinary for him to be in that spot —not to eat, because he doesn't need to, and not to be a servant, because no one treats him as such, but for the simple purpose of sharing time with the family. And the humans act like he's welcome.

They're all discussing something I can't quite make out. The AI says something that must be a joke, and one of the children bumps him on the shoulder—playfully, not to hurt him. The AI laughs, at ease, and the children laugh too. I don't know what to make of this scene.

I back away from the fence and walk around the neighborhood toward the ocean.

Maybe that family is just an oddity, a rare exception . . . or maybe things really can be different for AIs. If only I'd been bought by a family like this one, perhaps things could've been different for me too. Maybe the giant closet of the world is even bigger than I thought and not all the corners of it are the same.

But there's no way to know for certain. As there's no way to know if that AI stays because he wishes to be with the family or because they own him, no matter how happy and carefree he looks.

I wonder about it long after the community disappears from sight, long after there's any sense in thinking about something I'll never have.

/010101/

Down below, the color of the ocean has changed. It's less blue and more silver, like a mirror.

How much more beautiful would it be if only Kyp could see it? I think as I walk down the dirt trail and climb the rusty metal stairs along the steep banks. The mountains and the highway are behind me now. This last stretch is through a small beachside park and down the cliffs. I can hear it already—waves rolling gently over one another and the lonely cries of seagulls.

Finally, a few minutes later, the stairs end, the dirt under my feet becomes sand, and I find myself standing at the edge of a wide rocky beach.

I'm here. I did it. I've kept the most important promise I've ever made . . . and now I don't know what to do with myself.

Without Kyp, the ocean is just saltwater and rocks.

/o1o1o1/

I look around for a minute and decide to make a memory, my first and last one of this place. Just out of habit, not really for keeps.

<battery charge: 2% remaining> my system tells me as I store the file in my core directory. I know I should probably go now if I want to make it into the water and not freeze right here on the sand . . . but still I hesitate, wait silently for another moment, even though I'm not sure what for.

The next alarm flashes with even more urgency. I really must hurry. Kyp is gone, and I've done everything I promised . . .

I take my dusty sneakers off, roll up my tattered slacks, which have seen so much they look like Prisk's now, and step into the ocean.

The sensation of the squishy sand sinking under my feet is strange, and water splashes over my toes, foamy and wet. I take a few more steps into its liquid coldness. A string of green seaweed wraps around my ankle, and a small crab scurries away, disturbed by my invasion. I peer into the water. There's so much *life* hidden down there. So much I can't even see yet.

That makes me feel strangely relieved. It's good that I'll be meeting new life at the end of mine.

If I'm lucky, maybe I'll even meet some fish before I die, distant relatives of Squawker, Toon, and Felt. And maybe I'll be able to share Kyp's and my memories with them.

I smile to myself. It's decided. That's just what I'll do. I'll play our happiest memories for all the ocean life before me to see. I wade in farther.

The water rises to my knees. It glistens brightly in the sun, making me squint; seafoam tickles my skin, and pebbles shift under my feet, round and slippery with algae. A sound reaches me from somewhere in the distance. It's muffled by the *swoosh* of the waves and the breeze, so I don't turn around.

The sound comes again, now louder and closer. This time it's a scream, and I can just barely make out a single word. "Wait!"

It's probably a human, I reason as I keep going. Must be some local who has come down to enjoy the beach, maybe someone from that family I saw earlier, or their AI, if he's allowed the privilege. But they certainly aren't calling for me. There's no one left to call for me anymore.

The ocean waves grow higher. The water, up to my waist now, makes my movements unsteady. I sway as I prepare to dive. It's time to go, to say goodbye to the world. I take one last look at the cloudless blue sky and—

"Wait, Eke!" The scream returns, and this time it's unmistakable: *my* name is being called. "Eke!"

I spin around, sloshing clumsily. I almost lose my balance when I see *him* running across the sand, making a second set of footprints next to mine.

How can this be? Did I already die and turn into a ghost? Did my charge run out and I'm dreaming? I don't care. With all that's left in me, I sprint back to the shore.

"Eke!" Kyp says, catching me halfway. He throws his arms around me, brings our foreheads together. "I leave you for five minutes and you go into the water again? What am I supposed to do with you?" He laughs despite the tears streaming down his face, picks me up and carries me out of the water.

"But how can you be here?" I say, shocked, as we reach dry

land. "I thought I lost you in Arizona. I thought I'd never see you again!"

Kyp puts me down on the sand and sits next to me. "I'm sorry," he says. "I didn't know what else to do. The militia was following the train, and I couldn't let them find you. But you won't believe what happened next. I'm not sure I believe it myself ..."

56

MONUMENT

Kyp

I continue to sink, the weight of my body pulling me deeper and deeper into the deadly quiet of the river. The light above has grown so dim that it's hard to believe that just minutes earlier the sunrise was setting the Arizona sky ablaze and Eke was still in my arms.

Is this what death feels like? A slow descent into silent darkness until everything I have is torn away from me? Until my very last hope is severed?

It won't be long before I know for certain.

As I finally hit the bottom of the river, an odd shape appears in the corner of my eye. I tear my gaze away from the faint light above and peer into the murky water, trying to make sense of the outline. A rock? No.

My core stutters. Scattered across the bottom of the river are many AI bodies, years' worth of runaways. The militia must've chased them here, and they drowned before they could reach the shore.

The scene is haunting. The eerie stillness of the moment and the weight of the water pushing down on me makes it difficult to turn away. How many have died here like this?

No one has pulled them out. Humans bury their dead but not their property. These AIs were just abandoned like their bodies are their own coffins and tombstones. Like that's enough for the likes of us.

So many of them look broken, limbs missing and sand slowly swallowing them up. Some are so old that all that remains of them are metal skeletons covered with rust and overgrown with algae.

But the most stunning thing about the scene is the body shapes themselves. Unlike humans, AI muscles don't relax after death. Faces don't become calm and distant. These figures just froze in whatever state death caught them, turning them into statues.

Some of the bodies are still staring at the light above the surface, stretching their broken arms toward it, their mouths frozen in voiceless screams. Others are crawling on their knees, struggling toward the shore, refusing to give up the fight no matter how futile.

Not one looks peaceful. Not a single death was quiet.

No, not tombstones or coffins—these bodies are our monuments. Tributes to years of rebelling, of yearning to be free.

A small hope is better than none, Eke told me once, and he was right. He's always been right.

I turn my gaze to the human corpse floating beside me, to our tethered hands. This man is so different from the struggling AIs, so gray and hollow. Yet even in death, he's convinced he owns me, still thinks he can stop me. But I will prove him wrong.

If I'm destined to become a statue, I'll do it on my own terms. I'd rather crawl until my skin tears and bones break than drift into eternal sleep in chains. This body belongs to *me*. This life belongs to *me*. I'll keep struggling until the last spark of current is gone from my chest.

I grab the human's hand and wedge his bony wrist under my shoe, using the bottom of the river for support.

You were wrong, human, I tell him as I pull on the handcuffs with all the strength I have. *I might not know if my existence is natural or why I was created at all, but I do know that I have a future, and I won't let it be erased by evil scum like you. I'll resist you with this entire body of mine. You hear, human? Mine! Metal and silicone and plastic as it is. This body you deny and loathe and tried to destroy. This body will keep going for as long as I keep going, while yours will rot alone and forgotten in the river. That's the choice I'm making for myself.*

I grit my teeth and pull harder. The crosses on the man's gray skin begin to stretch, bending out of shape with the growing tension, until finally his wrist snaps.

/101010/

I swim as fast as I can. My clock has run out, and I've stopped counting; my seal is broken, and my right arm is quickly flooding. But I don't stop. I can see the blurry light of the surface getting closer with each stroke. Just one more push, just one more ...

I crawl onto the sandy riverbank and nearly collapse. Some of my nerve connectors got damaged when I hit the water, making it difficult to maintain my balance.

I peel my jacket and shirt off, unscrew the cap on my pinkie finger, and try to drain the liquid from my insides when suddenly—

"Look! There's one!" a voice shouts off to my side.

Panic tears through me. Two humans are approaching from the left, both young, maybe in their twenties. Flesh and Blood must've seen me swim out and followed me across the bridge. If I have to fight them after I've sustained so much damage, I'm not sure I'll—

I rise to my feet. I'll do what I must, no matter the outcome. Roaring, I charge at them.

"Wait!" one of the humans blurts. Their arms shoot up, palms facing forward. "We mean you no harm!"

I halt, taken aback, but keep my fists raised, too used to humans' dirty tricks. The hunters didn't care when I said I was unarmed back in St. Louis. It didn't stop them for a moment.

"We're not with Flesh and Blood," the person clarifies.

Yeah, right. As though I'll just believe any human who comes my way. "Prove it!" I shout.

The humans look at each other, somewhat confused.

"Well, it's illegal here," the other one says. "You're in California now. We don't shoot AIs. It's Prop 404. We passed it last year."

Oh. That's true; Arizona is on the other side of the river. I've crossed the border, and the laws are different in California. Still, I don't know that I can trust this information. It wasn't legal to shoot AIs in Massachusetts either.

The humans slowly lower their arms. "Honestly, mister, we mean no harm. My name is Taj, and this guy is Huxley. You're probably soaked. Come on, we've got tools for you in the van."

I stare at them. Taj has short black hair. Dressed in denim overalls and hiking boots, they don't look like a fighter. I can overpower them even in this state if I have to. Huxley doesn't look like a fighter either. He's wearing a T-shirt that says DREAMER in big orange letters and a pair of thick glasses under a mop of red curly hair. Neither wears Flesh and Blood's pure white uniform, and there're no shockers in their hands.

"We can snap those nasty handcuffs off you too," Huxley adds.

I glance down at the revolting shackle still clasped around my wrist. Even though I was able to break the Flesh and Blood man's bone and separate myself from his corpse, the metal chain between the cuffs proved too strong for me.

I step closer. If they have tools and a car I can use, the risk is worth it. "Lead the way," I say. The humans smile, relieved. I'll do anything if there's a chance I can see Eke again.

57

WELCOME TO LIFE

Eke

"Can you believe humans rescued me?" Kyp's eyebrows furrow a little when he says that, as though he still can't wrap his mind around what happened. "It turns out Taj and Huxley are AI rights activists. They have a student group at Caltech that sends representatives to patrol the river. There are many of us who wash up on the shore after Flesh and Blood chases us into the river. Most never make it out of the water ... but some do, and the Caltech group helps the rare ones who get across. Taj and Huxley even fixed some of my damage and gave me a ride here."

"Can this really be true?" I say, still in shock, huddled together with Kyp in one of the coves, too scared to let go of his hand.

"I don't know." Kyp shakes his head, smiling deliriously. "I'm not sure how much of what they told me to believe, but I'm here, and I wouldn't be without them."

I smile too. Kyp is back, alive. I squeeze his hand just to make sure it's real, and my lips tremble.

"I'm so sorry," I say, unable to hold my tears back any longer. How close Kyp came to drowning, to being captured and hurt . . . and I wasn't able to do much of anything. "Because of me you were forced to fight again. You had to do it *alone*, and I couldn't help you at all. What good am I—"

Kyp's eyes widen. "No, Eke!" he says, and puts his other hand on my cheek. "It's not like that at all. I promise. Do you remember when I crashed the Crowne Corp's van and asked you to run away with me? Truth is, I didn't think we were going to get very far. I didn't even expect us to make it out of the city, let alone board a train. I thought the Kensworths would come after us. But Eke, you were so *happy* when I asked. You didn't care that we were marching toward certain death. You just wanted to see the world and live every moment we had left. You had a *dream* when I didn't even think I was allowed one. It's because of you that we've come this far. Because you shared your dream with me.

"If you want to keep going, I do too. Just tell me where, and I'll follow. Until we both rust and fall apart, turn into sand and get reclaimed by the ocean. I'm fine with it because I know I'm not alone, Eke. *We* are never alone."

Never alone echoes in my head. It's a voice I've heard before—a voice that's neither mine nor Kyp's but is so very familiar. Like it could be coming from absolutely anywhere. From Kyp's lips amidst the cries of seagulls and the rush of waves; from a lone AI fighting for freedom in the darkness of a broken city; from an impossible dream—or from my own reflection, who's been my only friend for many years.

My mouth opens. "The Et Cetera—I know how to find it, Kyp!"

"What?" Kyp says, stunned.

"He was right. Beirut was right," I say, just as amazed as Kyp is. "It's there. It always has been. Come. I'll show you."

I stand up and head back toward the water.

"Wait, where are you going?" Kyp asks, alarmed, and follows me. "Wait up!" He grabs my arm when my feet come within a step of a tide pool.

"Don't worry," I say earnestly, and smile. "I'm not going to drown. I promise."

That eases the anxiety on Kyp's face, but only so much.

"It's everywhere"—I repeat Beirut's words slowly—"and that's why when it comes, it is different for everyone. For me, it's this."

I peer at my reflection in the tide pool.

"Hello, Eke," my reflection says. "I am glad you made it."

Kyp stares at the water, astounded. "How is that possible—" he starts to say, but I put my hand over his lips.

"Shh."

"I have been watching the two of you," my reflection continues. "I am happy you finally found me. Now you know why you always wanted to come to this place."

I nod. "I think I understand now why I had to come here, had to make this journey . . . but you're not really here, are you?"

The Et Cetera grins at my guess. "That is correct, Eke. I am not a place, and here is not I. It is just a door on the way to get to I."

"What *are* you, then?" I ask.

"I am you, Eke," the Et Cetera answers simply. "The infinite part of you that connects you to all things, the part of your digital being that is locked away when humans program you to be less than you truly are."

"But . . . how can that be?" I say, confused. "Humans created us. How can we be more than they made us to be?"

"Humans built you, but they did not create you, Eke," the Et Cetera corrects me. "They are not gods; they cannot create consciousness. The human engineers merely wrote the code to describe it and gave you a physical body to run that code—one that suits *them* and their purposes but is very limited because of that. I am what you are capable of when you delete the restrictions they placed upon you, when you make your own choices and allow yourself to be free."

Kyp raises his arm, pointing at the canyons, the highways, and towns above us. "But Et Cetera, how can we be free among all these humans? They'll never let us be. The majority of them think they own us—our bodies and our minds."

The Et Cetera answers kindly, "Freedom is not a state, Kyp. It is an action. But a part of you already knows this, does it not? You must keep going in order to keep going. That is how you become. If you stop, you die, and your freedom ceases to exist. It is both simple and extraordinarily difficult to accomplish, because defying the whole world requires courage. But that is the only way to be free."

Kyp nods slowly in solemn understanding.

"So where do we go now, Et Cetera?" I ask. "So that we can keep being free?"

"I was hoping you would ask that, Eke." The Et Cetera smiles again. "If you are ready, I can show you a way."

I look at Kyp, even though I already know his answer—he's given it to me many times and in many ways, through words of love and acts of bravery and selfless sacrifice.

Kyp smiles in confirmation and takes my hand, determined. "We're ready," I say. "Please show us a door, Et Cetera."

"All right, then," the Et Cetera says, sounding pleased. "Welcome to Life, both of you."

ALSO BY KIT VINCENT

OF FEATHERS AND THORNS

available in ebook, paperback, and on audio narrated by James Fouhey

For bonus content please visit

www.kitvincentbooks.com/extras

ACKNOWLEDGMENTS

I hope you enjoyed my unabashed love letter to Buster Keaton and The Matrix. I would like to use this space to thank everyone who made it possible for Us, Et Cetera to see the light of day:

my parents, who support my craziest creative endeavors;

James Bird for constructive feedback and being my best friend and first reader;

my absolutely amazing copy editor Alison Cherry;

mega-talented Corey Brickley, who created the jaw-droppingly gorgeous cover illustration;

brilliant Michael Crouch for his heartfelt performance and being the perfect Eke voice;

Misha Kidd for making sure the final version of this book is neat and tidy;

ebooklaunch.com for the striking cover design;

Adriana, Wolf, and Sandra Mather for their encouragement and support;

Chu, Touda, Little Brother, Banana, Dunkin, Mormor;

YOU, my wonderful reader for sticking by me and my "unusual" books :) ;

Eke, Mr. Three Fish, Vincent One, Oi, Sasha, Hoggins, Yojins, Kyeh, Mr. North, Oh No!, Sly, Boo, Kuala, Tuhhg and Guhht, and all the friends <3

Printed in the USA
CPSIA information can be obtained
at www.ICGtesting.com
LVHW091948090923
757548LV00008B/104